Helen Falconer was born in London. Her first novel *Primrose Hill*, published in 1999, was described by the *Guardian* as 'stunning . . . intense, intelligent and highly readable' and by *The Face* as 'inspirational . . . [Falconer] forces her characters to face moral dilemmas about avoidance and confrontation . . . a fantastic first novel'.

HELEN FALCONER

Sky High

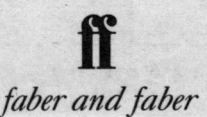

faber and faber

To Derek

First published in 2003
by Faber and Faber Limited
3 Queen Square London WC1N 3AU
This paperback edition first published in 2004

Typeset by Faber and Faber Limited
Printed in England by Bookmarque Ltd, Croydon

A CIP record for this book
is available from the British Library

ISBN 0-571-21762-1

2 4 6 8 10 9 7 5 3 1

Chapter One

I was stood at the sink, having a crafty toke, watching the filthy London rain come down, when a body hurtled past the kitchen window, hitting the ground with a horrifying crash.

Dropping the spliff, I sprang to the back door, and there was this half-naked bloke lying face down, motionless, empty bottles smashed around him. The only noise was the roaring of the downpour, hitting off his flesh and broken glass – water was streaming from his bare-skinned back and blackening his curly white-blond hair. His jeans were loose around his narrow hips; all he had on his feet were Arsenal socks; he clutched a Reebok Classic in each hand. I supposed he was dead, but I hadn't taken a step before he leapt up and fled through the soaking grass, making a sprint for the six-foot garden wall. 'Oi!' I shouted angrily, running after him. 'Stop!' He hurled his trainers over first, then sprang like a cat at the crumbling brick, making it to the top with a single bound. As he twisted to drop out of sight, into the tower-block wilderness beyond, I got a good look at his anxious face. 'I know who you are, you fucking wanker!' It was Jason, one of the crazy Peckhams, the toughest family on that shit estate. And, in particular, cousin to Gary Peckham, the most mind-numbingly irritating little hard-nut in my school.

I hurried back through the pouring rain, to try and figure how he'd broken in, and if he'd nicked any stuff or done any pointless damage. My spliff where I'd dropped it had browned a small spot on the lino. In the front room, last month's newspapers had been pushed off the sofa onto the wooden floor, but otherwise it looked the same as it ever did, piles of old pizza boxes towering undisturbed. Yet I had this weird feeling someone was still in the house, like the silence I heard was the silence of held breath. My dad's cat was snoring on the television, taking a break from shredding wallpaper and dragging long threads from sinking armchairs (it'd pretty much trashed the place over the past year while my mum lay slumped on the kitchen sofa, crying and smoking and slagging my dad for running off with some tart). But the presence I sensed wasn't Harry's napping cat.

I ran upstairs into my room. The window was wide open, curtains blowing, rain blackening the dusty carpet. In the bathroom, the talcum powdered floor was holed by footprints like thin snow. I thought I recognised Reebok soles. In my mother's room, the curtains were closed. Cigarette smoke filled the air. In the bed, I made out a body, deathly still, the green-striped duvet pulled up over its head. My heart gave a sickening bang. 'Mum?'

'Ferdia!' Annie shot bolt upright, clasping the duvet to her chest. 'Hi, honey!' She blinked at me through semi-darkness. 'Weren't you seeing your dad today?' She added, as I choked for breath, 'Ferdia, are you all right?'

After I'd recovered, I gasped out: 'No, I'm not all right! I just caught Jason Peckham in our *house* – I thought he'd *murdered* you!' I went to the window and yanked the curtains open. At the end of our neglected garden, concrete tower blocks marched across the sky, menacing our red-brick terraced house. I turned to see her in the dull grey light. Beside the bed a cigarette was smoking, not quite stubbed out in a volcanic pile of fag-ends. 'He was in our *house*, mum – we've got to call the police . . .'

'You saw him?' She seemed strangely doubtful, peering at me through black shaggy curls, chewing her plump pink bottom lip, round eyes bright but surreptitious. 'You're definitely sure it was him? You're dripping. Why don't you go and dry your hair?'

'What do you mean? Of course I'm sure! I chased the wanker over our wall!' On the floor was an empty bottle of champagne and two full glasses, bubbles rising fast. I said, frowning stupidly at the obvious, 'What . . .?'

'Look,' she murmured, lowering lashes, defensively raising her knees under the duvet. A packet of condoms plopped off onto the floor, spilling a handful of shiny squares. We stared at them, both of us open-mouthed, for ages.

'I can't believe it,' I said, when I could speak.

'I really thought you were seeing your father today . . .'

I wanted to vomit with disgust. 'I can't *believe* it. Mum. He's a *prick*.'

'I'm sorry you found out like this . . .'

'Mum, he's *half* your age.'

'He is *not!*' she squawked, suddenly outraged, freckled plump face flushing. 'He's twenty-*two*. And he's very mature!'

I couldn't stand to even think what she imagined she meant by mature. 'I've got to go now,' I said quickly. 'Sorry, I've got to go . . .'

She burst into guilty tears, intended to make me feel guilty too. 'No one thinks it's weird your dad's screwing a little bitch half *his* age!'

'I've got to go . . .'

'Don't go – you always walk away from things – don't go – we've got to talk about this . . . *Ferdia!*'

Outside in the red-brick Kilburn world, the rain eased off. September's leaves clogged up the gutters. I walked up our Victorian terraced street to Abbey Road, and stood at the bus stop with my hands jammed deep in the pockets of my leather coat, wearing my shades despite the dirty light, the other people at the stop careful not to even glance at me because I looked like a crack dealer. They must've wondered where my BMW was. I caught a 31 down the Abbey Road. I hadn't been meaning to see Harry that day, and I guess like Annie he hadn't been expecting me either, because when I let myself into his girlfriend's pricey first-floor flat in St John's

Wood, there was one hell of a row going on. I could see Abigail through the hinge of the living room door, stamping her sugar-pink trainers on the chocolate carpet, screeching, 'No, *you* look! I want a baby and I want it NOW! I'm sick of your feeble bloody excuses!' Abigail was one of those types who knows what they want and doesn't fuck about when it comes to getting it. She was annoyingly small and pretty, and she thought she was IT because she sang very poppy songs which she wrote herself and because she'd been on Top of the Pops. Bad snapshots of her posing half-cut at celebrity dos were always turning up in those teengirl mags precocious pre-teens love to read.

My dad kept crossing my line of vision, striding across the expensively empty room – one sofa, one sound system, one huge antique mirror – taking off his glasses to rub his large blue eyes, tossing his floppy fair hair aside. 'Look . . . Hang on . . . Why can't this wait?'

'I don't want to wait! It's not like you're getting any younger, Harry. The older you get, the less sperm you have, you know!'

Ouch! Poor Harry, terrified of turning forty. The last part he'd had on television, he'd been forced to play dad to a son *my* age ('How old do they think I am?' he'd asked me indignantly). 'Come on, Abby,' he pleaded. 'I've told you, Ferdia needs more time . . .'

'I'm not waiting years for some sulky, sneering teenage boy to decide to get a life!' She stopped shrieking and looked uncharacteristically depressed. Since I'd last seen her, her hair had turned to copper, like the leaves. 'Let's face it, Harry, he's *never* going to be OK about me. Like only last week, when I offered him a try-out for Dickie's new boyband? I mean, it's only every boy's *dream!* But he was so *rude* about it.'

(Rude? I hadn't said anything at all. In fact, I'd just laughed and laughed. She'd been playing some tweenie pop on her state of the art stereo, and she'd started dancing in front of me in her little bare feet, so I'd started *bopping* as it were, and

4

crooning, and then she said: 'Ferdie, you're so damn cute you should be in a boyband.' So I smirked a bit, and then she exploded, like a bottle of pop I'd shaken up: 'Hey! *Hey!* You know my old manager? He's thinking of putting this new boyband together, and he's bound to need a tall dark *smouldering* one! You're tall – you're dark – you've got gorgeous green eyes – god, you look nearly foreign . . .'

I pouted mockingly into her gilt-framed mirror, flicking back my *thick* black hair, fluttering my *extraordinarily* long eyelashes, and smouldered darkly, 'OK, what's it called then?'

She tried to remember, wrinkling her forehead, which meant she was thinking incredibly hard, and in the end said: '*Boybits.*'

Oh god, I laughed so violently I had to lie down and dribble on the carpet.)

'Ferdie in a boyband?' cried my dad, all enthusiastic. 'Great idea!' He'd always been an unprincipled breadhead – not one to starve himself for art.

'Harry, wouldn't you love us to have a cute little baby?' She wrapped him in her gym-hardened arms, knocking his glasses out of his hand to the floor.

'God, Abby – you know I would – to hell with Ferdie . . .' and he hoisted her up in her short blue dress, her kissing him with her feet off the floor, pink trainers cocked behind her, shadows crossing them as beyond her wrought-iron balcony, above the golden trees and vast white houses, heavy rain clouds came and went.

Then she saw me over his shoulder and dropped off him, crying brightly, 'Oh Harry, look, how lovely, it's *Ferdia*!'

'I'll be off then,' I said.

My dad fell to his knees, reaching for his glasses. 'Wait, wait . . .' he said. 'Wait . . .'

'No, really, I've got to go.'

'Wait . . .'

'No.'

'Oh god, give me a break,' he said, under his breath. As he stood up, putting his glasses on, she patted him sympathetically on the shoulder.

Outside the door, in a white-painted world, striding down the steps towards the pavement, I pulled my crack-dealer's coat around me and put my shades back on. He chased down after me, nearly breaking his neck on old spongy leaves. 'Don't walk out on me like this. We've got to talk. You're always walking away.'

'I'm not walking away,' I said. 'I've just got to go.'

'Ferdia, you only just got here.'

'Well, to hell with me,' I said.

He closed his huge blue long-lashed eyes, as he did whenever he wanted reality to stop happening to him. 'Come for a drive in the new car,' he said, with his eyes still shut.

'OK.' I watched his eyes crack open and the big white trademark smile break out. Normally I'd've said no, of course – it was just the rain was coming on again. Otherwise I would've said no.

Practically cheering, he unlocked his new little red two-seater, with the soft top and real wooden dashboard. 'Do you want to learn to drive?' he asked me. 'I'll buy you some lessons when you're seventeen. We can get you a provisional licence. What do you think?'

'OK.' When he'd bought it last month, saying he had to have a car because my mum'd kept the old one, I'd thought – why's he buying a car with only two seats? Maybe he hopes people will think he's been a long time single. (Family car? Volvo estate? Not Harry.)

'Great. I'll buy you lessons. It goes like the wind.' We crept up Abbey Road, bumper to bumper in the half-hearted rain. Waiting forever at the traffic lights, he asked, as he always did, 'How's Twinky?'

'Wrecking the place as usual.'

'Bloody cat,' he murmured, with an affectionate sigh. He'd left me behind in the rush, but I think he'd've liked to have taken the cat, if Abigail hadn't been so precious about her furniture. 'And how's Annie? Is she feeling all right?' I'd had a little trouble decoding this frequently asked question in the past, but now I knew it meant had she put the house on the market yet. He'd always been insecure about money, worrying there'd be no more parts for him, no handsome doctors nor long-lashed coppers after his heart-throb looks ran out. My mum claimed that's why he'd gone for Abigail – whenever he was standing close to her, he too got his pictures in teengirl magazines. He'd got his name in the tabloids, too, when he came out of a nightclub with her hand in hand, after her first appearance on Top of the Pops. The day of the tabloids was the day he left, snaking his suitcase-laden way through hungry hacks outside our house while I watched invisibly from behind my bedroom curtains and my mum did mad-dog howling in the kitchen. He told us he'd only known Abigail for a month, like that made everything all right – no deceptions, only snap decisions.

'Mum's fine, everything's fine,' I said. 'The new job's going great. She loves it.'

'Oh . . . that's great.' He tapped the polished steering wheel, staring at the red light, thinking gloomily about house prices. 'Is the new job going OK?'

'Yep.'

'That's great.'

He blew out through his teeth. 'Hmm.' Then he said: 'Actually, I'm surprised she's doing it.'

'What?'

'I know it's only for one day a week, but it must be incredibly depressing teaching at that fucking awful sink school.'

'Thanks, dad. I *go* to that fucking awful sink.'

'But *you* had no choice. If she sold that bloody red-brick pile you're rattling around in, she wouldn't need to work at all. Anyway, why doesn't she try out for some parts, instead of insisting on teaching drama to kids who couldn't give a shit?'

The fact was, she did do a load of auditions, but she didn't get anything, anywhere. That was the other high point of the year – Annie failing to pick up her career where she'd left it when I was born; Annie repeatedly cursing my birth and her lost life. She'd made me promise not to let on to Harry. 'Maybe she should. But we've got to eat, dad.'

He scowled, mouth handsomely hurt. 'I do pay maintenance, you know.' At the next set of lights he was smiling again, arguing persuasively for the hundredth time, 'That house is worth a fortune, Ferdia. When she sells it, she'll have loads of money of her own. We could even send you to a private school to do your A-levels.'

I've never liked the arrogant offspring of the rich. 'Come on, dad, where's your principles?'

Totally missing my screamingly obvious sarcasm, he answered proudly, lifting his dimpled chin, 'Ferdia, your education's even more important than my principles. I don't care what Annie says – your school's going to fail its inspection, and that'll be the end of it.'

'Drop me back home?' We'd got as far as Kilburn and the rain was getting heavier again, like the world was wetter at the poorer end. He turned into my road and pulled up outside the big dirty red-brick house where my mother smoked all day and ranted against my dad for leaving her, and cursed the government for paying today's teachers peanuts to raise the hooligans of tomorrow. I knew he was right – the house they'd bought fifteen years before was definitely worth a fortune now, and it was too big for us for sure, but only because he wasn't in it. I thought about going in and felt suddenly sick and tired at the thought of seeing Annie, so stayed sat in the car. My dad pinched at the top of his head and examined his fingers, checking if any of his fine fair floppy hair was coming away. Poor Harry, he feared the end of youth like it was something yet to happen.

'Ferdia,' he said, looking from his fingers to the pouring windscreen, 'this isn't your only home. My home is your home too. You should use your room at the flat more often.'

'Yeah, I know, I know,' I said.

'Abigail really likes you.'

'I'm sure she does.'

'She *does*,' he insisted, eagerly. 'You don't have to be so damned suspicious of her. She really wants the two of you to get on. You should talk to her.'

'I do talk to her.'

'*Nicely* . . . She told me she offered you a try-out for a boy-band. I thought you'd always fancied singing in a band?'

'Come on, dad, this is only Dickie she's talking about.' Dickie was Abigail's crap first manager, the one she'd ditched as soon as the going got good. She was still nervously nice to him though, because he was always threatening to publish a book about her 'early years'. 'He's a joke. She only talks to him because she's worried he'll write something nasty about her, and frighten off her six-year-old girlie fan base.' I started opening my door.

He sighed and clenched the wheel in his hands, irritated by me yet reluctant to let me go. 'So, your mum's really all right, yeah?'

'Yeah, great.' In the end, in the long unresolved pause, one foot out of the car, I couldn't help adding: 'Actually, she's got a new boyfriend.'

I think I was hoping he might be shocked or a bit sad or something – end of an era and all that – but instead he was annoyingly delighted, like this made everything OK at last. 'That's great – great,' he kept saying enthusiastically. 'That's terrific news.' He was all smiles. 'Thank god for that.' He really did think it made everything OK. He asked, Harry-like: 'Has he got any money?' I laughed, and he looked at me sharply. 'What's so funny?'

'Do you remember the Peckhams from the estate behind our house? Jason? The one with the silk shirts?'

He stared at me steadily.

'You must remember his cousin Gary? The one always chucking bottles into our garden from over the wall?'

'She's not . . . Gary?' He was having a problem getting his handsome head around what I was saying. 'She can't . . . he's far too . . .'

'Not Gary – *Jason*.' I added, unable to resist, 'It's OK, he's older than Gary. He's twenty-two.'

I got a shocked reaction then all right – he stared at me in speechless horror, and his face got tighter and tighter looking till he closed his eyes and rested his forehead on the wheel between his repeatedly clenching fists. 'Whatever makes her happy,' he murmured at last, almost too muffled for me to hear. 'Whatever makes . . .'

'Thanks, dad,' I said. Of course I wanted her to be happy. But the thought of Jason Peckham making my mother . . . *happy* . . . was frankly a little too much for me to bear.

Chapter Two

'Hey! Ferdia! My cousin's shaggin' your mum!'

I just kept on walking, walking, down the graffitied corridors of school. I didn't want to believe what I was hearing – no, wait – what the whole fucking *school* was hearing, courtesy of this foul-mouthed prick, this freckled five-foot-plus of solid muscle, this world-hating cat-killing worm-frying walking PA system with a number-one haircut and fists of steel.

'*Oi! Turdia!* Jason's shaggin' your mum!'

My mind flash-flooded with images of blood and mutilation, but my feet just kept on walking, walking, walking.

'Ferdia,' said my old mate Matt, hurrying to catch me up, indignantly red in the face and scrubby fair hair on end, 'do you want me to batter him? Just say the word.'

'*No.*' Matt could be brave to the point of pure stupidity, but since he'd grown about a foot in the past year he'd lost all touch with where his hands and feet were and spent most of his time crashing into things and falling over. I appreciated his offer but it was absolutely out of the question. He'd've been in hospital for a month. 'I don't give a shit about him. Come on, we're late.' Thank fuck we were – the classroom doors were shut. But Gary just kept on following us, Reeboks squealing on the worn-out lino, rattling the flaking radiators with his keys.

He started up again: 'Hey, Turdia! My cousin's shaggin' your mum! He says she's an animal in the sack! Like, a *dog*! Heh, heh!'

'Let me *batter* him, Ferdia – Ferdie, *please* . . .' I knew Matt was wondering why the fuck I was still walking away. He hopped along on his back foot in front of me, trying to get me to look him in the eye, then came to a halt, blocking me, spreading out his arms, practically pleading with me: 'I mean *Jason* for fuck's sake, it's like he's saying your mum's fucking a *donkey* or something, we've got to *do* something . . .' I shoved right past him and kept on walking.

'Oi! *Ferdia!* MY COUSIN'S SHAGGING YOUR MUM!'

I stopped dead a yard short of the classroom where we were headed and stood waiting, not moving, my back to the enemy, head lowered, my body bent sideways by the weight of my school bag. I had to shut that fucker's mouth before I went any further. Options rattled round my empty head, heavy books dragging my right side down, hearing the radiators jingling as he came. It was horrible, having to make this call. If I tried to batter him it would lead to extreme physical pain – mine. But it looked like he wanted to follow me right into my own classroom, shouting his salivating mouth off. If I didn't try to stop him, what would that look like? It'd look like my mum *was* fucking that arsehole's cousin. How could she do this to me? How could she *do* this to me? I could hear myself breathing, too loud, too fast.

'OI! TURDY!'

I raised my eyes. Someone had opened the classroom door. Faces were already turning in my direction, trying to figure out what was going on. The shriek of a thousand petty arguments was dying down. Those who hadn't already got a handle on the situation were beginning to wonder what everyone else was looking at. I glanced at Matt. He was standing at my side, also with his eyes on the floor, skinny shoulders squared, pink face gloomy behind his specs, feeling powerless, not watching me. I could hear Gary coming up right behind us.

'MY COUSIN'S SHAG–'

Bang! I caught him dead centre of his filthy mouth with my full bag of books. His shaved round head nearly popped off his neck and his freckled arms shot out sideways, keys spinning loudly through the air. Raising my bag above my head I smashed it down into his disbelieving face as he tried to get off his knees, and pure ecstasy flooded me as I decided to go on doing it until he was dead . . . a second later the fucker was up and had me by the hair and was dragging me about like a girl from side to side, banging me off walls while simultaneously kneeing me in the groin. Matt was hanging heroically onto the back of Gary's shirt, yelping 'Put him down!' or something equally pathetic. Luckily for him, Gary didn't even notice he was there. Behind me, I could hear excited voices screaming 'Get him, Ferdie!' from a very safe distance. Gary had me up against the side of the corridor with his hands around my throat. He was trying to nut me, but couldn't jump high enough. I went on feebly tapping at his bullet-proof torso with my fists, and without really meaning to closed my eyes.

An angry voice of authority ordered, 'Stop it at once! Or I'll call the police!'

Gary's hands unexpectedly left my throat, and he let rip a high-pitched squeal of pain like someone'd kicked him in the bollocks. I cautiously opened my eyes. Gary was spinning in agony on tiptoes, one bat-like ear stretched horribly towards the ceiling, suspended in the grip of a tall and serious woman. 'Have you calmed down now?' she kept asking, cool as ice, one hand on her hip, the other elongating his ear like putty.

'Get the fuck off of me, you silly bitch, or I'll 'av you for assault!' His face was blotched red with impotent fury – he windmilled his arms as murderously as he could, but he couldn't bring himself to punch her out, because she was so obviously official.

'Have you calmed down now?'

'I'm fuckin' calm, alrigh'?' he screamed. 'Lemme go! Lemme go!' Suddenly, she did. His ear snapped back with an elastic ping. Behind her, the entire classroom took one nervous step back. I braced myself. 'I'm out of here,' said Gary, panting. 'You'll be 'earing from my solicitor.' And, to my disbelieving relief, he just stalked off, grabbing up his keys from the floor as he went, giving her the finger behind his back, one ear delightfully, brutally scarlet.

'I'm reporting you to your head of year!' she shouted triumphantly after him. Then she handed me a tissue from her sleeve. 'Your lip's bleeding.' I dabbed at it, embarrassed. She asked, not taking her eyes from my bloodied mouth, 'So, what's your name?'

'Ferdia.' I was trying to figure who she was. She was skinny and tall, as tall as me, with long blonde hair pulled back in a green velvet ribbon. Her black-and-white checked skirt, knee-length, had got slightly twisted in the struggle; she tugged carefully it into place, thrusting her white blouse back inside its waistband, then grinned at me. There was a fine black gap between her front teeth. Behind her glasses, thin metal frames balanced on a long straight nose, her eyes were magnified.

'That's an Irish name, isn't it?'

'My mum's Irish.' But I was English, just stuck with this girly-sounding Irish name in modern thug-infested England, a walking target for all the rampant Peckham-types who naturally assumed I was gay and so, equally naturally, kept trying to break my arms.

'Wash your face, Ferdia, then come and *learn* something. You too,' she added to Matt, who'd simply been standing there, patiently absorbed. She stalked back into the classroom and slammed the door. Evidently, she was taking our lesson. We must've worn out our allotted English teacher already, only three weeks into the first term – fast going even by our standards.

'Shit,' said Matt slowly. 'Did you see the arse on that?'

I scoffed, 'Thinking of inviting her out to dinner, are you?'

It was another ten minutes messing about in the bogs before we finally made it into her class. Matt wasn't in the mood. 'We've nearly missed it,' he argued. 'Come down to the music room and I'll play you my new song.'

'Later,' I said. I was always up for hearing Matt's new tunes, but didn't want to risk Gary again, not yet, not till I'd figured out what to do about him.

'This one's fuckin' wicked, even if I do say so,' said Matt, marvelling at his own genius.

'Yeah, yeah – I can imagine.' They always were, naturally.

I found a window seat where I could take my wet coat off and pretend to dry my legs in the cold September sun. I started re-running the fight in my head. The memory was too wince-making, so I improved on it, arming myself with a machine-gun and blasting that fucker off his feet. Then I thought, anyway, how the fuck am I going to sort this one out *without* a machine-gun? It's not like he's going to stop his filthy mouth after one pathetic scuffle in the corridor. But if I fight him every time I see him, I'll be dead in a week. I thought, I have to explain it to my mum, I have to make the whole situation clear, she has to dump Jason – that, or I'll have to kill Gary Peckham. But if I try to kill him, the chances are he'll kill me. Or I could cut out the middle man by killing myself – quicker and easier and probably less painful.

'Do you like seventeenth-century love poetry, Ferdia?'

'Don't be ridiculous.'

'*I beg your pardon?*'

I woke up and realised I was in an English lesson, where one's contempt for love poetry of any sort was supposed to be temporarily suspended. It was that woman again, still looking at me like I was mad or something, eyes blinking slowly behind her glasses. 'Oh – right,' I said quickly. 'Yes, of course.'

She frowned, quickly flicking her upper lip with her tongue. 'Do you? *Really?*'

I hesitated. 'Well, no . . . not . . . *really.*'

'I see.'

She turned back to the rest of the class, but in the two seconds she had stopped paying attention to them they had forgotten all about her and were now going about the normal business of their lives – chatting, swapping items of clothing, emptying the bags of unsuspecting colleagues into the bin.

*

In the break, Matt insisted I came to hear the new song. I wanted to hear it, I liked Matt's raucous post-punk blasting, but also I wanted to be somewhere else, like outer space. But I was in school, where everyone can hear you scream but no one bothers to intervene. Even if I left the premises immediately, chances are Gary'd be waiting for me in the road.

We picked up the drummer Aristotle on the way down to the music room. He was a gangly, overstretched, thin-faced, half-Greek half-Ethiopian from the year below us, and I liked him, because he had one of those names, like mine, which made it like your parents had tattooed a target on your back at birth. Aristotle said to me, 'Hey, Ferdie – got yourself a bass yet?'

'No – have you?'

He replied smugly, 'Can't do without me drumming, man. I destroy those skins.'

The band, Matt's latest enthusiasm, was limping along a bit right then, thanks to the bass player going back to Bangladesh for a year. Matt'd tried advertising, but bass players, even the crappiest most hopeless ones, turned out to be gold dust on the music scene – everyone wants to play the sexy instrument, i.e. lead guitar, in order to waggle it suggestively at those mythical knicker-slinging girls. Aristotle's latest bright idea was for me to take up bass guitar and solve their problem.

Matt agreed with Aristotle. 'It's really easy,' he said. 'Don't worry about it. You just, like, plonk away at it a bit. You don't have to play like me.'

'Thank fuck for that.'

'No, I mean it, it's a piece of piss,' he said. 'Just try it, OK? You'll look good.'

I'd started hanging around with the band shortly after Matt got it together a few months ago, but only because I was a long-time friend of his, and it looked like they were having fun. I couldn't play an instrument, but sometimes I'd dance and sing along, although he took the piss out of my voice for not being bad enough. 'Gotta sing from your *heart*, man,' he said. 'This isn't some poncy little boyband, Ferdia. Think *grief*. Think *rage*. Not Top of the fucking Pops. '

Down in the music room, he struck a few chords and then played a whole lot of notes surprisingly fast, shouting: 'This is a cool riff, innit? Hit it, 'Stotle!' and they were off, shaking the remaining plaster from the walls, making the music stands in the corner jump like a jangling audience of pogo-ing punks. *'Gonna cut my throat, jump off the Empire State!'* bawled Matt. *'Gonna rip my head off, chuck it in a lake!'* At the end of the song he scowled at me over the end of his guitar, pink face sweating, fair hair on end. 'In my songs I let out my *dark* side.'

I laughed appreciatively. I thought his lyrics were fucking funny. Matt had always been into seriously black humour. When he was going to be the next best thing in TV comedy, his sitcom family hacked each other up with chainsaws; when he was going to be this famous cartoonist, his characters were disintegrating lepers. There was much pounding on the door. I opened it a crack. Several year-seven kids were outside, demanding to come in and listen. When I told them to fuck off, the little idiots tried to barge past me, so I slammed the door on them – literally slammed it on one of them, judging by the high-pitched squeal. I pushed a chair under the handle.

'Jesus, *groupies*, what a hassle,' sneered Matt, extremely chuffed. Then he bellowed at Aristotle: 'Hit the throttle, 'Stotle!' and burst into a different song (as far as I could tell): *'Wanna kill somebody – anyone will do! Wanna rip somebody's head off, yes it's true! Wanna chop them up and flush them down the loo!'* Screams of appreciation from outside.

'The thing about our music, yeah,' said Matt, adjusting the amp to continuous feedback mode, 'is that we tell it like it is, right, 'Stot? We hate that mindless house and garage, shallow electric dance shit.'

'Yeah, right. But I kind of like techno, man,' said Aristotle's voice, from floor level. 'Garage for crusties – *yeah*.' He was crawling around hunting for one of his drumsticks, which had gone missing in action.

'That's right, like it is,' repeated Matt to himself, dreamily. Then he asked me, hitting his strings softly, 'What's got into Gary, man? Do you think he's finally lost it?'

I looked at my watch. 'Got double history, man. You?'

'OK,' he said to himself, nodding his head. 'Let's go.' He was good at not asking about private stuff. He knew how to keep himself pretty close about the important things in life. I'd known him for three or four years before I found out his mother was such an alkie she could watch a whole episode of *Eastenders* without actually turning on the television, and it wasn't Matt but his little sister who told me that (Natasha thought it was an absolutely amazing skill that you only got when you were old enough).

Outside, the year-seven kids had dispersed, though as I stood looking out for Gary I could hear a shrill chorus in the distance of '*Wanna chop them up and flush them down the loo-oo-oo-oo-oo!*'

Swinging down the corridor towards me was the tall woman in her checked skirt, long black legs in sharp black shoes snapping and clicking like scissors. Her blonde pony-tail hung to her waist. She stopped and smiled at me, pointing at the door behind me. 'Was that you with the music just now?' She wasn't wearing her glasses; her eyes were round and full, an odd indefinite marbled blue-green colour; she'd underscored them with a thin black line.

'Music? You mean . . . that, just now?'

'Do you play a lot? Is it your band? You certainly look like a pop star. What's it called?'

Matt and Aristotle loved constantly changing the name of the band. It'd been called Dangerous Dogs, then Coked-up Cats, then Dangerous Badgers, then a whole load of other names I'd stopped bothering to remember. For the sake of something to say, I told her it was called Boybits, and she cracked up laughing, creasing around her peculiar-coloured eyes. Her front teeth were definitely gappy. I was pleased she liked Matt's music.

'That is so perfect,' she said. 'That's the ultimate ironic name. Who came up with that one?'

'It was kind of a joint effort,' I said.

'Good one. See you at your next gig,' she said, clicking away.

I spent history still musing how in hell I was going to get around the Peckham problem. I wished it was Friday, but Friday was tomorrow. At the end of the day I went home to my mother's house, looking behind me all the time, falling leaves making me jump like a scaredy girl. No Gary Peckham; no nobody. I was even tempted to risk the short cut I sometimes took across a corner of his estate, which could save me twenty minutes. But as I slipped under the shadow of the tower blocks I spotted one of Peckham's mates, another vicious arsehole, a fat brain-dead specimen I hadn't seen in school for a while, hair like fireworks, skin like red brick, eyes like dots, mugging a year-seven kid for his pocket money up against the wall of the Evil Eye, a coke-head music dive which I'd never seen not seriously boarded up. I stood on the edge of his dirty concrete world and yelled, 'Oi! Wanker!' as loud as I could until he heard me and dropped his poor little victim to come chasing after me, a mound of slow rippling fat. I turned and ran a few yards ahead of him, away from the flats, down a couple of terraced roads, keeping a steady distance so he'd keep running till he collapsed, which he did fairly soon, hopefully having a heart attack or something. It struck me that it would be best for me if he'd left school for good, not just been off skiving for a couple of weeks – I wasn't too sure which was the case.

I found Annie in the kitchen, curled up on the old rust-coloured sofa pushed back against the wall, wearing only a sleeveless vest and old torn leggings, smoking intensely, staring at her naked feet, while Harry's cat sat watching her from the floor, purring and thinking about jumping up. 'Hi,' she said in a faraway voice, without raising her eyes.

I dropped my books on the table, and stood between her and the sink. 'Mum,' I said determinedly, 'I'm really worried about this Jason thing.' I waited for a response, but she didn't look up. Ash fell unchecked from the end of her fag, splashing white on the knee of her grey-black leggings. I frowned and raised my voice. 'Look, Mum. He's gone and shouted his mouth off about it to his cousin Gary, and now Gary's telling the whole bloody school. Think about it, mum – it's *incredibly* embarrassing. You've got to get rid of him.' She leant her forehead wearily in her hand, and smoke seeped upwards through her rough black curls. Exasperation at her limpness mounted in my chest, but I tried to push it away, like I'd spent all year pushing it away, while Annie sobbed and ranted in the kitchen, and Harry pretended everything was OK because these things happen and why was she so upset. And both of them told me in passing I'd be fine, they loved me and nothing important would change for me. 'Listen. The Peckhams are a load of . . .'

'*Fuck!*' The Siamese had jumped and dug its claws in. 'Bugger off, Twinkie, you little shit!' Her anger freed from its box, she snapped at me, ramming her fag out in a dirty plate, 'Stop! Relax! He's not coming back, OK?'

I was delighted. 'Yeah? Thank god for that!' I smiled in pure triumph out of the window, over the wall to the towers of his estate. With their backs to the afternoon sun, they were pasting vast black shadows over our house. I felt a moment of misgiving. 'Sure?'

'Of course I'm sure – look at me, for heaven's sake!' I faced her again, puzzled by the pain in her voice. 'Of course he's not coming back. Look at these lines!' She was jabbing angrily at her freckled forehead, green eyes bulging with tears. 'Look how fat I am – look here – and here!' She waggled the soft flesh of her upper arms and grabbed her stomach through her vest. 'Why *would* he come back, when I'm so fat and disgusting?'

I gasped, shocked, burning up inside, ready to go to war for her, 'Where is he? I'll fucking *kill* the dirty bastard.'

She laughed mournfully, reaching for another fag. 'It's OK, honey, you don't have to be my knight in shining armour. Jason wouldn't say anything so rude.' She lit her cigarette with trembling hands. 'But then, he doesn't need to, does he? The fact is, I'm just too bloody old.' Slumping deeper into misery, she alternately dragged on the fag and bit at her blunt right thumbnail. 'No wonder I can't get any acting parts. Why would anyone want me? Your father didn't, and he's the same bloody *age* as me. There was me stupidly thinking he still loved me, and the first chance he gets he runs off with some skinny bimbo.' She groaned, 'I suppose I can't blame him. Why would anyone put up with an ugly old hag like me?'

'Don't be ridiculous.' I felt embarrassed by her self-pity. 'You're beautiful.' I actually thought she probably was, but how could I tell? All I could see when I looked at her was my mum – exactly the same woman I'd seen since the day I was born.

Chapter Three

In the end, I decided to crash at Matt's place for the night. I think Annie would rather I'd stuck around, but all that pointless self-loathing was doing my head in. The high point of her evening was a cathartic screaming match with Harry down the phone about money and my school (she defended it); later she sank back and drank a bottle of wine, and wept inconsolably for lost youth.

Matt lived in the nearest tower block to our house, and the quickest way to his place was over my garden wall, the same route Peckham had used the day before. Making my way down the garden by the light from the kitchen window, I hauled myself cautiously up on the cold mouldy brick, ready to drop back if Gary or other hooligans like Fatboy were hanging about in the night with nothing to do. But the only sign of life was directly below me – a crouching monkey-like gang of five- or six-year-olds, with fierce concentration making a very small fire with two sticks, a cornflakes packet and a whole box of matches. I got into a sitting position and sprang out from the wall, landing in hard among them. They scattered like sparrows, then drifted back, little fingers a forest of v-signs. I threw them some change out of my pocket; they dived on it then rushed away again, squeaking and jabbering into the jungle. It struck me as a bad version of Narnia, really – over the wall, another world. The night here was lit by a thousand windows streaking up towards the stars. I hurried across the rubbish-strewn tarmac to the big glass entrance doors of Matt's block. I prayed the piss-ridden lifts were working. Horizontally speaking, Matt and I were next-door neighbours, but vertically, if the lifts were out, he lived a long and weary way away, marooned at the top on the twentieth floor in a disturbingly flaky flat – the ceiling in the bog was covered in black bubbles, and there was a long crack in the kitchen wall which would've been fine at ground level but was kind of scary that high up, like noticing the wing is coming off your plane.

I was out of luck. What seemed like hours later, I arrived exhausted at his door. Later, lying wrapped in sheets on the floor of his room, I could feel the building rocking in the wind, soothing us, twenty layers of sleeping bodies, gently all to sleep.

In the morning, Matt had another go at me about learning bass guitar. 'For the good of the band. For the future. For the *music*, man.' We were stood side by side on his long concrete box of a balcony, sharing one last already-smoked fag, gazing mesmerised over the flat-topped metal railing at the stomach-churning drop below, two hundred feet down to the rubbishy glass-strewn floor. Cloud-capped towers were stacked to left and right, useful storage for unwanted people; squatting beneath us was the Evil Eye, and my red-brick house, and the terraced map beyond. We were too high up for birds, but a black-dotted cloud of starlings rose and fell several floors below us, screamingly riding the roller-coaster air, then swept out boldly over the low-rise world to shit collectively on the tiny cars which buzzed impatiently in mile-long queues.

'I suppose it'll be a laugh,' I said at last.

He answered sharply, flicking his cigarette through the miles of air, 'It's not supposed to be a *laugh*. The music gods need you, right?'

I hoped he meant that as a joke, but at the same time it struck me he'd been getting a bit heavy lately – still hyper, but in a less happy, more nervy way. I realised he was taking the band thing pretty seriously, more than the cartoons and the TV comedy. I reassured him, 'The band's good, man – you tell it like it is. Like Nirvana.'

Matt smirked, short fair hair on end, West Ham T-shirt

back to front, jeans ripped and no laces in his trainers, grunge beyond grunge. 'We ain't.'

'The Sex Pistols? The Ramones?' I hesitated. 'The Fall?'

He shook his head, pleased and pissed off in one go. 'Naaah.'

A police helicopter roared past at the level of our feet, skirting the high estate, blades whipping up the thin blue air, ruffling our hair and making it impossible to talk for a minute. When it had gone I asked, 'Well, what then?'

'Well . . .' He thought about it, leaning his arms on the balcony rail, scratching his manky head. 'Y'know – riot-chant pop?'

'Like, punk?'

'Hmm. Something like that. Different though. Needs its own label. KnowhatImean?'

I said cautiously, 'Tower-block rock?'

He was delighted, gesturing with both hands at the other blocks to left and right. 'Exactly! Urban menace but up in the air! Music with a view and a nearly-always-broken lift! Sky-high music for people who can't *afford* a fucking garage!'

I interrupted even more cautiously, 'And I just have to, like, plonk away at it a bit?'

'Voices of the poor trapped in their tiny fuckin' council cages miles above the rich fuckin' ground!' cried Matt proudly, leaning dangerously out and saluting the dirty red city beneath his feet. 'Serenading all you fuckin' ground-dwellers, stuck down there in your Victorian terraces with your mortgages and your burglars and your chicken-shit security locks! Tell it like it is, mate! Breakfast?'

'Uh, yeah – what you got?'

I followed him into the cracked kitchen, a small desolate place, and he went through his usual futile routine of opening one empty cupboard after another and finally looking in the fridge. A single pint of milk pleased him, until he took a mouthful and gagged violently over the sink. Matt's five-year-old sister was sat on a stool at the counter, colouring pictures in with a blue biro, very carefully, right to the edges. She looked at her brother twisting his head at a neck-breaking *Exorcist* angle to gulp groaning straight out of the cold tap and commented, 'That milk tastes really disgusting, doesn't it?'

He came up dripping. 'You *drank* some?'

'*No,*' she said, like – d'you think I'm stupid or what? 'I *sniffed* it, you moron.' She was just like him, with her round pink face and soft nose and fair hair stuck to her cheeks. Her teeth were dark blue from too much biro-chewing. She had a bit of a sarky streak.

He searched the back pockets of his jeans and even went as far as checking the inside of his ripped denim jacket, and when he'd proved that he'd really tried his best, he turned to me and asked politely, 'Got any cash, Ferdia?'

I did have a couple of quid, but it was back in my other jacket in my embarrassingly ground-level house. I offered to go get it, but Matt decided that was too much hassle and started a full-scale search of the flat, rummaging through his mother's jeans (she was still in them, unconscious, face-down on her bed), digging down the back of the sofa and armchairs (five pence) and finally trying to crack the combination on Natasha's plastic piggy-bank.

'You'll *never* do it,' Natasha said scornfully, and then burst into tears when he forced it. Somehow she'd saved up over two pounds. 'I'll call the police!' she screamed hysterically.

'We can get milk *and* cornflakes,' begged Matt. 'Come on, Natty, I'll pay you back tomorrow.'

'No you'll never!'

'We gotta *eat*!'

'What's the point of me saving money if you're going to *steal* it all?' she shrieked.

'What's the point of you being a miser if we're all going to *starve* to death?'

'I'll pay you back, Natasha,' I said. 'I'll pay you back this afternoon. I promise. Please.'

25

She stopped screaming, glared at me hard from under quivering tear-tipped lashes, then went back to her one-colour colouring.

Amazingly, the lift was working. By the time we'd made our sick-making way, jerking and clanking, down the bottomless shaft, we were stinking of other people's piss and feeling it. A fierce fresh wind was blowing outside, perking us up, crisp packets whirling round our heads. We hurried along the edge of his estate, human dots in the shadow of a vertical concrete world, past psychedelic walls made brilliant to head-height by graffiti in fluorescent paint; we skirted the rotting mass of the Evil Eye, a red-brick pile with fireplaces exposed on either side, and peeling wallpaper on its outer walls – the rest of its Victorian terrace long since bombed in the war, then bulldozed down. Me and Matt used to hang about to play here when we were younger, but then it got so every time we'd get some bother, a lot of it down to Gary and his gang. We were at that age when boys tried to kill other boys for a laugh, especially pathetic non-macho types like us. It was Matt's bad luck he didn't fit in where he belonged – a spliff-toking ragbag of indie-hippy-punk, when all the kids round there dressed ultra-clean, did coke as drug of choice and danced all night to house and garage. Bad luck and also something suicidal about the way he was – like, always wearing a West Ham shirt when every family on his estate, from grannies to babies, followed the Arsenal. (Thanks to his influence, I was West Ham too – but unlike him I tried to keep it quiet.) We ran over muddy concrete up to the nearest road, and instantly the air was calm again – something weird to do with the strange aerodynamics of tower blocks; like Matt always said, they stood in the eye of the storm.

Just outside the shop, Matt grabbed my arm and hissed, 'Don't move!' He was staring at the pavement between his legs as if an escaped tarantula was going to run up his trouser leg. It was a black leather wallet.

'Get it, quick!' Like it'd scuttle away.

'Just pray,' said Matt, in American. 'Just pray to the Lord.' Because of course they're never wallets that someone has just that moment lost – they're always pre-stolen wallets with everything taken and then thrown out the top of the bus. He picked it up and kissed it for luck before opening it.

The money was still in it. Whoever it was lost it was probably still only a few yards ahead of us up the road. There was only one guy in sight – youngish, suited, walking on fast.

We'd an excellent time loading the basket with thirty quid's worth of bacon, eggs, sausages, tomatoes, mushrooms, beans, sliced bread, butter, yoghurt, orange juice, tea, milk, sugar, fags, the works. Just as we handed over the money, the guy in the suit turned up in a hurry. He said to the bloke behind the counter, 'I'm sorry, did I leave my wallet here?'

'Nope,' said the bloke, counting out our change, not looking up.

'Black leather? I was in here just a moment ago and I bought . . .'

'Nope,' said the bloke, zinging the till shut and handing Matt the remainder.

'I definitely had it with me when I . . .'

'Nope.'

Matt said, 'Is this it by any chance?' holding it out. I couldn't help making a slight dying noise in my throat. The guy grabbed the wallet, nearly in tears of relief. Matt said kindly, 'It's all right, mate. I found it in the road just now. I was going hand it in at the station later.'

'Thank you. Thank you so much. Look, let me give you something . . .' He opened it, and his face dropped slightly. 'Shit.' He glanced up at Matt, who looked straight back at him, clutching his huge bags of shopping, eyebrows raised in concern.

'Everything OK?'

'Sorry, kids, I was going to give you a fiver . . .' Still searching, he relaxed and smiled. 'All the plastic's still there, that's

27

what I was really worried about. I'm just sorry I can't . . .' He looked again at Matt's shopping and at me standing behind Matt with two more stretching bags gouging deep red lines into my fingers. His eyes flickered and darted away. 'Thanks anyway.' And he went.

'I'm going to write a song about that,' said Matt, as we staggered back into the graffitied jungle. 'You know, all those bastards who are so fucking rich they're only worried about the plastic. If you mug them and just take the notes, they think they're so fucking lucky, they're over the fucking moon; cash is just their spare fucking change.' And he sang (using the word 'sang' pretty damn loosely) all the way back to the block: '*Gonna chop his cards up yes I really am, it's the only way to hurt the plastic man* . . .' etc until the bottom of both his shopping bags fell out suddenly and I had to race back to the shop for some more, leaving him fighting off the usual marauding gang of shaven six-year-olds which had poured instantaneously out of the nearest block. The lifts were out again, but all in all it was worth having to climb slowly back up the twenty floors, panting past the struggling teenage girls with their buggies – ('I'm gonna write a song about that,' said Matt, 'called "Babes in the Air"') – worth it and probably safer than taking the dodgy lift anyway.

We gave Natasha her money back. She was gobsmacked, and went off to hide her combination safe under the bed she shared with her mum, where Matt would never find it again. She wandered back when the smell of sizzling bacon had filled up the bare little kitchen. She stuck her fingers into the empty bacon packet.

'Matt?'

'Go *away*.'

'What's bacon made of?'

He looked at her and then at me. I was hacking into a tin of baked beans with a dodgy can opener, and raised my eyebrows at him. After a long pause, he muttered uncomfortably, 'Pigs.'

'*Really?*'

'Yep.'

'*Policemen?*'

'No, for god's sake – pigs like you see on the telly.'

'Pigs with *tails*?'

'Yep.'

'And *skin*?'

'Yep.'

She sniffed the air. 'Mmm. Tasty.'

Tessa came in as the three of us were half way through scoffing the lot. Her hair was tied back and she looked as thin as a model in her yellow shirt and baggy jeans. She was a lot prettier than her kids – clearly she'd hung with some really ugly man. She still had the pillow's creases stamped into her left cheek. She pulled a face. 'I don't know how you lot can eat that shit,' she said. 'Just the smell of it makes me feel sick. Oh god . . .' She went into the bathroom and shut the door.

Me and Matt decided it was too late to go to school and instead spent a happy afternoon feeling rather ill with overeating, and wandering about Kentish Town, standing in doorways while showers full of rain and yellow leaves blew over, looking in windows for cheap guitars. We were loitering outside Priceslashers (rock-bottom prices, no refunds even if it explodes in the shop just after you've paid for it) when a very cute girl with long black rained-on curls came up, sub-Saharan skin and Taiwan eyes, tucking her arm through Matt's like she had the right.

'Hi, Matt,' she said, 'how's it hanging? How's the band?'

'Just checking out some strings for our new bass player,' he said. 'Ferdia, this is Lily – she wants to come and sing with us some time. Whadyathink?'

I thought she was incredibly cute. I'd met her before once or twice because my mother knew hers – they'd started out together on their low-level luvvie careers – but we hadn't seen them in a couple of years, what with one thing and another and the divorce, so I hadn't bumped into her in a while. She nodded and smiled at me, remembering me. She'd got quite a bit taller, but was still pretty short. She had on a purple zipped top with a hood and pockets and genuine seventies 501s trailing over her platforms, damp along the bottom. She tucked her head into Matt's upper arm like she didn't realise he was an ugly bastard. It always amazed me how Matt managed to pick up these really beautiful looking rich girls. 'Fine by me,' I said. 'You can sing, right?'

Lily rolled her huge black eyes at me. 'This *is* Matt's band we're talking about? I bet you're really crap on the bass, right?'

'Yeah. Well, I'm getting there,' I said. 'I'm . . . maybe even going to buy one. Eventually.'

'Jesus,' she said. 'I take it back.'

Matt went bright pink. 'Hey, Lily,' he said. 'Crap's the new black, right?'

'He means the new brown,' I explained to her.

Matt raised his voice. 'We tower-block maestros *vomit* on all these modern fucking production values, all smoothed-over fucking edges, everything patted down, it's like . . . it's like processed *ham*, man, like music as fucking mechanically retrieved *meat*. We like it *rough*, we want it *real*.'

'Like running over a cat?' she suggested.

'That one's only seventy quid,' said Matt, pointing in the window. 'Will your dad get it for you, d'you think?'

I was doubtful. 'He's not shelling out as much guilt money as he was. He keeps going on about being skint.'

'Did he leave your mum?' asked Lily, interested. 'How long's it been?'

'About a year.'

'Oh, come on,' she said, sticking her hands in her purple pockets. 'That's still got to be worth seventy fucking quid.'

'And an amp,' said Matt. 'But that'll only be another fifty quid, max.'

'I d'know . . .'

'No, really,' Lily reassured me, nodding wisely. 'Trust me. It'll make him feel better. You have no *idea* how bad he feels right now. Use it. It sounds like a mean thing to do, but basically it's the best way.'

'Like fox hunting?'

'Exactly.'

But I found out later she hadn't seen her dad since he'd left six months ago to be a banker in Taiwan, only getting expensive presents through the post, so she was bitter against the species and thought they were only there to be screwed for cash. We walked on towards Chalk Farm, down the Prince of Wales Road. Lily was still being very familiar with Matt. She asked him, 'Written any more great songs?'

'One or two,' he said. 'Y'know, they just keep on coming.' He said to me, over her wet black head, his arm comfortable on her narrow shoulders, 'Talking about songs, y'know like I was talking about writing one called "Babes in the Air" today, when we were passing all them girls with their buggies on the stairs? You know, my mum was one of them. It must've been fucking tough for her when the lifts were out, lugging me all the way up to the flat. I was a fucking massive baby, man. I'm gonna write a song about it.'

'About what a gross baby you were?'

'*Hush, baby, hush, we're so fucking high; me on my valium, you in the sky.*'

Lily said, 'You should call it "Stairway to Hell".' Then she shut him up by sticking her tongue in his mouth, pulling his face down to her level (he couldn't avoid going cross-eyed at me past her ear while this was happening, faking horror but actually *incredibly* smug) and sauntered off down some sideroad towards home, waving her hand above her head without looking back.

'She's pretty fit,' I said, after we'd walked on in silence for a while.

'Not bad,' he said, wiping his mouth thoughtfully with the back of his hand.

'Where'd you meet her?'

He looked over at me and smirked. 'You 'member when me and Aristotle and Vivek had only just gotten together, and that posh girl Claire' – another of his beautiful rich girls – 'asked us to play at her party?'

'Vivek said that was a total disaster?' I hadn't been there, thank Christ. I hadn't been involved with the band in its first few weeks.

'No – what? It was fucking brilliant, man! They were real ground-dwellers. I mean, we played them out of the fucking *house,* they all had to go and stand in the garden, it was excellent.' He paused, entertained by the memory, then added wonderingly, 'But *Lily*, man, she didn't just stay in the house, she stayed in the *room.* It was amazing. I bumped into her again a couple of weeks ago, and we kind of took it from there.'

'Have you got, like, a thing going with her then?'

'Depends what you mean by a *thing*,' he said doubtfully. 'I mean, she's cute but it's not like we're talking long term or anything, knowhatImean? You know me – I don't like to be tied down . . . I mean, what? Are you interested, man?'

'No – no. I just thought she seemed nice.' It was true, she was nice, but she didn't sort of get to me; she didn't give me that feeling where you felt you had to touch someone, even touch them just a little bit, making out as if you were picking a cat hair off their arm.

He strummed a stick along the railings, playing them like mighty strings. 'Are you gonna check with your dad about the bass today?'

I thought about Annie yesterday, weeping and showing me the fatness of her arms, as I slid with a false 'see-you-later' out of her door. 'I've got to go back to my mum's, really – she's been in a bit of a bad way lately. I'll check with him tomorrow.'

'You know we've got a crucial gig coming up in a couple of weeks,' said Matt anxiously. 'I mean it'd be really handy if you at least knew which way up to hold the fucking thing by then.'

'A gig?' I tried to sound cool, but my voice came out a bit strangled.

'Lily's mum's having a party.'

'Her *mum*? Are you *mad*?'

'Lily arranged it. She's going to be singing, so her mum'll love it anyway. It'll be a real laugh. And – get this – she's going to *pay* us.'

I thought another Matt-style success, i.e. total fuck-up, was definitely on the agenda, and decided then and there to get totally fucking bollocksed before we got up to play, so at least whatever happened next I wouldn't have to remember it for the rest of my life.

We caught a bus back to Kilburn and Matt walked me down the road to Annie's house, under the peeling planes. The light was fading; leaves kept falling like flat yellow snow, dissolving in puddles on the uneven pavement. Matt came in for a cup of tea.

In the kitchen, on the rusty sofa, Annie sat with a stupid grin on her round freckled face drinking red wine while Jason Peckham, his white silk-shirted arm around her, rested his head on her shoulder, blond curls brushing her black ones, his slender feet in clean Arsenal socks stretched out before him. Two bright red drops of wine had stained the left breast of his shirt. The split second I saw them – the split second they saw me – I turned to leave, but slammed straight into Matt who was still coming through the door and who, not getting it, kept on coming, making me edge back further into the room, nearly forcing me to step backwards over Peckham's blatantly shoeless feet. And then, when Matt saw the two of them for himself, he was so shocked he didn't know what to do and just stayed there staring, blushing pink, mouth open, blocking my exit. All I could do was walk round to the far side of the table and stand looking out over the sink. Crouched on the windowsill, staring back at me, was Harry's sodden cat. An upturned wheelbarrow rattled in a surge of rain, lying half-hidden in the sodden lawn which had raged uncut since the day my father left. Beyond the wall the tower blocks in the west blocked out the falling orange sun and threatened us with early night.

I heard Annie say, awkwardly, 'Hi, how are you?'

A long stunned silence. I thought, Just leave the room.

She said, made bold by booze, 'Do you know Jason? He lives on your estate.'

'Hi,' said Matt, at last, disbelievingly.

And then Peckham had the nerve to open his mouth in my house. 'You're at school with my cousin Gary, right?' He laughed, like this was a normal conversation. 'He's a right little wanker, innee?'

Another silence. Don't answer the arsehole, Matt – just leave the room.

'A *total* fucking wanker,' said Matt, with great depth of feeling.

Peckham said, not laughing anymore, 'Yeah, well, like they say, it takes all sorts.'

Annie jumped in quickly, placatingly (placating a *Peckham*), 'Matt's got a band – Ferdia sings with him some-times – isn't that great? I bet they're going to be famous.'

I knew Peckham was looking in my direction. The skin of my back rippled as if a bucketful of cold wet maggots was crawling under it. He said, 'Sweet. You want a gig at the Evil Eye?'

Are you *kidding?* That cheapo wierdo electric dance shit-hole? That seriously life-threateningly dangerous coke-sniff-ing *dump*? Matt – mate – hear me – *leave the room.*

But on Matt the word *gig* had a hypnotising effect. His voice came over all excited: 'The Evil Eye? A gig? How could you swing that one?'

Jason laughed again, lightly, self-consciously. 'I'm the sound engineer. It's a weird sort of place. But I could have a word if you like.'

'Sound engineer? Cool. Can you really sort us a gig?'

34

'Oh, that's kind of you,' said Annie, with sickly adoration. 'That's so nice.'

I ran back round the other side of the table, grabbed Matt's arm and dragged him out of the room. Annie turned away embarrassed as I was doing it, but Peckham just kept on looking straight at my very best friend, his silk-shirted arm still tight round my mum, acting like everything was totally OK, saying casually, 'No probs . . .' till I slammed the door on his blue-eyed stare as loudly and bitterly as I could.

'What the fuck are you doing?' I was practically choking. 'Do you realise who that *was*?'

'The Evil Eye, man . . . That's exactly the right kinda place for us to play. Everyone from my estate hangs about there . . . We could play tower-block rock for tower-block people . . .'

I couldn't understand what Matt was on about. I thought he'd always despised that shit estate where he was forced to live. I know I did. 'They're into garage, man – mindless shallow crap, remember?' I hissed, as I hustled him up the stairs. 'They ain't like you . . .'

'Wait till they hear us, mate, they're gonna love it. We could wake 'em up – inspire a few of them out of their stupors . . .'

'Fuck's sake!' We were in my room. 'Are you out of your *mind*?'

'I always wanted to play to my own kinda people . . .'

I sneered, 'Oh yeah, right, Jason Peckham's your kind of people?'

He winced, looking embarrassed, folding his lanky arms, perching his arse on the table where I occasionally did my school work. I stood contemptuously waiting for him to back down. Then he said, experimentally, 'Yeah but, if your mum thinks he's OK . . .'

Blood poured like burning petrol through my veins. I rushed at him and slammed him in the chest, knocking him off the table onto the bed, shouting and screaming, jumping on top of him, still crazily punching, 'Don't you dare fucking say that, don't you dare say that . . . I'll fucking kill you . . . you . . . you fucking . . .'

'Easy, easy,' he yelped, grabbing hold of my wrists as I battered him, pushing my fists away, hanging on tight. 'Easy, man . . . stop . . . stop . . . Chill the fuck out! Ferdia? Ferdie, man? It's me, Matt . . .' Gradually his words got through to me. I stopped trying to murder him; he let me go. I straightened up and moved away from him, coughing with the effort of violence and rubbing my face.

'Jesus,' Matt kept groaning behind me. 'Jesus.' Still breathing noisily, I glared at him. He was lying on his back on the bed, sweaty hair stuck up even more than usual, expression totally shocked and confused, a jelly-like string of snotty blood stretching from nose to open mouth. 'Jesus, man. Relax. What the fuck's got into you?' He sat up and wiped his lip with the back of his hand, studied the browning smear of his insides. 'Who d'you think I am – Gary?'

I snarled heavily, 'Fuck Gary.'

Matt raised his hands mockingly, like, Don't hit me again. 'Is the anger management course not working, man?'

But I was keeping it under control. 'Look,' I said, willing my blood to cool, 'I'm sorry, OK? It's just . . . fuck it.'

'It's alright, mate.' He waved away possibly embarrassing explanations. 'You don't need to tell me. Forget it. You know what to do? Write a fucking song about it. That's what I do.'

Chapter Four

I caught the bus down to St John's Wood for the second time that morning and stood for a while under the golden trees, scabby pigeons hustling my feet, autumn leaves collecting in my hair, before setting off walking (no more money for bus fares) back along the endless road to Kilburn. Three bus journeys and now this weary walk – up and down the Abbey Road, my long grey road of indecision.

All last night I'd sat in my room, trying not to hear what was going on downstairs, waiting for Reebok Man to leave the premises. Annie kept coming up, tapping on my door, asking was I all right, did I want anything to eat. I should've left her house straight away and slept at my dad's, but at the same time I didn't want to leave until Peckham had left; it was like I didn't want to back off; it was my home; I didn't want to leave him in sole possession. I woke up not knowing if he'd gone or stayed, and afraid to check. Then all I could think about was seeing my dad. I remembered what he'd said – his home was my home too. But as my bus left Kilburn in the early light, pulling out of the dirty red terraces into the clean white world of the rich, I could only think of how where I was going was really Abigail's flat and if they were there how she'd be lying legs cocked on her great white sofa, with my dad sat humbly on the floor, fixated on her like she made great television. That is, if they weren't busy trying for her trophy baby. So up and down the Abbey Road I went.

In fact, I could have gone on like that all day, but as I reached Kilburn again on foot, my dilemma was thrown into violent perspective and my mind made up for me: I was taking a short cut across the corner of the estate behind our house when Gary's personal pack of Peckham lesser-cousins plus god-knows-how-many prepubescent hangers-on came pouring out of one of the tower blocks and streamed like wildebeests towards me.

I turned and ran back to the Abbey Road, vaulted into someone's posh front garden and knelt in mud among their dying roses, hoping they hadn't seen which way I'd gone. Too late – Peckham's breaking voice rose high above the soprano yowling of his herd: 'Oi, Turdia! Come back 'ere or I'll rip ya!' (Like if I did he wouldn't.) Unclimbable fir trees lined the boundaries; the triple padlocked side gate bristled with broken glass and barbed wire (typical ground-dweller warding off the tower block hordes). Peckham's Classics churned yellow gravel as he thundered round the circular drive, and right in front of me two wet-nosed kids leapt the low wall into the roses, fists in the air.

'Oi, Gary! He's . . .' Jumping up I punched one out among the bushes and pushed the other so hard the wall caught the back of his knees and he cracked his head stunningly on the pavement. But then another forty-eight twelve-year-olds came panting up, squealing outrage and streaming snot, and Gary was thrusting his way through the waist-high thorns. No way out but to outrun the pack. I burst out and hit the pavement running, small sticky hands grabbing at my coat, shrill shrieks of 'Turdia!' in my ears, and raced as fast as I could back down towards St John's Wood, with Abigail's flat looking more and more to me like home sweet home. They gave up chasing with half a mile to go, but by then I was too tired to think about which place to go to and just carried on, staggering up the steps to her flat, feeling a stitch like a gash in my side, my lungs dried up and silver whirlpools in my eyes.

In my exhaustion, I couldn't find my key and pressed the bell instead. Abigail answered the door in a bright pink dress, and to my surprise looked delighted to see me, calling over her shoulder 'Here he is now!' and dragging me along behind her into her front room. A man was sat crossed-legged on the sofa, both arms resting along the back of it. He was small, shaven-headed to hide his baldness, lean but thuggish in a dodgy kind of a way. He wore a tartan shirt with sleeves rolled half way up his muscular forearms. His shabby suede jacket was folded over his knee. 'Dickie, this is Ferdia . . .'

'Ah yes, the tall, dark, *sultry* one,' murmured the short, bald, dodgy one in a fake East End accent, glancing up at me under his creased pink eyelids.

'Isn't he lovely?' She hadn't yet looked at me – face sweating, knees trembling, jeans muddy, tucking my hair behind my ears with shaking hands. She cried, 'We were dancing to one of my songs the other day, and I just thought – my god, he'd be so perfect for Dickie's boyband! All those twelve-year-old girls are going to scream themselves *sick!*'

'What happened to *you*?' asked the man, who'd been taking me in all this time, fishy eyes swimming up and down, looking slyly amused at the state of me.

Abigail turned to me, and her smile fell flat. She said, 'Oh.'

When I got my breath, I gasped, pulling off my coat, 'It's OK. I just ran a couple of miles, that's all.'

The man grinned. One of his canine teeth was dead. 'Pursued by screaming twelve-year-olds, one hopes?'

'Actually, yes.'

He gave me a slow calculating look, lingering to consider if I was serious. Then he thrust his baldy head in my direction, and softly urged, 'Come on, Ferdia – don't you *want* to be famous? Don't you *want* to make it to the top?' His yellow teeth hovered simpering near my crotch. I stepped sharply back a couple of paces. 'Don't you think you're hot? Abby says you are.'

'Too right I'm hot, mate – I just ran two fucking miles.'

'Oh, Ferdie,' simpered Abigail, kicking me lightly on the tip of my anklebone. 'You're such a *kidder*.' I don't know how she managed it, but I nearly crumpled to the floor with the pain. 'Honestly, Dickie, I swear, he's such fun, Harry and me love having him around.'

Dickie sank slowly back into the great white couch, and

nibbled a broad half-eaten nail. 'Why don't you sing something then?'

Abby was totally thrilled. Clearly she'd been seriously pimping me to her ex-manager – I guessed I was part of her scheme to ingratiate herself with him, just in case he ever did make good his threat to write that book about her. 'Yeah, why not?' She prodded me in the back with a sharp little finger. 'Sing something, Ferdie. Something good.'

Grinning down at her, I chanted the opening lines of Matt's recent number, '*Gonna cut my throat, jump off the Empire State! Gonna rip my head off, chuck it in a lake!*'

Dickie gave me a funny look, which I couldn't interpret. Abigail gave me a look which was pretty easy to interpret. 'No! Not one of Matt's . . .' She rolled up her eyes, perching her hands on her hips. 'Come on, be serious – I've told Dickie so much about you. And I *promised* your dad to encourage you . . . *I know*' – like she'd only just thought – 'why don't you sing "Sunshine Baby"?' She'd written it last month for the album she was working on and made me go through it with her a few times. 'You remember it, don't you?' I remembered it all right, no problem – like all her stuff, it was the sort of tune you couldn't get out of your head for months on end. 'Go on then, Ferdie. Come on. Be a darling boy.'

I was shattered from running, I didn't like her songs, I didn't like Dickie and I thought she had a real nerve, offering me up to him just to stay on his good side. *And*, she'd just nearly broken my ankle. Yet when I looked at her to say no, she was so full of puppy-bright eyes and hopeful smile, so sweetly fucking waggy-tailed desperate for me to play along, I just groaned. She took that as a yes, scampering about hunting for her demo tape, giggling and flirting and acting so babyish, so *Abby*-like, I just felt obliged to give it a go. It wasn't exactly Matt, of course – more *Sunshine baby, maybe maybe, will you be my sunshine baby* etc. just lob in a few *doo-be-doos*, some *hey-babies*, shake your boy-bits and hey, caramba! St Joseph's primary school *rocks*.

When I finished, he was beating his fingers in his trouser pockets, legs flopped apart at the knee. 'Nice voice,' he said, throatily, not to me but to Abigail.

She simpered, 'He's great, isn't he? Doesn't he look the part?'

For a moment I was seriously chuffed to be the centre of their breadhead attention, and did a twirl.

'He's a genuine pretty-boy, all right.'

Then I felt ashamed, and thought how right Matt was about my voice, my poppy commercial middle-of-the-road boyband voice. 'I'm not a singer, actually,' I said, resentfully. 'I'm a bass guitarist.'

Abigail laughed hysterically. She'd tried to teach me guitar once or twice. 'You are *not.*'

'I am. I'm in a band already.'

'Really?' asked Dickie, with bland uninterest.

Abby groaned, flopping down beside him, one slender leg chucked over the sofa's arm. 'He only means he hangs around with some weird ugly druggie kid, with sticky-up hair.' She'd had a downer on Matt since he came round to her flat and insisted on singing her his songs till he blew up her chronically expensive amp (he was more than a bit stoned and pissed at the time, and I think despite himself he wanted to impress her because she was so terribly cute and had been on Top of the Pops – he had this thing about beautiful rich girls which totally went against everything he said). She complained to Dickie, 'He played me some of his stuff. Terrible racket.'

I knew Matt wouldn't give a shit what shaven suits like Dickie or subtly cunning airheads like Abigail thought about his music, but I was still feeling kind of dirty and sordid after letting myself be paraded around like some tart. 'He's pretty fucking good, actually,' I said loudly. 'He's really . . . um . . . good.'

The bald man quirked his eyebrows at Abigail, intending to make her laugh. She sniggered behind her tiny hand.

'Come on, Ferdie, I know he's your best friend and all that, but Dickie's talking about a *serious* proposition here.'

I sniggered right back. 'Serious? That's serious? Music for tweeny-girls to wet their pants by?'

'Ferdia!'

'Whereas *your* band,' said Dickie rudely, sitting up and squaring his short thick legs, reverting in irritation to his original accent, dropping from East End into public school, 'is . . . oh, god, is it . . . don't tell me . . . could it be . . . *cutting edge*?'

'At least it's real,' I said, turning away from him towards the mirror. To my horror, my face looked hurt like a stupid kid's. 'We tell it like it is, OK? At least it's new.'

'Oh, of course. A garage band. How very' – he crooked his fingers round the word – '"*original*".'

'Not *garage*,' I said, scowling at him over the shoulder of my reflection. 'Not electric dance shit.'

He laughed, made a wanking gesture with his hand. 'I mean *punk*, for god's sake – *garage* bands – how old are you? – all those seventies suburban boys whacking away at their dicks in daddy's garage.'

'Not punk.' Now he'd said that, I finally got what Matt had meant. I cried, with a stab at his conviction: 'Tower block rock! Music in the sky for people who can't *afford* a fucking garage! Urban menace but up in the air!'

He said sarkily, 'I *see*. You mean a punk band several floors up.'

'Lovely,' said Abigail, with a pink delicate yawn.

Jumping up, he strolled over and stood to the left of me, examining his face in the mirror, one rough round cheek after the other. Then he held my eyes in the glass till I looked away, displaying his dead tooth ingratiatingly. 'Am I right?'

What did I know? I was only mouthing Matt's rant. I couldn't be arsed to argue the toss with some soulless bread-head who wanted to fake the next-best-thing. I thought about Tessa struggling on those endless stairs, bouncing gross baby Matt in his buggy up every step, desperate for a drink from the bottle in her bag. Stairway to hell, like Lily said. 'Nearer to hell than punk,' I muttered. But then I pictured myself standing on Matt's balcony, just him and me in the middle of the thin blue sky, far above the pigeons, little white clouds and delicate glass bubbles of helicopters floating by at our level, and thought: Closer to heaven.

Dickie was muttering softly, 'Tower-block rock.' And he repeated, like he was checking the sound of the words, 'Tower-block . . . rock.'

I felt a moment of panic for telling him, as if he was going to go off and use it for himself. 'That's just what *we* call it,' I said hastily. 'Just us.'

'Yeah, I'd kinda noticed it wasn't a household name,' he said, switching back to fake East End. He went ambling back to the sofa, picked up his brown suede jacket and paused with it over his arm. 'Be seeing you, Abby. Million and one things.' Abigail followed him to the front door, and I heard him say, 'He's a definite possible. Thanks for the tip.'

'No problem . . .' When she got back in the living room she did a forward somersault in the air without touching the carpet with her hands, pink dress flying up and showing her sugar-pink knickers, and jumped around screaming at the top of her girly voice, 'Yes! Yes! *Yes!* YES! *YES!*'

'Yes what?' I dead-panned.

She flung herself at me and covered my t-shirt with bright lipstick kisses. 'Ferdie! Darling! You beautiful boy! I always felt bad about ditching poor old Dickie, but he can't complain about me now, can he?' She slammed on her demo again, and started singing 'Sunshine Baby' in her high, slightly silly voice, catching me by the hands and whirling me around the room, pouting kisses at me from time to time until I stopped leaning backwards in stiff rejection and swayed along smiling with her, thinking she was mad and funny when everything was going just the way she wanted it. 'You're going to make loads of money and Dickie's going to forgive me everything!'

She'd done me one favour – she'd set me off thinking about

getting properly involved in a band. My dad was right, I had always fancied it. I circled my arms around her as we danced the room. 'So, do I, er, get anything in return for all this?'

Hugging me tightly in her gym-hardened arms, she purred, 'Just name your price, my handsome prince.'

'Bass guitar?' I chanced, chin on her smooth copper hair.

She giggled. 'I knew you hadn't even got one. What were you on about, making out you were serious about Matt's silly band?'

'No, honestly, I am. I'm going to play bass. I really want to start learning . . . please?'

'Certainly not – I'm going to make you a millionnaire, not a bad-hair drop-out.'

I pulled back slightly. 'Abby, I'm not . . .' I couldn't sell all dignity for a million pounds.

She squeezed me back to her and sighed, ear on my heart beat, spinning me round. 'You are, you are. You are, you are.'

'Abigail?' asked Harry coldly. 'What's going on?'

I knew straight away I'd stepped out of her embrace a touch too fast.

'*Harry!*' Abigail whizzed over to him, high-pitched about her plans for my debasement, and he nodded and patted her continuously as she squealed, but all the time he couldn't quite take his eyes off me; even when I turned my back on him, and sat on the sofa, I knew he was there still, gazing on.

'Dickie absolutely loved him, he's going to make an absolute fortune, I just know it. And you should've seen Ferdia,' she shrieked. 'He looked *so* sexy and beautiful, and he sounded absolutely fantastic. He'll be on every poster in every girl's bedroom in the world!' There was a pleased little pause while she expected his thoughts on her genius.

'Will he?' said Harry, at last.

She shrieked and cried excitedly, 'Yes! Dickie absolutely loved him!' And so on and so on, about her dodgy shaven mate.

I twisted round on the sofa a little so I could find him over my shoulder, and see what he was at. He was still staring at me with his big blue eyes, in his handsome clothes, black overcoat draped open, arm around his girlfriend, his face inert and calm. In the end he said, cutting straight across her flow, 'You're right, you know – Ferdia *has* grown up gorgeous. And he looks *so* like Annie.' It was the first time I'd heard him mention my mother in front of his new girlfriend. And he spoke her name with such tenderness, to show he was contemplating how great she was, how beautiful, how recently his. I got the bad impression it was meant as a serious punishment for Abby.

Abigail certainly looked slapped for a split second, until she said as if she was really intrigued, 'Oh, *does* he? That explains where he gets his lovely thick hair from – and he hasn't got your colouring at all either, has he, Harry? Does he get his height from her as well? Come on, Ferdia, let's go get you that bass guitar.'

I had to go with her, I couldn't pass up on the bass, even though it was a revenge attack on Harry. As I trailed the triumphant girl out of her flat, Harry walked past us across the front room, ripping off his coat, eyes immediately hooked to the mirror, struck dumb by miserable outrage, not saying or even indicating goodbye. It annoyed me, his insecure suspicions, his fears, his wish to keep his stranglehold on youth. Anyway, he needn't've worried about me and Abby – she was too much of a bitch for my liking, and pretty fucking shallow with it.

She drove me in her little pink Fiat to Kentish Town, where she spent hours trying to park as close to the shops as she could, finally darting with delight into an empty space where some hopeful character had painted No Parking in white on their garage gate. She bought me quite a flash bass and an amp as well; every assistant in the shop, male and female, trailed her around, but she was well used to being followed. I didn't really know how to test my strings, so she stood there in the music shop, one foot up on the amp, hard bronze leg bare under her pink hem, resting the bass on her knee, tuning it, then plucking out "Sunshine Baby" fast and easily. A few punters who were stood gawping at her instantly started humming along, like they thought they must know the song already, and she smirked at me, arching one neat copper-dyed brow.

On the way back she suddenly started making a lot of mileage out of Harry having let Annie's name out of its box in my presence. 'Has Annie got a boyfriend?' She'd never dared mention my mother to me before.

I had the guitar between my legs, and kept tapping vaguely at the strings with the plectrum. I thought my dad had probably told her Annie had a boyfriend – *So that's all right then*. But I wanted to deny it; I didn't even want to think about Jason, and I didn't want Abigail making out like Annie and Harry were now evens. Yet for the sake of my mother's dignity, I couldn't have Abigail imagining she was sitting around defeated by life, soaked in misery, on the trail of lung cancer, waiting for Harry to slope back home. 'Yeah, she's got a boyfriend.'

'Great!' She seemed surprised, like my dad hadn't told her. 'So, she's all right then?'

'Yep.'

'That's great.' She reached to flick off the music she'd had on, as if we were suddenly having this intimate conversation. 'What's he like? Is he nice? Is he rich? Is he her age or what?'

'No.'

'Why do women always go for older men?' she wondered, accelerating violently away from the lights until she hit traffic ten yards on and screeched to a halt. 'I suppose it's a father-figure thing, like me and Harry.'

I grinned. I tried tightening the strings, then loosened them quickly, afraid of snapping them. I wondered why Harry hadn't told her about Jason. I didn't want her running away with the idea my mum could only pick up some poor old decrepit bugger of ninety. I said, 'He's twenty-two.'

Her little lipsticked mouth popped wide open. She was twenty-four. '*What?* Jesus. Really? My god, and Harry said . . .' She stopped herself instantly. It wasn't a tease line, she really hadn't meant it to slip out.

Said what? That my mum couldn't get anyone but him? That she was a horrible old hag with fat arms who no one'd look twice at? What? 'Said what?'

'Nothing.'

'Said *what*?'

'Oh god, nothing, just . . .' she undertook a juggernaut at two miles an hour, while glancing at me anxiously, puzzled, on and off. She couldn't help herself in the end, because she was Abby and Abby didn't do discreet. 'You know, like, that she wasn't really *into*, like, that . . . sort of thing . . .'

Chapter Five

Talking of Harry and his unusual take on the world, by the time we arrived back he'd got over his bizarre hissy fit and was now very insistent on my making a living out of thrusting my groin at cherubic fainting children. 'But you'll make *money*,' he said by way of explanation, standing in the kitchen drinking red wine and smashing garlic with a hammer.

'Dickie's a great manager, he won't make you do anything sordid,' lied Abigail. 'He might not be big time but . . .'

'He took you to the big time!' cried Harry, shaking the hammer fondly at her. 'Well, part of the way . . .'

Abigail muttered sourly, pouring herself a glass, 'I got where I am today by standing on the shoulders of pygmies.'

I went off to strum my bass in my room, a tidy white rectangle with a bed in it. At the beginning, they'd bought me loads of things to put in it – gifts of guilt, like expensive computer games – but I always brought them back to my mum's. I knew Abby hated that, which was why I didn't just take my new bass straight round to Matt's. But after I'd spent several hours that evening and all next morning practising how to play 'I'm Forever Blowing Bubbles' she practically hurled the bass down the front steps herself (she was an Arsenal fan with a musical ear, of course) and voilà, problem solved.

Matt's living room was the best place for the band to practice, because if Tessa was in she was usually out of it, and his neighbours, poor bastards, never complained because they weren't supposed to be there – they were supposed to be living in Russia and were pretending to be some old nutter who'd died unnoticed over three years ago.

The only problem was Natasha, who drove us mad running about with her hands over her ears screaming, '*Stop that noise!*'

'Fuck *off*, Natasha.'

'Stop that noise! I can't hear the Tweenies!'

'Turn the telly up.'

'I can't hear them! *Stop that noise!*'

Matt said, 'Come here . . .' Which she did, suspiciously. He howled into the mike, *'Wanna wake the dead, but the little girl said . . .'* and stuck the mike under her nose just as she bellowed furiously *'Stop that noise!'* so loud she got feedback, jumped out of her own skin and burst into tears. After she'd calmed down a bit, Matt tried again, *'Wanna fuck with your heads, but the little girl said . . .'* and this time she shouted really expertly into the mike *'Stop that noise!'* and thought it was a great laugh, and from then on we couldn't get rid of her – she wanted to be a permanent fixture.

I was really enjoying my shiny brand new bass. I spent the first half hour trying to jump off Matt's bed and play riffs at the same time, but it was fucking difficult. To be honest, I had to stand completely still before I could play shit.

Matt was a bit troubled by doing Lily's mum's party, not because he realised we were going to ruin it, but because he thought it might classify as selling out – Sisi's friends were serious ground-dwellers. He was very gracious about my own low-level life-style, saying I spent enough time at his place to qualify as a true tower-block rocker. 'Anyway,' he said, 'you've got the soul of a sky-high man.'

'Cheers, Matt.'

We worked on some new stuff, aimed at keeping the ground-dwellers at the party from feeling too smug. *'Hey, you on the ground, watch out for the hungry poor! Gonna squash you flat when we jump from the twentieth floor!'* And Matt added, *'Gonna jump to my death, take my very last breath, mid-air . . .'*, bouncing dangerously high out on to the balcony and back again.

Lily turned up for the practice wearing some kind of Camden Lock sixties dress with a fringe made of beads, and an old leather flying jacket. Natasha was completely bowled over by her and insisted on performing 'Stop that Noise' immediately. Lily thought it was absolutely brilliant, petal-shaped eyes going bright black in her enthusiasm.

'We've *got* to do that at the party,' she said. 'You've got to *come*.'

Natasha threw her little pink arms round her and kissed the jacket devotedly.

Matt said quickly, 'No. It'll, like, go on all night, it's way past her bedtime.'

'I haven't got a bedtime,' countered Natasha, giving him a real evil look.

'No. *No*. I'll have to look *after* you . . .'

'You *never* . . .'

'Bring your mum,' said Lily.

Matt blurted out, trying not to look too horrified, 'NO – I mean, no, she won't know anyone there.' I didn't look at Matt, but I knew what his mental picture was all right – Tessa seeing how fast she could put away free booze, slugging wine by the neck in a mad headlong race against unconsciousness.

Lily said, innocently, 'She can keep an eye on Nat and meet some nice people at the same time.'

Matt said, 'Hmmm . . .' It was kind of awkward to explain.

'Great, I'll tell mum she's coming – she'll be really pleased,' said Lily.

In Matt's red silence, I felt an urge to sing his latest song, and burst out, '*Hush, baby, hush, we're so fucking high; me on my valium, you in the sky*,' then randomly whacked the strings of my bass, which by chance gave the whole thing a suitably fucked-up ending, as of people falling down on their faces among broken bottles.

'Fuck's sake, don't smash it before you can play a single note,' complained Matt.

Lily said, a lot more politely, turning out to be a really nice girl, 'Why don't you let Ferdia sing instead of playing? His voice is really good.'

'We don't need a fucking boy-babe pop singer – we need a fucking bass guitarist,' snapped Matt, temperamentally.

'Couldn't he sing along with you as well?'

'Lily,' he said, stressing most of his words, still pissed at the implication he wasn't the greatest singer around, 'Ferdia can't possibly sing and play guitar at the same time. He can't even breathe and play guitar at the same time. He can't even fucking *blink* and . . .'

I was feeling seriously hurt. 'You want me to play this thing or not? And I'm not a fucking boy-babe singer – I just got touted a job in a fucking boyband and I turned it down, OK? Because I want to play with *this* band. So don't have a fucking go at me!'

'You got offered a *what*?' asked Matt, astonished.

'Hey, guys, hi Natasha,' drawled Aristotle, walking in wearing a pair of black flares frayed and muddy from dragging along the ground. 'You wanna give me a hand with the drums? My mum's waiting in the car downstairs, and she's scared shitless someone's gonna mug her.' As we followed him out of the the flat, he added casually, 'The lift's out, so it's gonna take a few trips.' The lift wasn't out, it was just his incredibly bad idea of a joke.

As we crashed dangerously from floor to floor, Matt asked again, 'You got offered a job in a *boy*band? Jesus Christ. How come?'

I filled them in on the story, and Lily acted really impressed that I'd gone for the bass guitar instead. 'That's, like, really principled, you know.'

'You really told him about the tower-block rock thing?' asked Matt, with a hint of heavily suppressed interest.

'Like I said, he's a complete dickhead. Abigail ditched him the minute she started making any serious money.'

Aristotle said meditatively, 'You know, when I was a little kid I used to think I'd make a great job of being the tall, dark, sultry one, but now I'm older and, like, developed into this hot sexual being, I've realised you have to be a real dickless pretty-boy to qualify for being in a boyband. Zero sex appeal and that. No offence, Ferdia.'

'None taken.'

When we got to the car outside the block, we had to shoo away the usual annoying pack of five-year-olds who were swarming all over it, testing its windscreen wipers and the nuts on its wheels – acting like a bunch of monkeys in a game park. Aristotle's mum was shaking, big eyes swollen with tears – Aristotle sat in the car with her and held her hand till she calmed down enough to let him stay with us. She was a tall Ethiopian woman who'd married the shortest fattest Greek guy you ever saw, with a chain of barber shops and a nice house – like all ground-dwellers, she was scared out of her wits by the unexpected wildlife of the concrete jungle.

Aristotle's drums took up most of the small living room floor. Amazingly, Natasha didn't complain, even though it ruined any chance of her even watching her Tweenie video, let alone hearing it. But she fancied herself as a pop diva now, a sort of tower-block Spice Girl, and she was besotted with Lily who seemed to her like the real thing. She decided to be our audience, sitting on the floor with her hands clamped expectantly over her ears. Lily reopened the balcony doors, which we'd closed against the cold, and sighed, 'It's so fucking beautiful up here, Matt, I'm never going down again.' She'd the soul of a sky-high woman. It was late afternoon and the city was dark sad shadow, but from our height the day had not gone down. We could see the whole wide world, gold-rimmed; the one white star was at our fingertips; beneath our feet, home-coming starlings roared in screaming waves.

'You're right,' said Matt. 'It's only up here it feels really pure. Up here, you know, close to the music gods. Sometimes I think going down there is like taking a journey into hell.'

'Yeah, man, you're so right,' remarked Aristotle, winking one brown eye at me and cheerfully jabbing his temple with his finger.

We finally settled down to some serious practice, blasting the passing planes out of the sky through the open balcony doors. Lily was a great aquisition. She laid a sort of smooth bright up-in-the-air black-girl hip-hop over Matt's hoarse white-thug riot-chant, Aristotle's totally self-centred head-in-the-clouds drumming, and my laborious yet tuneless plink-plonking, giving the whole thing a sort of 'what-a-mess' chaotic unity, as Matt described it later, with cautious satisfaction.

Going on for midnight, Matt's balcony now in darkness under the moon, Lily walked me home. I'd assumed she was going to stay over with Matt, but after we'd passed a spliff around he'd gone lurching off into his bedroom alone, muttering about his bloody music gods. Aristotle decided to kip on the sofa, rather than land his mum in another scary situation. Lily phoned a cab as we scurried nervously off the estate, then relaxed and started chatting about music, Matt and other stuff that came into her head. 'Don't be upset about what Aristotle said, about sex appeal,' she reassured me kindly. 'You're, like, really really attractive.'

'Don't worry about that – that's just Stotle being Stotle. You've got two choices – live with it or kill him.' I borrowed her mobile to phone home.

My mum when she answered sounded bored and miserable. She said, 'Ferdia, I'm so lonely without you.' I thought, Peckham's gone again – good. When Lily followed me into the house, Annie tried to smile bravely and offered us pizza, but there was none left in the freezer. 'Nothing ever goes right for me anymore,' said Annie, like someone'd just announced the start of World War Three, round face a circle of gloom, black curls drooping.

'No, really, I've got a cab coming any minute,' said Lily. Then she got talking really enthusiastically about Sisi's party, and how we were playing a gig, 'Ferdie's fantastic, Annie!' (How did she make that out?) 'You've got to come!' (Fantastic at what?).

And Annie, Lily's upbeat happiness gradually penetrating her sulky sadness, took a good look at her and recognised her as Sisi and Vin's daughter. 'Oh – you're *that* Lily – Jesus, I haven't seen you for – what? two years? – and you've got so beautiful and grown up – how *are* Vin and Sisi? Is Sisi still getting good parts?'

The doorbell rang, and I went to answer it, and it was Lily's cab, and then it went again, and I thought she'd forgotten something, but this time it was Jason, shivering slightly with no coat, holding a couple of beautiful hungry-smelling pizzas in his arms. 'All right?' he said, staying put outside on the step. His eyes shone strongly in the light behind me. He was two or three inches shorter than me, in dark blue shirt and faded jeans. 'Is Annie in?'

Recovering from the shock, I slammed into the front room and switched on the television. Before I could track down the remote to blast up the protective sound, I heard her call 'Who was that?' and him say 'Delivery boy, madam . . .' and then she degenerated into joy. Oh yes, he knew how to make her happy all right. I fell back onto the sofa, nearly sitting on the bloody cat which in revenge began dismantling a cushion.

A few minutes later, the door opened and I heard him come in, taking only two steps into the room. Tantalisingly, the pizza came with him. 'All right?' he repeated. 'Annie says, do you want something to eat?'

I fixed on the adverts and tried to keep my anger silent. I didn't want to waste my energy on scum.

After a while, he said, 'Anyway, I need to say something to you about my cousin Gary.'

I sighed and started channel-surfing, an unimpressive-looking occupation when you haven't got cable.

He said slowly, 'Annie told me what he's been up to. He's a wanker and he was right out of order, and I'm really sorry he got to know about Annie and me. Look, trust me, he didn't get it from me, right?'

I couldn't help glancing over at him for a split second, but with my eyes only, not moving my head. He'd one hand still on the handle of the door, and in the other a plate with a couple of pizza slices on it. I wanted to say, What d'you mean *hear* about it like it was by fucking accident, you arsehole? And what do you mean, Annie and *me?* But I couldn't bring myself to speak to him.

'Like, I didn't tell *him*,' he insisted, knowing exactly what I meant. 'Look, I know, all right, I kind of mentioned it to my sister, that's all, and I'm really gutted I did now because I thought she'd keep her mouth shut and you know girls, she went and mouthed off to her best mate . . .' He stopped and mused almost dreamily, ' Fuck me . . . that girl's got a bigger mouth than the Dartford Tunnel . . .', then picked up again, saying loudly, 'Ferdia, I'm sorry, look, the guy's a muppet – what can I say? I'm going to kick his arse for him, right? I'm gonna kick *all* their arses, right?' He hung around. 'Right?' Then he came forward, balanced the pizza on top of the telly, and went out closing the door carefully, like I'd fallen asleep.

Fantastic. The whole world knows. The whole fucking world knows my mum is . . . with a Peckham.

All I needed in the morning was to run straight into Gary, pissed as hell for getting his arse kicked and looking for revenge. On the plus side, I didn't. On the down side, the first person I met as I came through the school doors was the monstrous ginger-haired arsehole I'd called a wanker last Thursday. I tried sliding past him innocently, but it was pretty obvious he remembered me, especially after he'd grabbed me by the coat, slammed me up against the wall and screamed at full pitch in my face, 'Hey, Ferdia, I'm gonna murder yer!' – a positively Matt-style lyric which instantly stuck in my head like a finger in the eye.

As I was waiting for Fatboy to stop infecting me with his spit and just settle down to breaking my arms, I heard Gary in the distance running and shouting, 'Oi! Fatboy! Wait for me!' Great.

Fatboy was over the moon. 'Yeah, and my mate here's got something to say to you as well, you stuck-up shithead . . .'

'Don't touch him!' yelled Gary.

Fatboy was fucking confused. He said, not letting go of my coat, 'He's not touching me, Gazza, I'm touching him.'

'Don't fuckin' touch him then!'

'What? You want me to hold him for yer?'

'No – just fuck off and let him alone.' He was panting, almost panicky, but then pulled himself together, pale-faced, open-eyed, smoothing down his number-one cut, straightening his pale purple sleeves. 'You all right?' he said to me, looking me over for damage. All I could do was stare at him, propped up with my back against the wall where Fatboy had reluctantly set me down. 'You all right?'

I said, 'Yeah . . .'

'Sweet.' He was genuinely relieved. He said to Fatboy, who towered over him, 'You touch him again and I'll kick your fuckin'ead in, get me?'

Fatboy didn't get it; he just hung there speechless.

'D'y'get me?'

'Er . . . yeah.'

Gary turned back to me and acted like he wanted to say something. In the end he stuck his hand in his breast pocket, pulled out a packet of John Players, and offered me a fag. I took it just to smooth the moment. 'So,' he said. 'You all right?'

'Yeah . . . a bit . . . but . . . fine, yeah.'

'Listen, mate,' he said, lighting my fag, 'anyone like Fatboy here give you any trouble in future, any trouble *at all*, right, you just say you're Gary Peckham's best fucking friend, right? *Right?*'

'Right,' I said. 'Uh . . . thanks.'

'No problem.' He inhaled, ripped the fag out of his mouth while he coughed and spat gunge into the corner by the door, then stuck the fag back in and grinned. 'Hey, don't thank me, thank Jason – if the man says you're my best fuckin' mate, that's the way it's gonna be. Ain't nobody gonna touch you now. Right, Fatboy?' And off he went.

Frozen, me and Fatboy stared at one another, until suddenly he lowered his tiny eyes and muttered into his mighty chest, 'Sorry about that, mate – you all right?'

'Fine.'

'Be seeing you then.' He shuffled away, shaking his head like he'd been hit over it.

Briefly, I wanted to do a war dance, but almost at the same time I thought, stunned, staring at the cigarette pinched between my fingers: This is complete and utter shit – what the fuck is happening to me? This is the direct result of my dad deserting us – one minute everything's normal, and the next minute some future serial-killer is my new best friend. Then Matt and Aristotle came smashing through the swing doors, and I couldn't help boasting to them, 'Hey, watch this . . .', and yelling after Fatboy, 'Oi! Fatboy! Fuck off, you fat ginger cunt!', and while my fellow musicians skidded to a shocked speechless halt, all Fatboy did was glance back at me with grim hatred and walk on.

Every time they tried to get the real story out of me, I just bugged the hell out of them by saying in a serious totally-naive-parent type of voice, 'Stand up to a bully and you'll find he's a coward at heart.'

Chapter Six

Lily's mum's party thundered towards us at unbelievable speed, like we were a gang of rabbits crossing a motorway. The more I practised, the more I found out I couldn't actually play, not unless we were going nice and slow – like, I could manage 'Babes in the Air', because it had a nice chilled beat. But when we got onto the other stuff like 'Wanna Rip Somebody's Head Off' or 'Watch Out for the Hungry Poor', I was pretty shit. I'm not saying it wasn't a good laugh, and it was a great way of getting life off your chest; you didn't have to talk stuff through, all you had to do was make up a few words and scream them out at the top of your voice, like in honour of the party I came up with *'Your life is on the skids, when you're sleeping with kids'* ; and Lily added *'One pound of flesh and your life is a mess'* because apparently her mum was not very secretly convinced that Vin had deserted her because she was one whole pound over her ideal weight. Matt was right – write a song about it.

Annie was looking forward to the party – she was hoping the place would be full of handy luvvie contacts, and she'd wangle herself a couple of auditions. She squeezed on a long green velvet dress and stood in front of the wardrobe mirror making herself up repeatedly and brushing out her hundreds of black curls until they fizzed and crackled under the plastic bristles. 'Have I lost weight?' she kept on asking, unhappily poking dents in her lightly freckled arms. 'Do you think I'm showing too much breast? I'm sure this dress has shrunk. Do you think I've lost weight? Oh god, look at the state of me. I'm an *elephant.*'

'You look OK to me.'

She kicked away the cat, which was trying to rip holes in

the velvet dress, and commented irritatingly, 'Men.'

Yet she did look OK to me; I didn't know why she couldn't just believe me. Anyway, I was having difficulty concentrating on what she wanted me to say, because there was a seriously major problem about the party that I'd only found out about a week before, and I'd been kind of hoping would go away without me having to deal with it. It hadn't. It was a much worse problem than being shit at bass guitar. 'Mum,' I said.

'What now?' She was still a bit pissed off.

'You know tonight?'

'Hmmm?' She was doing bright red lipstick, rubbing her wide full lips over each other.

'Dad's coming. With Ab . . . *her*.'

She reached so fast for the gin and tonic perched on the shelf that she knocked it into the sink, the glass smashed, and she started screaming and shouting, 'Typical! That's typical! That's bloody fucking typical!' – I didn't know whether about Harry or about the crappy fucking behaviour of gin glasses when you most needed them. I did the smart thing and literally ran to get her another drink. When I came back her hand was bleeding from picking the broken glass out of the sink; she was just standing there looking lost, letting the blood drip off the ends of her soft plump fingers down the drain. I wrapped her hand up in bog roll and gave her her gin. 'I can't believe you only just told me,' she said, dazed sounding. 'I can't *believe* it.'

'I only found out today – Lily only just told me,' I said. 'Honestly.'

'How?' Her voice got higher and more panicky. '*Why?*'

'Oh god, you know – Lily says her mum met him in the street and she asked him was he coming with you, and she didn't even know you were split up, that's what the problem was, she wouldn't've asked him otherwise, I swear.'

'But didn't Lily know – didn't she tell her? Don't kids today ever *talk* to their parents?'

59

'Maybe she thought it'd upset her, what with her dad having left them and all.'

'Vin left Sisi? For Christ's sake . . . Ferdia, ring your dad now and tell him I'll be at the party, then he'll know not to come.'

'Right.'

'Now! *Quickly*, before he leaves the house.'

The thing was, I'd already mentioned it to him, and he'd refused to back down. He said he'd asked could he bring his girlfriend and Sisi'd said, Fine, so he said she was obviously fine with it. (Lily said, no, it wasn't like that, it was the shock of the moment.) Harry said it was time everyone started behaving like adults – Annie had a new boyfriend now, so she could hardly go around pretending to be upset about him anymore, and that was good because we could all be friends, which would be better for me as well.

'*Quickly!*'

'Why are you bringing this up again?' complained Harry, making out he couldn't understand why there was a problem in the first place. 'I thought we'd talked about this.'

'I just think it'll be kind of awkward.'

He laughed, actually hurt-sounding. 'I thought kids were always trying to get their parents back together, like engineering accidental meetings and stuff, isn't that the idea?'

Obviously I was keen for them to get back together. Who wouldn't be? 'I just think it'll be kind of difficult, with Abigail there.'

'Come on, Ferdie – Annie's going to be turning up with some twelve-year-old boy in tow – what's the issue here?'

Because I didn't answer right away, he said, now a bit smug instead of pissed off, 'Well, I *assume* he's going to be there.'

He was waiting for me now to say Peckham wasn't coming. He wasn't. The reason he wasn't was because I'd made it pretty damn clear to Annie that it was him or me at the party, non-negotiable, and I was in the band. I didn't want Harry feeling glad or sympathetic that my mum hadn't got a date. 'I think that'll be kind of difficult too,' I said. 'I mean, how'll *you* feel about it?'

He took time out. 'Great,' he said at last, but I think he meant not. 'I'll see you there then. Can't wait to hear you play.' Sometimes he had this annoying habit of *'confronting the issue'*, i.e. making life fucking difficult for everyone.

'That's it,' said my mum. 'I'm calling Jason.'

'Oh god, no, can't we just *none* of us go?'

'If you think I'm having that smug bastard . . . Anyway, you've got to go – you're in the band.'

'No, I don't. They play better without me. He's not smug.'

'*Please*, Ferdia.'

'Mum, I just . . .'

'*Please* . . .'

'Jesus *Christ*.'

The place was choking with true ground-dwellers – actor types, sixties clothes and red booze. Me and Matt and Lily floated round the room, drinking wine like it was shandy and listening to all those egos with their bored expressions, showering each other with loud trivial facts about their low-level thespian careers. Sisi stood swaying like a newly planted tree, six foot of super-slim super-cool, her Kenyan body wrapped up head to toe in red, green, black. She kept telling everyone this party was a divorce celebration party, her personal inde pendence day (but she'd only one piece of sushi on her plate – she was trying to starve herself more beautiful). My dad came in and looked around him tensely, his fingers dug into Abigail's arm (her eyes glazing over automatically at the sight of such unimportant little people) and, seeing me, came over and wanted to know, 'Your mother not here yet?'

'Not yet.'

'*Ferdia!*' I hadn't noticed him, but Dickie was nodding his shaven head at me from the kitchen doorway. Abby flicked a forced smile in his direction.

'Isn't she coming?' asked Harry, not noticing.

'Maybe.' I drained my glass.

'Don't drink too much before you're on, Ferdie,' he said.

I was trying hard to get out of my tree before the big event, but I must've been pumped, because things had barely begun to blur around the edges.

'Ferdia . . .' It was Dickie again, his bitten fingers patting my upper arm. 'Abigail . . . Harry . . .'

Abigail nodded sweetly but kept scanning the party, trying to find someone worth talking to in the sea of small-time faces bobbing round her. Harry shook Dickie slavishly by the hand. 'So, I hear you're going to make my son a star?'

'Abby told me Ferdia's band was playing tonight,' said Dickie, twiddling his unshaven eyebrows at me.

'Oh that,' said Harry knowingly, laughing his handsome blond head off.

'It's a very good band,' said a loud firm voice as I was turning away in irritation. Standing behind us was the woman who'd stopped Gary Peckham killing me in the school corridor. I'd only seen her at a distance since – our usual English teacher had crawled nervously back in again, determined to last the course, and this one must have returned to her own class. She was wearing a red dress, tight and short, black tights and red very high-heeled shoes.

I must've been a bit pissed after all, because I cried without hesitation, 'Hey, great to see you! What're you doing here?'

'You know my son? I'm Ferdia's father,' interrupted Harry, moving in fast beside her, looking slightly up at her long pale profile.

'Hello there.' But she said to me over his head, 'I've come to see you.' Her long blonde hair was tied up in a knot, twisted round in a thin silver scarf, the ends of which touched one shoulder.

'Me? Why?' I was completely thrown.

'What, you know Ferdia?' repeated Harry, rising on his toes.

'I said I'd come to your next gig, didn't I?' she said, again just to me. She started slipping away, turning her head to smile a little smile at me along her red-strapped shoulder, winking one blue-green eye.

Stunned, I followed her, leaving Harry and Dickie standing together, both following her too, but only with their slavering expressions. 'But how did you . . .?'

Still drifting through the clinking crowd, she went into this long, slow, husky, slightly unnecessary explanation, about having known Sisi forever, and how they'd been talking about . . . this and that, and my name had come up (she didn't say *why* exactly) and so on until Sisi told her a boy called Ferdia was in her daughter's band which was playing at her party. 'I'd've been here anyway,' she said. 'I didn't really need to say I'd come to see you, I was just trying to surprise you.'

'No, that's fine,' I said, still following her doggedly. 'I like surprises. Surprises are good.'

Then she said, pausing, so I clumsily bumped shoulders with her, 'That sounds wrong. Of course I *do* want to see you play.'

I winced. 'I'm pretty shit, really.'

'Oh, I'm sure you're not,' she said, putting her red-lip-sticked mouth close to my ear so I could feel her breath and hear her clearly. 'I bet you're great.'

My mum shouted, 'Hey, Ferdia!', waving warmly. Peckham, white shirt, black trousers, black shoes, was pressed up against her by the thickening crowd, hard blue stare jumping from face to face. My dad, yet unseen, was glaring bug-eyed at him across the room.

I didn't need this shit. I said to the woman, 'Come into the kitchen.' I took her by the hand to pull her sideways through the boasting people. She closed her fingers firmly round my own, which pleased me.

On the other side of the kitchen was another big room with most of the furniture cleared out of it for dancing. I was interested to catch sight of Aristotle in there, setting up his drum kit with Matt's help. Lily came up and put her arms around me from behind and hung on me drunkenly while I tried to pour out two drinks, red wine splashing all over the table. 'Where'd you get to?' she mumbled. 'We can't start without you. We're first on.'

'Just getting a drink, all right?' She slid off and into the other room.

The woman watched her go with a curious expression. 'Sisi's daughter's very pretty, isn't she?'

'Yeah – hey, anyway, what's your name?'

She took her drink and looked at me carefully over it, taking a sip which stained the centre of her top lip before she answered, 'Cassandra.'

I smiled at her enthusiastically. 'Yeah? That's great.'

She laughed, tilting back her head. I'd forgotten the hairline gap between her white front teeth. 'Well, Ferdia, I'm glad you approve. I like your name too.' One streak of blonde hair had slid out of the silver scarf and clung to the side of her mouth, fluttering feather-like with her breath; she caught it and tucked it loosely behind her ear.

In her heels she was taller than me. I thought, with that hair and those legs, she could be a model. 'Nice scarf,' I added, taking a swig from my cheap plastic glass.

'I'm glad you like it.' Then she asked, kind of jokingly, 'How about the dress?'

'Very sexy.' Which was the moment I realised the drink must've finally numbed my brain and that I was now definitely pissed enough to get up and play in front of a crowd. I hurried across the kitchen and stuck my head into the other room. 'Hey, Matt man! Are we on yet?'

'Whenever.'

I went to fetch my guitar. Sisi followed me back to the room and said anxiously, 'Just two or three songs, Lily, that's all, before the main band comes on, OK?'

'"Babes in the Air",' I said to Matt. It was the only one I'd any chance of keeping up with.

'No, it's too slow, it's fucking boring,' he said. After Sisi left, and Lily went into the kitchen for another drink, he complained, 'Two or three songs only? I can't believe we're just the support band. Who's she got coming on after us – the Stone fucking Roses comeback special?'

I thought Sisi'd made a pretty smart move, actually. '*Please*, Matt, the slow one.'

Aristotle said, rattling his kit airily, 'Come on, or Ferdia'll show us up before we even get started.'

'This lot don't deserve the best of us, anyway,' said Matt moodily, as Lily returned looking dangerously unsteady.

I took the mike and shouted to the empty room, 'All right then, you wonderful people! Let's get ready for . . .' – and then realised I didn't know what the band was actually called this week. Cassandra leaned lankily in the doorway and Dickie had suddenly appeared, forcing his way past the tumultuous drinks table, poking his bald white head around her shoulder, and I couldn't help myself: 'Get ready for . . . *Boybits!*'

Matt said, '*What?* But we're called . . .'

Lily screeched, 'That's *disgusting*.'

Aristotle nodded, 'Wicked! Much better than Coked-up Badgers . . .'

Cassandra was laughing, but as far as I could make out Dickie's expression didn't even flicker, so Abigail must've just got the name wrong anyway, which I'd kind of suspected she might've.

Aristotle crashed into 'Babes in the Air', and off we went. There wasn't a crowd exactly, but Cassandra kindly tapped her foot, and Dickie stood expressionless with his hands in his pockets, and the occasional alarmed-looking face checked round the door. It was great being pissed – even if I wasn't playing the right notes, it felt like I was; it was kind of nice nobody was watching; I even glanced up from my guitar a couple of times, and risked bopping around a bit; I hardly panicked when Matt launched straight into 'Watch Out for the Hungry Poor'. Some ground-dwelling bastard closed the kitchen door on us at that point but Cassandra calmly forced it open, and propped her long thin body firmly against it. Jason appeared in the centre of the doorway, arms folded, hips tilted, head cocked, fag in mouth. I hardly cared.

Natasha came scampering across the floor as we were ending the second song. I'd completely forgotten Tessa was bringing her. She grabbed the mike off Matt and shrieked into it, *'Stop that noise!'*, bringing a round of applause from the kitchen, which was considerably less packed than it had been, despite the lure of the drinks table.

So Matt sang, *'Gonna wake the dead, but the little girl said . . .'*
' . . . Stop that noise!'

Predictably, we then developed cute factor, and eight or nine people actually came in to watch, pushing past Jason, who faded away, and when we stopped they *applauded,* which made the whole gig seem one hell of a lot more successful, and also made it much less embarrassing for us to hand over to Sisi's star attraction, a bunch of greasy beards who only had to bash out the first bar of 'House of the Rising Sun' before the whole room filled up with relieved-looking bad dancers.

On my way back into the kitchen, Cassandra clapped her long thin hands and cried, 'Great, you were great!', and Dickie grabbed my elbow and murmured into my ear, 'Stick to singing, that's my advice,' while pushing something into the back pocket of my jeans. It bugged me, him taking the piss, so I ignored him, even though I was kind of interested to know what he'd slipped me. I was thinking about nipping up to the bog to check it out, but when I got into the front room I saw a sight so bizarre that Dickie went completely out of my head. Harry was relaxing on the sofa, chatting away to my mum, his head slightly inclined towards her, his fingers stroking the green velvet dress where it stretched tightly round her thigh. Annie's soft freckled face was pink with pleasure – she was smiling vaguely into her wine, as if she was admiring her reflection in it. Confused, I went out into the hall and found Abigail with her face pressed to the coats, in tears.

I nearly turned and left her to it, but she was crying so hard I ended up saying, 'Abby?'

'Ferdie!' and she threw herself sobbing into my arms. Then she pushed me away and said miserably, 'I suppose you're happy now – *look* at your dad, all over that fucking woman.'

I answered, feeling like a bad stand-up, 'That's not a woman, you moron, that's my mum.'

'I know!' she wailed, like I was missing the point. 'What's he *doing* with her? He's trying to get back with her, that's what! What am I going to *do*?'

It was pretty weird, her complaining about that to me. I wondered if she was right, and felt both surprised and glad. But at the same time it was odd to see hard little Abby cry; so much so, I found myself comforting her. 'They're just talking, it doesn't mean anything . . .'

But she wouldn't stop crying, screwing up her sad wet face. 'It does! He loves her more than he loves me!'

'No, he doesn't . . .' Oh god, this was fucking ridiculous.

'He *does*!' she blubbed and hiccuped. 'He never really wanted to leave her in the first place! Do you know how long it took him to do it? Two whole bloody years! There was me waiting like an idiot all that time – *me*! waiting for *him*! – and now look at him! He's all over her!'

My head rang faintly with her revelation. Two years? 'Didn't he only just meet you when . . .?' Just one poxy month before he went running off with her?

She cried, mopping her cheeks with somebody's grey fake fur, 'D'you know, the bastard nearly wouldn't come and see me on Top of the Pops, in case anyone realised about us? Cowardly bastard. He'd never have left her at all, if our picture hadn't made it into the papers.'

Two years? And he'd always claimed it was a rush decision, his long-drawn-out departure from my home. I couldn't believe what Abigail was telling me. Two whole years while he *made up his fucking mind*? Two whole fucking years spent working out was his family worth staying for, while I drifted around thinking it was enough just to watch football with him on the telly or make stupid little bonfires in the autumn, or grunt into my cornflakes when I saw him in the morning. Why hadn't that calculating bastard warned me, if all that time I was actually *failing the test*? I could've made an effort. I could've learned to juggle. I can be a laugh. I could've told a few fucking jokes.

The urge to throttle him with my bare hands swept me back powerless into the party. I stormed with difficulty through the jammed-together people, knocking big red splashes of wine out their glasses, getting a fag burn in my shirt, but when I reached the sofa several minutes later, Harry had shifted even closer to Annie, talking and laughing in her ear while she sat and smiled blearily at her lap. I couldn't think how to break it up, and opted to stand there glaring, being ignored. Jason popped up beside me, caught my eye and jerked his head slightly in my parents' direction, eyebrows raised, like, What's going on here, mate? I moved away sharpish. As if I would know, or tell him if I did. Looking back as I pushed across the room, I saw him sit down on Annie's other side, pick up her spare, non-drinking hand, and sandwich it tightly in his lap. She looked pleased to see him, making a kissy shape with her mouth.

Two years! The noise and smoke was like an accident; I grabbed a passing glass and drank it down, then thought nauseously that I needed more and waded shoulder-deep into the kitchen. Cassandra, looking like a long streak of lipstick, was chatting to Dickie of all people. I realised I was singing to myself: 'Wanna kill somebody, yes I really do . . . Wanna chop them up and flush them down the loo-oo-oo-oo-oo.' I found Matt. 'All right?' I asked him loudly. 'How d'you think it went?'

'Listen to those wankers,' he scorned, pointing into the gig room. 'They're playing fucking Rolling Stones covers. How sad can you get?' I could just make out, across the wild tossing tide of drunks, the band's lead singer strutting his stuff as a short-arsed fat-bellied bushy-bearded Jagger. Behind Matt, his mum was working her way methodically along the drinks table. A couple of blokes were trying to chat her up because she looked so pretty and skinny in jeans and a yellow shirt, but Tessa was barely bothering to acknowledge them. Matt's little sister was stood between the table and the fridge, eating crisps with an absent-minded expression, cultivating a bland Matt-style detachment.

'All right, Nat?'

'Yep.'

'You were wicked.'

'Thanks.'

'God,' said Matt. 'Please. Don't encourage her.'

I had a bottle of wine by the neck, and Cassandra stuck her glass under my nose and grinned her gap-toothed grin, coming close to me to make herself heard over the party's roar. 'Loved the set. Did that man I was talking to just now – Dickie – did he catch up with you? He told me he's thinking of signing your band!' She shouted, 'He tells me you're made for stardom!'

'He liked Matt's band?' That was interesting news. I looked around to share it with Matt, but couldn't make him out in the crush.

'You and the band . . . He's *very* keen on you . . . Well, of course, you do look like a famous pop star already . . .' Her face kept smiling and smiling at me, bobbing gently about, a balloon on a string, as all the happy party people forced their way around and between us. I smiled back, suddenly feeling good. 'Actually, he told me he discovered some singer–song writer who's here tonight –' She craned around the room. 'I don't really know which one she is, I don't watch Top of the Pops . . .'

Great – just as I was enjoying myself, back came the rage

again. Thanks for the information, Abigail – nice one. Closing my eyes, I pressed the heel of my right hand into my right eye-socket, hard, until my inner lights flashed on. Two whole years *before* Harry finally left us. I suddenly realised how much younger I'd been three years ago – really, someone entirely different – when he'd first started screwing that silly bloody airhead.

'What did you say?' She was peering at me. 'Ferdia? Have you got a headache?'

I thought, Shit, I've got to leave this party. 'Sorry, I've really got to go.'

'You've got to go *now*?' Cassandra reached out a staying hand. 'But shouldn't you talk to Dickie first?' Holding my sleeve, she quickly hunted the loud self-congratulatory crowd. 'Hang on, he was here just a moment ago . . .'

'I'll catch him later – my dad knows him – shit, sorry, I've got to go . . .' Elbowing hastily towards the exit, I lost her voice behind me in the crowd.

In the hall, Abby was gone, thankfully. But when I opened the front door it was tipping it down, long shafts of water out of the inky sky, car roofs resonating, pavements spangled yellow under the street lights. I wasn't expecting it to be raining – Sisi's raucous party had drowned the sound of it. It was past tube time, and a long way home, whichever home I chose. I took a step back into the hall, set down the bottle I was still holding on the telephone table, and breathed deep, turning up my collar and working my sleeves down over my hands, getting my energy together to walk out head down into the freezing wet.

'You're not walking home in that?' she asked from behind me.

I glanced at her in her tight red dress. 'I s'pose.'

'Why don't you call a cab?'

'No, it's all right.' I would've needed to tap one of my parents, and I couldn't have gone near them right then.

'Ferdia,' she said, in this very caring way, 'are you OK?'

'Of course I'm OK. Why wouldn't I be?'

'I don't think you are.' She slipped her long hand under my arm. 'Do you want to talk about it?'

I answered miserably, gazing into the hissing night, 'I just want to go home. I'm tired of all this shit.'

'Then at least let me give you a lift,' she said.

Relief. 'No, you're not going yet. Don't worry about me. Stay and enjoy yourself.'

'Don't be stupid.' She pulled her short fake fur coat from the top of the pile, no doubt still wet with Abby's tears. 'Come on.' Her old Ford car was parked about fifty yards up the street, and we had to leg it through the angled rain, her high red shoes scattering the shiny puddles. I'd brought the wine bottle with us and was running trying not to spill it. 'Quick, get in,' she shouted over the top of the car as she unlocked it on the driver's side. Once we were in, doors slammed, the pitch of the rain turned soft and vibrant. I lay back into the seat, shivering a bit from the cold out there. Cassandra was giggling, her grey fur showering water like a dog as she stripped it off and threw it in the back. She winked at me, throwing the car in gear, and asked cheerfully, 'Where to?'

As she drove up the narrow street between parked cars with the extreme care of the only slightly pissed, I slowly scraped away the hair which trickled down into my eyes, and thought about it.

She paused at the corner, waiting for directions. 'Terdia – talk to me – where's home?'

Oh god. Too many homes to go to, and right then I couldn't think where I'd rather be – Kilburn and my mum rolling in drunk and satisfied, arm in arm with that arsehole Peckham, or St John's Wood to watch Harry being chased round the flat by a furious tearful axe-wielding Abby. Some choice.

'Where's home?' she repeated, patiently.

I answered, rather unhelpfully, 'Mmmm . . .'

'Well?'

'Hang on a sec . . .'

71

She took the corner and pulled into a space made by some-body's driveway, killing the engine and switching on the inside light. 'Ferdia,' she said, looking intently in my face. 'What's happening here? You have *got* a home, haven't you?'

I said lightly, twisting the bottle in my lap, 'Yeah.' I thought, He was seeing Abby for two whole years, not four fucking weeks, before he made up his mind. You never know what's going on in someone's head. You never know what anyone is thinking. You think you know everything about them. You think they're boring. It always comes as a shock.

'You do want to *go* home, don't you? Is something wrong?'

'No. Well..' My parents were always urging me to talk to them, not walk away, but they only really wanted me to tell them what they wanted to hear (All right, Ferdia? Yeah, I'm fine. You know we both love you? Yep, I do). It was actually nice to have someone asking questions who looked prepared to listen to an answer. 'You see . . .'

After a long silence, she sighed and said, 'Look, I only live five minutes' drive away – do you want to come round to my place for a bit while you make up your mind what you're doing?' She said, 'We could drink the wine in that bottle, and I'll call you a cab.'

It seemed like a good idea at the time, being rescued.

Chapter Seven

I did feel rescued by her, warm and dry in her intimate space, relieved not to have to walk miles through the pouring rain. But only a minute after setting off, a police car passed us going the other way and she decided abruptly she was too drunk to drive. We parked and hurried on through the miserable night, getting piss-wet through after all.

'You seem a bit unsteady – do you want to take my arm?' she shouted above the noise of the rain.

I took my eyes off the uneven pavement to answer indignantly, 'No, I'm fine . . .', tripped over a broken paving stone and fell dramatically flat on my face. My nearly full bottle of wine sloshed out on the ground, disappearing into the liquid world without a trace.

'Oh god.' She sounded alarmed but amused. 'Are you all right?'

'Fine!' I croaked, when I got some air back into my lungs. I was seriously embarrassed. She helped me to my feet, then insisted on taking my arm for my own safety, making it actually harder for me to walk without lurching. I lobbed the annoyingly empty bottle over a passing wall. I wondered what the fuck I was doing with her, struggling along in the wrong direction. I thought bad-temperedly: Should've stayed and gone home with Matt.

Her place was a first-floor flat in Camden Town – a tall Victorian red-brick building with iron railings round the basement, packed kebab shops on either side. She shed her coat with a satisfied sigh to be back, and carried on into the far room. I stayed back in the hall, still feeling humiliated, trying to dry off against the radiator. I could see her going to the high front windows, lanky body outlined by city lights,

73

drawing the curtains, then switching on a couple of low-level lamps. Then, while I was still watching, she bent over with her narrow but rounded arse sticking out towards me and popped off her red high-heeled shoes. Her dress rode up at the back, high enough to see that she was wearing stockings (*stockings!* for fuck's sake), and, next thing, she slipped her fingers under the hem of the dress and dragged down first one and then the other, arranging them neatly over the back of a chair. 'Come in,' she called, swivelling towards me.

Shaken, I stayed glued to the radiator as if I'd melted slightly.

'Come *in*.' She adopted her voice of authority, like she was teaching a class. Obediently, trainers squelching, I entered the room, coming to a halt just inside the door. The long space was nicely done up – gold curtains, dark yellow walls, shelves of books, dried flowers in the fireplace, a polished wood orna-ment on the mantlepiece. She stood calmly waiting, one hand resting on the back of the curved metal chair where she'd hung her wet stockings. Her legs were incredibly long, even without the heels; she stood with her toes spread wide on the stripped pine floor. 'Don't look so anxious,' she said, with a dazzling gap-toothed smile. 'I'm not going to *eat* you.'

I forced a laugh to show I'd got the joke, but it popped out more like a squawk, because I couldn't help wondering what she'd do when she noticed her dress was wet as well, from where her coat had flapped open in the rain. I pictured her rolling it off over her head like a stocking, leaving her naked . . . skinny . . . A Naked Cassandra . . .

'What are you looking at? Oh god.' She was staring down at herself. 'I'm *completely* soaked.'

Head bowed, concentrating furiously on my shoes, I felt myself getting a long slow helpless hard-on, and thanked Christ I was still wearing my coat.

'I'm going to get changed – Ferdia, pay attention! Go in the kitchen and find us some wine. There's plenty in the rack. Choose a nice one.' Passing me, her bare arm swept the raindrops from my coat – a touch I didn't feel through the thick leather but which made my body-hairs stand up on end all over, like cold air blowing up inside my clothes.

When I could walk without hobbling, I went to check the kitchen. There were seven bottles in her wine rack – I pulled them out one by one, but had no idea which was 'nice'. I knew one thing only about wine – it was what you got pissed on at parties. I hunted around for a corkscrew, opening and closing drawers. Now my prick had deflated, I was dying for a piss, but I didn't want to go looking for the toilet in case I burst in on her without her clothes . . . *Don't think about it . . .*

'Still in here?' She had changed into a baggy black T-shirt and green leggings, and was rubbing her long hair furiously with a towel. Her feet were still bare. She gave off a new sweet scent. She'd washed off the party make-up, leaving her mouth clean and pale. Her eyes looked large and naked without mascara. 'For pity's sake, take off that coat. You look really uncomfortable.'

'Cassandra, can I use your loo?'

She pointed me down the hall. Her bedroom door was open as I passed it, the wet dress hunched on the floor, carelessly shed. I checked in briefly, without crossing the threshold. No men's shoes or jackets or anything. I carried on into the bathroom and had my piss. The alcohol in my blood must've suddenly dropped below a certain point, because my knee began to hurt. I lowered my rain-soaked trousers to take a look. It was mashed and slightly bloody – I must have hit the ground with it first, maybe landed on something sharp, the edge of the broken paving stone. I dabbed at it with wet toilet roll. The place was heavy with the scent she'd come back wearing. Curious, rebuttoning my jeans, I opened the glass cabinet over the sink, and uncapped the only bottle of perfume, spraying it on my wrist. That was the one. I turned the bottle in the light. Pricey. She said through the door, 'Take a towel from the airing cupboard, if you want to dry your hair.'

Guiltily, I shoved the perfume back on the shelf. 'Just having a wash!' I ran the tap hard. I didn't want her to think I was taking a crap. While I was rinsing the scent off my wrist, I registered some naff brand of aftershave, right at the back of the cabinet. Quickly, I checked out the other shelves, pushing her things around at fingertip. A razor, but it could've been hers, for her legs. Condoms. Shit. But I saw there was only one toothbrush in the glass.

Pulling a thick purple towel out of the cupboard, I went back into the living room. She called from the kitchen, 'I'll be with you in a minute!' I sat down on a yellow sofa by the fireplace, its grate heaped up with dried metallic flowers. The stockings still hung there, taunting me with the memory of that moment. My knee was hurting under my stiff wet jeans. In my saturated trainers, my socks were deep puddles. Shivering, I scrubbed at my hair with the big soft towel. Hearing her come in, I kept the towel over my head, still slowly rubbing, watching her dry naked feet walk around, making soft kissing noises off the boards. Some music came on, late-night sounds to chill to, a bit of Bristol-based rhythm and bass. I heard the chink of glass on glass. The next minute, she was loudly panting and groaning, and I threw up my head, startled, not knowing what the hell she was doing. She was squatted with her rounded arse on the edge of the armchair opposite, grappling with a wine bottle, gripping it between her legs while she dragged at the corkscrew. My own body tensed up watching her struggle, like I was also straining at the cork. The towel slid down my back.

I offered, 'Do you want me to . . .?'

And she gasped, 'No, no, not yet . . . It's coming . . .' It popped, and she grunted with relief. While pouring, she sank her teeth lightly into her tongue. 'Try it. It's good.' She leaned out towards me with a glass. Her T-shirt bagged, and her breasts fell forwards within it, making clear blunt peaks in the soft material. She wasn't wearing a bra. 'Did you enjoy the party?'

I thought, Mustn't stare at her tits . . . Mustn't stare . . . *Stop it.*

Her voice grew fractionally louder: 'Ferdia?'

With a start, I sucked my eyes from her breasts – they came away with what felt like an audible plop. She pointed at my glass. 'Aren't you going to try it?' The wine was untouched in my hand. I tasted it, but it was pretty evil. My heart was beating a little, but slowing down. She repeated, curling up in her chair, playing with her freshly fuzzy towel-dried hair, studying me over her drink. 'Did you like the party?'

I glued my eyes to her face, determined to stop them slipping. 'It was OK – bit full of ground-dwellers, though.'

She was brightly interested. 'Full of what?'

I took another sip of the wine. Still disgusting, but maybe it'd kill this growing throbbing in my knee. I set it down carefully on the bookshelf bedside me. 'What Matt calls people who live at ground level. Big houses with mortgages and that. Like, he thinks we should all live in tower blocks.'

She looked hopeful. 'Is a flat on the first floor high enough?'

I laughed. 'Not really.'

She made a humorous disappointed face.

I added hastily, 'I mean, your flat's really nice.' I meant it, too. Matt would've ripped the piss out of me for being OK with all her stuff, most of it probably bought down Camden Lock – the rip-off twist of polished wood, the printed cotton throws, the chunky rug of llama wool woven at fifteen hundred feet above sea level by some pissed-off peasant. But I appreciated the way her place wasn't full of depressing shit like my house had got over the past year – half-opened bills, junk mail and last month's tabloids, like every day flaked off a paper skin. It was warm in Cassandra's place. And clean. The rain sounded cosy at the windows. I thought suddenly, relaxing into my chair, this feels like a real home.

'But I don't *want* to be a ground-dweller,' she protested, smiling, looking inquiringly at me like I could sort this out for her.

I shrugged, still feeling chilled, relaxed on the sofa. 'Don't worry about it. I'm one too. Matt's the genuine sky-high man. I've just been drafted in cos there's no one else.'

She gathered the mass of her long blonde hair into one hand and twisted it into a rope, pulling it over her shoulder and – *Stop! You're looking at her tits again!* 'Ferdia?' I stared determinedly at her face. She was giving me this wide, sweet, motherly smile. 'You look so uncomfortable – do take off your coat.' Reluctantly, praying she'd do nothing to give me another boner, I shuffled my arms out of their leather sleeves. 'That's better' – but staring at my lap, her eyes grew huge and anxious: 'Oh, god, *look* at the state of you!' Terrified, I glanced down at myself.

She jumped to her feet, 'I can't believe you've been sitting there in such wet clothes – you'll die of pneumonia! Take off those jeans and trainers and I'll stick them in the tumble dryer.'

I thought she meant undress there and then, in front of her in her living room, and was filled with panic and confusion. 'Look, Cassandra, maybe I should go. I'll dry off at home . . .'

But, ignoring me, she sprinted out of the room and returned almost at once with a long white silky dressing gown, embroidered on the pocket with golden flowers. 'Sorry – best I could do. You can put this on before you take off your trousers.' She put on her teacher's voice again – 'Come on, now! Don't be shy!' – making me pathetically unable to say No. Feeling a total and utter prat, I took the dressing gown and turned my back on her to undress. To be honest, it was a relief rolling off my socks. Working soggy denim down my legs, I winced as it scraped across my mashed-up knee. She murmured, almost breathing down my neck, 'Are your boxers dry enough to keep on?'

I gasped, flinching under the too-close brush of her breath, 'Yes! Fine!'

She was laughing at me, crouching down behind me, reaching round my ankles to pick up my clothes and shoes from the floor where I'd dropped them. 'Listen, I said before, I'm not going to bite you!' Clutching the feminine dressing gown around me, I turned to see what she was up to. Standing up, moving away, she started going through my jeans pockets. 'We don't want to tumble-dry your keys,' she said, pulling them out. 'Oh, look, that man gave you his business card – I thought you didn't get to speak to him? He gave me one too – I was going to let you have it.' So that was what Dickie had slipped into my pocket. I sat back down on the yellow sofa by the fireplace of flowers, watching her messing with my clothes, arranging the stuff from my pockets on the seat of the stocking-hung chair; I kind of liked the way she was mothering me. My knee was bugging me again, pulsing away like a frantic separate heart. Distracted, faintly nauseous, I parted the dressing gown to take a look. Cassandra exclaimed, 'Ferdia, are you *hurt*? Why didn't you say?'. Throwing down my stuff, her right breast with a big black patch of wet on it from clasping my trainers under her arm, she hurried over to examine the spongy mess, now embedded with tiny scraps of bog roll. Her tits, one damp, became longer again, swaying close to my face. 'Wait there, I'll get something.' When she came back with the Dettol, she murmured, sinking slowly to her knees before me, 'Don't worry, I'll be really gentle.' Then she gripped me firmly behind the knee and dabbed ferociously at the roughed-up wound.

'Jesus!' I writhed around inside, fighting to keep my outer body still, concentrating hard on the muffled sound of the rain, the yellow walls, the blonde ruffled top of her head, while Cassandra twirled bloodied balls of cottonwool between her fingers, lining them up beside her on the floor, all the time humming brightly under her breath.

'Am I hurting you?'

'No!' But it hurt like hell, her fingering me through my unzipped skin.

She pressed harder. 'Am I hurting you now?'

'*No!*'

She laughed, still gripping the back of my knee. 'Do you mind my asking,' she said, 'what was the issue with going home tonight?'

'Nothing . . .' This was terrible, now there were tears in my voice. I was seriously under assault – pain in my leg, now this pain in my head.

'Come on, Ferdia, *something*'s wrong. Why don't you tell me? Maybe I can help.'

'I'm fine . . .' I said. 'That's fine.' I was pushing her hand away; she looked up expectantly. 'It's nothing, it's just, my dad went off . . .' Absurdly, I broke up. 'I'm sorry . . .'

Letting go my leg, she knelt up and wrapped her arms around me, murmuring in my ear, 'It's all right, it's OK,' pressing her cheek very hard to mine.

It wasn't OK. My nose was filling with snot – I sniffed to block the overflow, and made this disgusting jokey noise like a pig snoring. I couldn't believe I was making such an arsehole of myself. I made to pull away, but she tightened her hug, not letting me go. I pulled one arm free, twisting my head to wipe my face on my sleeve, trying to clear my throat, swallowing slime. 'I'm sorry.' My voice was thick with gunk. 'I'm sorry,' I bubbled pathetically.

She whispered, 'Don't be,' and kissed my cheek, then sat back on her heels and reached me down a handful of tissues from the box on the mantelpiece.

I blew my nose as quietly as I could and carefully wiped my mouth and eyes.

'Better now?'

'Yeah.' I took a deep jerky breath.

She hugged me again. 'Sure?'

'Yeah. Sorry. Yeah.'

'Good.' She lowered her head, her forehead resting heavily on my shoulder.

I would've liked to've gone to the bathroom to wash my face properly, but for a while I stayed. There was a comfort in being held I'd almost forgotten now I was growing old. Her hair was bushy against my chin; she smelt so sweet of that sharp scent: I breathed her in. Her body temperature seeped like thick warm liquid through my clothes. I moved slightly, but again she tightened her arms around me. In the background I could hear my heart start up, slowly in my ears like distant drums, and realised I needed to get away from her quick. Yet I put my hand on her back, stroking the hard raised ribs beneath the cotton. 'Cassandra . . .' When she didn't answer, I touched my lips to the hot pink triangle of her ear.

She whispered, 'You'd better stop now,' wriggling against me. Her body-weight was softly pressing me back into the sofa cushions. Her breasts were flattened between us. My heart increased its speed, thumping so hard I was physically shaken by each stroke, deafened by the whoomph of blood. I moved my hand up and down her bumpy spine. The dressing gown was coming apart; I could feel the material of her leggings against my naked thighs. She pulled away suddenly, scrambling to her feet, and I was left stranded crookedly in the cushions, coming down fast, skin rapidly draining of her heat, groggily pulling the silky white material tight around me. I thought, Oh shit, oh shit, I was trying it on with a *teacher*.

'I'd better put your things in the dryer.' She picked them off the floor, sounding cool and authoritative. 'It's getting late.' Not meeting my eyes, she stalked out of the room.

I slammed my head into my hands. If she hadn't taken my trousers I would've left at once, not even said Goodbye. I curled up tightly in her yellow chair, in her silly gold-flowered dressing gown, trying to look as small and unridiculous as I could. I heard her come back, but didn't risk looking up. She said nothing to me, only gave a near-silent sigh. I heard the creak of cushions as she sat. Then, after a bit, the rustle of turning paper. I checked her out from behind my fingers. She had on her thin-framed reading glasses, a sharp expression on her face, a fine-lined concentrating frown, going through some kid's essay with a pen. The music was still playing, the lamps still lit. Trying it on with a *teacher* . . . seriously mad! – and yet . . .'Cassandra,' I croaked. 'Look. I'm sorry.'

For a while she sat there, pen raised over the words. Then she lifted her eyes and asked in a quiet rough voice, 'For what?'

'Just . . . sorry.' What I really wanted to say was, Hang on, this isn't fair, it wasn't just me, I didn't mean to piss you off, I thought you liked me, I like you too – I just forgot you were off limits – if I had my jeans, I'd leave you alone at once. She startled me by standing up, taking off her glasses and resting them carefully on the mantelpiece. Leaning over the sofa, she pulled my face up with her hand, fingers denting the soft front of my throat. Her top teeth pinched the wide lower lip of her mouth; her marbled blue-green eyes shifted repeatedly across my face; her blonde hair showered around her shoulders. I thought, thick-headedly, She's beautiful.

Dropping my chin again, she remarked, 'It's me that should be sorry.'

'No, I am, I'm sorry . . .'

'I didn't mean to upset you like that . . . You seemed OK with your dad at the party . . . Have your parents split up recently, is that it?'

I muttered, embarrassed by having cried, 'Well, no, it's been a year . . .'

'Divorce. What a *mess*.' She turned away with a weary expression. 'Why can't people stay in love forever?' She threw herself back down in the armchair, long thin green thighs falling apart. 'Look,' she said, with another, deeper, sigh, fiddling with the hem of her T-shirt in her open lap. 'Let's face it. It's late. You're upset. The jeans will take a while. I need to get to bed. Would you like to stay here for the night?'

Chapter Eight

Monday morning, on my way to school, Matt shot furtively out of the newsagents as I neared it and hurried ahead of me up the dripping street. I knew he'd seen me; I didn't shout after him but plodded slowly on; the remains of last night's foul weather glugging down the drains, leaving a smell of petrol and October. When I eventually turned the corner he was stood under a plane tree waiting for me, reading the *NME* and tutting each time a small balloon of rain burst on his page from the branches overhead.

'McCartney on the front *again*,' he said. 'Is it his fucking centenary or what? I don't know why I buy this thing, it's so totally fucking middle of the road.'

'I didn't think you did buy it,' I said. 'I thought you nicked it.'

'Still a waste of my time – where're you going?'

I was surprised. 'Where d'you think? . . . what – is it, like, a bank holiday or something?'

'Today's Monday?' He sighed. 'Shit.' He folded up the paper and stuck it back under his ragged denim jacket. Everything he had on was torn to shreds that was the way he wore his clothes, a bit of a late seventies punk throwback thing, to be honest, though it was getting a bit excessive these days, like he'd fallen repeatedly under a lawnmower.

'You coming or what?'

For a moment there he'd looked ready to roll; now he stood glancing vaguely up and down the red-brick road. 'I dunno . . .'

'Make up your mind.' I pulled away gradually, backwards, forcing him to follow me. 'What's the problem? You something better to do?'

He fell in step beside me; I turned to face the way we were

going. He kept glancing at me, pink face repeatedly changing expression under his badly-cut hair, like he kept thinking if he answered I might start taking the piss. Finally he said, 'It's just, I'm beginning to have some serious fucking doubts about this whole education thing, man.'

'Issit.' I was a bit heavy on the sarcasm.

'No, listen, I'm serious . . .' He paused. He seemed genuinely troubled. 'I think they might be fucking with our minds.'

I gasped and staggered. 'Wha . . . you mean? . . . they're creating a race of . . . *zombie kids*?'

'Something like that, yeah.' He was pleased I'd caught on so quick. 'You noticed too?'

'Sucking our blood and bottling our brains in jars and that?'

'*Exactly.*'

Now I was seriously fucking worried. 'What jar did you leave your brain in this morning, man?'

He became oddly distressed. 'Come on, it's no fucking joke – I'm working on a song about it.'

'Yeah?' I was relieved. 'How's it go?'

'It's this national curriculum thing, it's really bothering me.'

'Needs some work, man – even Pink Floyd came up with snappier fucking lyrics than that.'

'Fuck off . . . No, listen, it really does bother me. It's like we're being moulded to this government ideal, man. Everyone reading exactly the *same books*. Everyone being taught exactly the *same answers*. What's that all about, man?'

What indeed? I took a while to think about it. My school bag scraped along a privet hedge, sending an unpleasant shower down my neck. Sparrows were easing out long worms from concrete cracks; I tipped one damp bird with my trainer, and it shuffled out of my way, blinking sharp little eyes. 'You think some of us should be taught the wrong answers? For variety's sake, like?'

He said pityingly, 'Fuck's sake, Ferdia – challenge the system, man. Teachers are your enemy. Truth is the big lie.'

Like some hypnotist had snapped their fingers, I fell in a dream of being in Cassandra's flat – the warmth of it; her skinny white arms around me; the cleanliness of her possessions; the feel of her leggings on my naked thighs . . . Waking up with a sigh, I said, 'Y'know, I don't think you need worry too much about our school teaching us all the right answers – my dad says it's going to fail its . . . something report, government inspection thing?'

'That's good. The lamer the teachers, the less they'll fuck us up. No one needs smart enemies.'

'I suppose they try their best,' I said, thinking again of Cassandra, then heard myself, and groaned.

Matt laughed. He'd assumed I was taking the piss. 'Listen to this, man,' he said, letting his head fall back and staring at the dirty sky. After a few more yards, he yelled out suddenly, sending the sparrows leaping for the trees, '*I'm a zombie kid, I'm weird because I'm dead; it's not my fault my teacher ate my head.*'

To which, delighted, I added, '*She ripped my head off, yes she really did; but I'm not bitter – I'M THE ZOMBIE KID!!!!*'

We were outside the school gates. Stopping me on the pavement, Matt squeezed my shoulders through my coat, his small blue pale-lashed eyes suddenly as intense and frustrated as if he was that madman in Hyde Park prophesying the end of the world and I was the cheerful been-there-done-that crowd. 'I'm serious, man. Don't believe in the answers. Their truth isn't ours, d'you see? I mean, there's a million different universes out there, right?'

I laughed. 'All right, all right . . .'

Out of the blue he came over all agitated, nearly shaking me about. 'Come on, I'm serious, man. You gotta be careful out there. Don't let them eat your head.'

'Oi, you! Matt the Twat!'

Matt slumped. 'Oh fucking great.'

Gary Peckham was legging it across the stinking road, brakes screeching and drivers screaming silently behind sealed windows.

'Oi, Twat! Leave my mate alone!'

What mate? Shit! I looked wildly around me for the Gary-mob. 'He giving you grief, Fez?' – seizing two handfuls of Matt's tattered jacket – 'You want a fuckin' dig, or what? Oi!' He jerked Matt's totally gob-smacked face down to his level. 'Nobody fuckin' fucks with my mate Fezza!' It took me a second to figure who Fezza was. Yep, for a minute there, it'd totally slipped my mind that Gazza Peckham was my new best friend, my mate, my mucker, my sharp-suited guardian angel from hell.

Matt was *speechless*. It took a lot to shut him up.

'It's all right, Gary,' I said, smoothly, like everything was in proper order. 'Just a friendly discussion. You can leave him alone.'

He was disappointed. He didn't want to believe me. 'You sure, mate?'

'Yep. Chill.'

His neck muscles deflated. 'Fair enough.' He let go Matt's jacket and took one step back. 'Jus' checkin'.'

Matt was slowly straightening up, shaking his head like he'd water in the ears, rearranging the holes in his clothes. After a bit he recovered enough to say rather pointedly, 'Ferdia, your *pal* just ripped my threads.'

Peckham was still with us, mooching around in my body space, being wordlessly friendly, stuffing his mouth with handfuls of cheesy wotsits and rattling the open packet under my chin. After Matt spoke, he continued to crunch violently while at the same time rotating his eyes towards him, making this big thing of looking him up and down. 'How can you tell?' he asked, at last. Then he went and cracked up, slapping me on the back, nearly snapping my ribs with his elbow, spraying my coat with bright orange cheesy-snack-flavoured gob-drops. '*How can you tell?* Geddit? For fuck's sake . . .'

After he'd calmed down, he said to Matt sadly, carefully smoothing his shaven head, 'I don't know about you, bruv, but my mum'd *die* rather than send me to school looking like that.' And off he skipped, with an airy wave to me ('See ya, Fezza!'), pristine and proud in his fresh-off-the-hanger Ralph Lauren shirt and lovingly ironed Versace jeans.

'Yeah. So. Right,' said Matt, staring after him, 'Look, it's fucking obvious if you think about it, there isn't just one universe but loads of parallel ones splitting off the whole time, like, time is constantly splitting, right? And in each universe things take a slightly different direction, like turning right instead of left and a tree falls on you instead of you meeting the woman of your dreams, right? So this whole thing about the *truth* is total shite, because, like, who's to say which universe is the right one? What's the right answer? There isn't one, right?'

'OK,' I repeated, cautiously. I wondered, what universe was he in – if any?

'I mean, I get out of bed this morning and you and Peckham are best mates, right?'

'So? We've always been real close.'

He didn't laugh. He barely reacted at all, just spread his hands with an unshockable shrug. 'See? Different universe.'

Year-seven kids were piling off the bus. I rode their flood through the gates, rafting the short-arsed squealing mob. Matt surfed with me, gazing around him over their tossing heads, humming 'Zombie Kid', suddenly chilled – surprisingly laid back, actually, for someone who believed he'd got out of bed that morning into the wrong world, especially one where I was friends with Gary Peckham.

'What d'you think of the gig, Saturday?' I shouted him over the tidal roar.

'Where d'you get to, anyway?' he yelled.

'*What?*'

'You disappeared on us – I was looking for you – what happened?'

We washed up on the steps of C Block, shaken, ears ringing. 'What?'

'It must've been important, to dump your bass like that.'

'Oh shit – yeah – I completely forgot about that – it must still be at Lily's.'

'You *forgot*?' And suddenly he was all strung out again, full of unnatural anguish. 'How could you *do* that, man?'

Puzzled, I tried to lighten the mood. 'Come on, Matt, it's a possession – aren't we supposed to be free of possessions and stuff?'

'Aagh!' He punched himself on the forehead. 'Your guitar's not a fucking *possession*, man..You gotta take *care* of it . . . it's supposed to be *important* to you, man. It's not *stuff*, it's like leaving your *soul* behind . . . the music gods . . .'

I was open-mouthed. I was, like, *What are you on?* 'All right, Jesus. I'll pick it up later, OK?'

'You've gotta take care of your *soul*, man, don't be a zombie kid . . .'

'Matt! Hello? Wakey wakey, mate! Remember the teacher that stopped Gary kicking the shit out of me?'

That brought him back to earth, sharpish. 'Too right. She was at the party, wasn't she? Unbelievable arse.'

'That's where I was, Saturday night. I stayed at hers.' I carried on up the steps into the building.

He came chasing after me, jerking me by the strap of my school bag. 'What . . . hang on a minute . . .'

'Yeah, I stayed at her place, man.' I was working hard on sounding super-cool. 'She's called Cassandra.'

'*Shit*. How the fuck did you manage that? What happened?'

I shrugged, like it happened all the time. 'She asked me back.'

He whistled. 'So, you stayed the night then?'

'Yep. That's what I said.'

Disbelieving. 'You *slept* with her?'

'Leave it out' – my mind flashed to that short ambiguous embrace – 'she's a teacher, for fuck's sake.'

He dropped his voice, murmuring suggestively. 'Maybe she wanted to give you *extra lessons*?'

I giggled like a fucking girl. 'Jesus . . . That ain't funny, by the way . . .'

'Go on then,' he said, meaningfully, giving me a sharp shove as we walked the filthy corridors under the high meshed windows. 'Spill the beans.'

'No beans to be spilt, Matt.'

'She can't've taken you back to hers for no fucking reason.'

'We just chatted, that's all there was to it.'

'She must be starved for fucking conversation then.'

'Cheers, mate.'

He cornered me determinedly beside the crumbling stairs. 'So – what d'you talk about? Fucking Shakespeare?'

'The band, of course!' I cried, with a flash of brilliance. I pulled out Dickie's business card and waved it under his nose. 'Remember that dodgy boyband bloke I was telling you about? He was at the party and he maybe wants to manage *us*. He told Cassandra he's interested – weird, innit?' As we climbed the stairs, Matt read the card at least a hundred times, upside down, back to front, holding it up to the distant daylight, like he could milk a million sentences out of a handful of trivial boring words. I warned him, 'He's a bit of a twat, though – that's why Abigail dumped him. You wouldn't like him much.' But Matt said nothing, turning and twisting the card, absorbed.

Lolling in the classroom, resting against a desk before the yawning morning crowd, long legs crossed at the ankles in little black boots, hair falling forward, her finger parting the pages of her textbook, was Cassandra. My stomach did a forward roll and a backwards flip. 'Hi, boys,' she said. She glanced up at me, expressionless behind her glasses, running her finger down the page. 'So glad you could make it.'

I took my usual window seat, easing off my coat, staring open-mouthed at her. Matt kept poking me in the side and hissing, like maybe I hadn't noticed her being there. Wincing,

I twisted to watch the pigeons shitting on the sill.

'Hamlet's sexual desire for his mother,' said Cassandra, clearly, tucking her hair behind one ear.

Immediately Matt exploded, choking and spluttering, sliding down in his chair, only his scrubby fair hair above table-height. She raised her voice: 'Everything all right back there?'

Unable not to react to her irritation, I looked up at her. She raised her eyebrows at me over her thin wire frames and gave me a tiny, restrained smile. I couldn't look away again. It was odd – she appeared completely different from how I'd already begun to remember her. I'd been thinking about her so much since I last saw her, Sunday morning, that by Monday she'd sort of evolved through generations in my mind and now I was thrown by the sight of the original. She was wearing a short dark purple skirt with a fluffy lilac cardigan buttoned to the top. Her tights were black. As she shifted her arse on the desktop, I tried to figure out if they were stockings, searching obsessively for a shot of skin.

Yesterday morning, she'd woken me on the sofa, patting my duvet, handing me my dried-out trainers and socks and jeans, promising toast and scrambled eggs and juice. I'd this weird suspicion she'd very lightly stroked my hair before I opened my eyes. I didn't stay long, just ate and went, because she seemed so far away; I left her sitting in her dressing gown at the high counter in her kitchen, reading Sunday papers in a puddle of sunshine.

'Do you think it's possible to fancy your mother?' she asked the room.

The boys convulsed in stomach-hugging protest, retching fake vomit into their bags, shrieking and howling, 'That's fucking disgusting!' The girls, marooned at the front, wrinkled their noses and folded their arms, exchanging sympathetic glances with the one among them that was a mother already.

'You in the blue shirt – can you explain why you find that so disgusting?'

He was rolling his eyes, looking anywhere but her, trying to rally his mates. 'It's just it's disgusting, innit?'

'And that,' said Cassandra, acting superior, poking her spectacles up her long thin nose, 'is the power of the incest taboo. We don't even want to think about it – the very idea of it fills us with disgust.'

'Nah, miss,' said blue-shirt's immediate neighbour, 'it's not that. It's just, you should see the state of his mum.'

Which led to such an outraged brawl, even a storming Cassandra found it hard to break it up.

Me and Matt were still laughing when the bell went. But when it came to leaving the classroom I couldn't just pass her by, but came to a halt at the corner of her desk, hanging around watching her shuffle her books briskly together into her bag. 'Hi,' she said to me, warmly, like she was pleased to see me, taking her glasses off and slotting them into a slim silver case. 'How are you?'

'I'm fine.' I stood trying to think of something else to say. Matt came up behind us, interrupting my pathetic silence, 'So, Cassandra, how d'you like the band?'

She grinned from ear to ear, the gap between her front teeth showing in her wide, parted mouth. 'Best thing at the party.'

Matt preened himself automatically, like he always did in the presence of sexual beauty, rubbing his filthy hair backwards across his head and shuffling his shoulders under his ripped denim jacket. 'Yeah? Cheers . . .'

'Pity about the ground-dwellers . . .'

Matt laughed, impressed. 'You know about ground-dwellers?'

'Ferdia filled me in,' she said, tugging hard on the straps of her bulky leather case, buckling them at the very tips.

And Matt said, grinning and flapping his sandy eyebrows at me, '*Did* he now . . .'

'I'm going round to Lily's after school to collect my bass,' I said, raising my voice, trying to cover up his cringe-making innuendo. 'You coming, Matt?'

'See you then.' Cassandra grabbed her bag and left the room with a stiff angry back.

'You *moron*,' I hissed at him. 'What the *fuck* d'you say that for?'

'What?' Innocent.

'About – Jesus – *filling her in*, you wanker. She probably thinks I've been bragging about it . . .'

'Oh, I don't think that was it,' he said, smugly. 'She was just fucked off when you started banging on about Lily, innit.'

'I wasn't banging on about Lily.'

'Yep, you're in there, all right . . . Bragging about what, anyway?'

'She didn't like you talking about *me*?' Lily was pleased and intrigued. 'What the fuck's the matter with you talking about me?' She was standing on her bed, holding an Eminem poster up to the wall, her wedge-heeled shoes driving down into the mattress.

'Hell hath no fury,' said Matt, lighting one of Lily's cigarettes. Letting the fag droop from the corner of his mouth, he shook a joss stick out of a packet and lit that too, jamming the metal end of it into the window frame. 'She's got the hots for him, all right. She took her stockings off when he was in the room.'

I was beginning to wish I hadn't told him that.

'The old tart. Isn't that illegal or something?'

'Ignore him, Lil,' I said. 'All we did was talk about the band.' I was lying back in her easy chair, an ancient Barbie annual on my lap, rolling a generous spliff from her plentiful supply.

'Well, I'm gonna call that Dickie guy,' said Lily, warming old Blu-Tack in her fingers, trying to get it to stick to the shiny poster, squishing it against the wall with the heel of her hand. 'We might become famous.'

'Look,' I warned her, sucking back and swallowing my spit, then licking drily along the length of the spliff, 'don't get too excited, OK? It's probably all bullshit. I'm only saying, Cassandra said he was keen . . . Like, he gave her his card . . .'

'Oh, *Cassandra* said,' said Lily, rather bitchily. Eminem slid down the wall, and she repositioned him. 'Anyway, we should. He managed your dad's . . . I mean, Abigail, didn't he? And she's been on Top of the Pops. That makes her *famous*.' She slammed her palms against the wall; the plaster cracked; the poster stuck. '*I* want to be famous.'

'Famous – what for?' asked Matt, a bit irritably. He started walking up and down the length of Lily's bed, swinging on his heel every few seconds. 'What d'you want to be famous for?' He pulled noisily on his fag. 'Fame is shit.'

'Bollocks,' she said, basically unbothered. 'Everyone wants to be famous. And I want to be rich. '

'*You* want to be rich?' He stopped, fag tilted in his fingers.

Hearing genuine surprise, Lily also stopped dead, and turned to follow the puzzled trail his eyes left over her lifetime of acquisitions: tall empty CD racks with heaps of CDs piled up around them; her Playstation and its games, unplugged; layer upon layer, wall to wall, of once-worn clothes from all the shops down Chalk Farm Road; shelves of Famous Five and china dolls and other toys, her silly pointless souvenirs of childhood. Matt's flat was as empty as a balloon, floating in the sky without weight, a mere space above the streets, completely free of all possessions no string to hold it down.

'Famous people are just zombies, man,' he said, recovering and getting back to his point. 'It's like the aborigines say – every photo takes a bite out of your soul. Every time your picture's in the paper . . . Haven't you seen them on the telly? Their eyes are totally fucking empty.' He added to himself, with a sudden frown, obviously beginning to believe his own shit, 'Fuck me, man. Even their skin looks weird – have you seen Richard and Judy lately?'

Lily sighed, plopping down on the bed, waving her hand

towards me for the spliff, 'Of course their skin looks weird, they've all had face-lifts.'

I yawned. 'Come on, Matt, what's with the cold feet? Let Lily call him. It might be a laugh.'

He stalked over and plucked the spliff from Lily's hand. She sat with her back to the wall, smiling vaguely up at him. He stood over us both, big, pink-faced, with unwashed hair, brooding and smoking. 'A laugh? You're saying we can't make it? You saying my stuff's not good enough?'

I groaned. 'Fuck's sake. Whatever.'

He jabbed his finger at me. 'I don't mind just having a chat with this bloke. But I'm not letting some material bastard stop me telling it like it is.'

'Good. Wouldn't want you to.'

'I'm not into authority figures, man.'

'All right, OK, you're not into authority figures . . .'

He passed the spliff back to Lily, pulling her down beside him on the bed, running his arm around her waist while she held the smoke in her lungs for a count of five before releasing it. He said to me, airily, 'Like, it's not me wants to knob my *English* teacher.'

'She's not my teacher . . .'

And they both went, 'Ah-HAAAA!!!'

Chapter Nine

But, as it turned out, she was my teacher now.

The reason was, the woman we'd started the term with crashed and burned surprisingly fast. We knew she'd crack sooner rather than later, just didn't realise it was going to be that sudden. Those types usually managed a term or two of crazed enthusiasm before they descended into weeping looniness – and sometimes even then they might carry on for months, keeping us both shocked and entertained, before they finally jacked it in (they were never *made* to leave – even when dangerous, teachers were irreplaceable).

So we had Cassandra now, or, as she was known to our ecstatic class, the *Motherfucker*. She certainly had a way of getting them going; everyone in Shakespeare apparently was fucking a relative, or – much more provocatively – gay. Even Shakespeare was gay, OK? Then she went and claimed *all* the best men were gay, and the boys went mental, even the obviously gay one. She had my attention all right. I couldn't stop trying to see up those short tight skirts. Luckily, she never asked me a question or wanted me to read anything out. In fact for nearly a week she totally ignored me. Then on Thursday she stopped me on my way out the door. It was the last lesson of the day. She wanted to know where I was going after school. 'Are you doing anything special?' she asked.

Matt was waiting for me in the corridor. 'Not really.' I had band practice.

'No Matt? No Lily?'

'Nope.'

'Who's the other one – Aristotle?'

'No. I mean, yeah, I'm not meeting him, no.'

'I just thought I'd buy you a cup of coffee. See how you were. If that's OK?'

'Er – yeah.'

'I've got to take this back to the staffroom – meet you in fifteen minutes in . . .?' and she described for me how to get to some obscure place in a back street even I hadn't heard of, and I was happy with relief, realising I wouldn't have to walk out of school with her, or sit in an enormous window like in a showroom being pointed out by junior morons to their moronic little mates. I was glad she understood all that.

'What was all that about?' asked Matt.

'Something I should've handed in – listen, I'm gonna be another half hour, I've got something to do.'

He was impatient. 'Like, what?'

'Nothing – I'll see you at your place, half hour max.'

'You better be knobbing Cassandra,' he said. He was really fucking peeved.

Outside the school gates the day was grey; damp to the skin; smelt of recently rained-on gardens. I walked along shifting my bag from shoulder to shoulder, looking at street names, feeling vaguely guilty about letting Matt down, and puzzled about what was going to happen next. But then it came into my head I'd been walking much too long up this particular endless road, under these relentless peeling planes. I was much too late, she'd be gone, and I went like *that* from feeling kind of cautious about the whole thing to being in a shit-shit-shit panic about missing her. I started to run, in what I felt fucking sure was the wrong direction. And then I saw it, a little coffee shop called Pleasant Aromas, a place you could see straight off was a failing dream. I took five to catch my breath and confidence, standing outside a hairdresser's, reading a sign saying *Qualified Stylist Needed* (and judging by the woman just coming out, they were). Then I looked into the café, through the rainbows painted on the glass. Nothing but empty wooden tables.

I went in anyway, as if I'd nothing better to do, and I was so convinced she wasn't there it took a while to bring her into focus. But she was there – the only person – sat at the back on a yellow-painted chair, a red leather bag on the floor beside her, drinking from a painted mug, a jam jar of real flowers at her elbow, her hand half-lifted in an idle wave. 'God, I'm sorry,' she said, when I sat down. 'You've been running. I forgot how far it was. I came in the car. What d'you want to drink?'

When I got my brain in gear, I said, 'Hi.'

'Hi. D'you want a coffee?'

'Oh – right – no, just a Coke.'

'Fine.' She nodded at the lonely aproned woman behind the counter. 'Anything to eat? They do nice carrot cake.' She'd been eating some – she shoved away a plate of big damp orange crumbs. The woman, maybe the one who'd had the dream, smiled hopefully at me over her homemade heaps. She'd her hair in a bun, to give it that country kitchen feel.

'No, just Coke – thanks.'

'I've been thinking about you, since Saturday,' said Cassandra, as the woman set down my drink. 'I wanted to know how you were feeling about everything.'

I said nothing, sucking up Coke. I thought how beautiful she looked today, in a green cardigan, and her hair done up in a black velvet bow.

'I just thought you might want to talk about it.' Then she added, 'My parents divorced when I was still at school – it's a really hard thing to have happen, isn't it?'

Of course I wasn't stupid enough to think she meant talk about *us*. Yet I couldn't help feeling disappointed; it showed on my face, I guess. I said to the yellow table between us, 'I'm fine, thanks.' On the table, her white hand was creeping slowly towards me across the painted wood.

'I'm sorry – I didn't mean to upset you,' she said, as her fingers reached mine, gently stroking me with her thumb. 'I just wanted you to know I was here for you if you needed me. That's what teachers are for, you know. We're not just here to teach. We're here to listen as well.'

'I'm OK,' I said. I was so sensitive to the moving touch of her thumb, the back of my hand grew slightly sore beneath it.

She dropped her voice throatily. 'I'm concerned about you. I want you to be happy.'

I remembered Matt saying, *Maybe she wants to give you extra lessons*, and she asked, curiously, 'What are you smiling at?'

'So – how come you're taking us for English?'

'Someone had to take over. I volunteered.'

'Are you *serious*?'

She became oddly self-conscious, whipping her hand away, not meeting my eyes, lifting the end of her ponytail over her shoulder. 'It makes a change from year seven. And it's easier to get supply teachers for the young ones.'

I didn't even know that's where she'd been. 'My mum teaches year-seven drama once a week,' I said, without thinking, and then wished I hadn't. I didn't want to give her the impression I thought she was like my mum.

She seemed pretty damned shocked. 'Your *mum*? Goodness. What's her name?'

I really wished I hadn't mentioned it. 'Annie. She's a supply teacher.' I added hopefully, 'You might not know her . . .'

'*Annie*? Oh my god . . .' She frowned and started pinching and tugging at the front of her green cardigan. 'Of course I know her – she started the beginning of this term, like me – *Annie*? Are you sure?' And then she laughed, breathlessly. 'Of course you're sure – I mean, you're not going to make a mistake about your own mother's name, are you? Do you want another Coke?' She flapped her hand at the counter. 'Anything to eat? Hey – didn't I see Annie at Sisi's party? Oh, but wasn't your dad there? They get on OK then? That makes things easier. My parents fought like animals.'

'Yeah?' I didn't want to get into this conversation.

'I must say,' said Cassandra, staring intently at my fresh fizzing Coke, 'she must have had you when she was very *young*.'

'Well . . . I don't think she was *that* young,' I said.

She seemed a bit pained. 'We're all old to you, I suppose.'

Sometimes she was hard to follow. 'I didn't mean . . .'

'Of course you didn't,' she said, with one of her massive stretchy smiles.

Not sure if I'd understood her meaning, I said nothing, and nor did she. In the silence, we both watched her pulling petals off the thin white flowers in the jam jar and scattering them across the yellow wood. Then she folded her left hand under her chin, and stirred the mess she'd made with her long right fingertip. I brushed the petals into my hand and dumped them into the clean glass ashtray.

'Neurotically tidy?' she asked, tearing off some more.

'That's neurotic,' I said. 'That flower-pulling thing.'

'I've thought about you a lot since Saturday night,' she said.

Was that the same as what she'd said before? I didn't really know. 'Thanks.' Ridiculous answer.

She looked very directly at me, with her big pencilled eyes. 'It's a pity you had to rush off on Sunday so soon.'

'Sorry.' Then I thought she was being unfair to me – I hadn't rushed off anywhere, it was her who'd acted all distant, sitting in the kitchen with her back to me, head in a newspaper, saying nothing. 'But you were reading the papers.'

'Well . . .' She shrugged, squirming around on her chair with a little unapologetic grin. 'You could've read them with me.'

'Really?' I said. 'I thought you wanted to be alone. Sorry.'

She smiled, arching her neck a bit, as if she was feeling smug, as if she'd scored one over on me. 'Don't be sorry. At least you stayed for breakfast.'

'Have you got a boyfriend?'

She burst out laughing. 'What sort of a question is that?'

'Just . . . a question.'

'Does he stay for breakfast, you mean?'

Of course that's what I'd meant. I'd seen the condoms, hadn't I? The naff aftershave in her bathroom cabinet. She sat waiting for me to answer, smiling sympathetically. I finished my Coke.

She pushed my glass aside. 'Do you have a girlfriend?'

'No.'

'I don't believe you.' She was enjoying teasing me. 'A lovely-looking boy like you. Tall, dark and handsome. What girl could resist those huge green eyes?'

I felt myself blush, and wriggled in my seat. 'I don't have a girlfriend.' Then I said quickly, 'Do you have a boyfriend?'

She tensed up and sighed, tugging bits out of her cardigan again, chin down, acting like she'd really not wanted to go down this road. 'Look, I'm not going to pretend I never see anyone, Ferdia.'

'Does he stay for breakfast?' Why did I ask that? And, oh god, I suddenly, mortifyingly realised – the woman behind the counter was really loving this.

Cassandra hesitated, stretching out the soft green wool. 'Come on. What do you think? I'm not a nun.'

The woman genuinely was watching us; she'd both hands on the glass top and her eyes on Cassandra, totally lost in listening. I jumped up, grabbed my bag, and stormed out of the shop. It felt liberating yet guilty, like running out of a lesson.

A wind'd got up and patches of sun were racing down the road, catching on side mirrors. Leaves scratched and hopped along the pavements. It was a quiet wide street; a car drove by, braked, double-parked, and she jumped out, legs and arms everywhere, hair ruffling in the wind. 'Ferdia – wait! What's the matter with you? Don't you want a lift?'

Too weak to leave again, I stood waiting with my school bag.

She came right up to me, running her eyes over me, and then her hands – she gasped and pulled my hair and kissed me furiously on the mouth; she rammed her knee between my thighs; I caught her round the waist before she went off balance; I closed my eyes; the bag slid off my shoulder with a bang; she kept on kissing me, her wide lips spreading out, softer and wetter; she squirmed and kept taking deep delicate breaths. 'I didn't pay,' she murmured suddenly into my mouth. 'I didn't pay.' Her puzzling words buzzed on my lips.

I pulled away, burning, shaking, thrown. 'What?'

'The woman in the shop – I just ran out after you, I so much didn't want you to run away from me. I didn't pay.'

'Shit.' We both looked helplessly up the road, but only dead leaves came rasping after us down the long empty pavement.

She started to giggle, shivering. 'And I bet we were her only customers all afternoon. Poor woman.'

'Forget about her.' I hugged her, and for a minute she went soft in my arms, boneless under the cool green wool. Then she hardened and pushed me away; I whined in fright, grabbing at her like a blind man.

'Not here,' she said clearly. 'Not where people can see.'

'I don't care. I don't care.'

She was as alert as I was drugged, a tight grip on my arm, checking out our surroundings. We were stood on the pavement outside a locked-up second-hand furniture place, insanely paranoid grills over door and windows, crammed to the ceiling with unsellable junk. A narrow open passageway ran down the side of it, pitted and puddled. 'Down here.' She urged me with her, into the yard behind. A van was there, with no front wheels; pallets leaning up against the walls; dangerous piles of splintered furniture; a splash of broken plates. Holding me by both hands she pulled me after her over the dirty broken ground till she was stood with her back to the back wall of the shop, sheltered from the wind, and then she stopped, and just waited, large shiny eyes fixed over my shoulder. I thought she seemed anxious looking, as if she was as vulnerable as me. I thought – she wants me to be a man or something. I didn't know what to do with her, but I pushed her back hard into the flaky whitewashed plaster; a shower came down on her hair like dandruff; she smiled and tilted up her pale, thin face; I kissed her open mouth and leant

against her till I felt like I must be crushing her and support-
ed my weight with my hands on the crumbling wall, sweating, touching my forehead lightly to hers, then resting my
cheek against hers, feeling this was it, this was the moment.

'Come on, then,' she whispered.

Startled by the impatience in her voice, I stood back. She
came after me, frowning intently, her fingers popping me
open, coat, belt, jeans.

'Ah . . .' She pushed her hands up under my T-shirt. I
flinched at their hard coldness. 'Sssh . . .' She pushed them
down into my boxers.

'Cassandra . . .'

'Ssh . . .'

I lost my head and shoved her down onto the ripped-up
muddy tarmac and pulled up her skirt. She was wearing
stockings. I froze and stared. Christ. Did she always wear
them?

'Ferdia . . .' She meant, get on with it.

Believe me, I wanted to. I was so keen to fuck her my body
was pumping – not just my dick, which was about to burst.
But I'd never got this far before, except last year with my ex-
girlfriend's ex-best mate (not worth it). Taking a deep determined breath, I tugged down Cassandra's loose silky pants.
She rose up on one elbow, serious-looking, blonde hair over
her face, and dragged them off over one foot, letting them
hang from the other ankle. Then she opened her slippery
stockinged legs, worked down my trousers, pulled me on top
of her, took a firm grip of my dick and forced it inside her
cunt. For a moment I thought it wasn't going to go, then in it
sunk, easy as anything, so warm and wet I nearly cried, it was
that much better and more welcoming than a wank.
'Cassandra . . . Cassandra . . .'

She said something incomprehensible, bit me on the shoulder and dug her fingernails in my arse. Nothing hurt me: not
her teeth nor her nails nor the icy air on my thighs nor the
sharp little stones embedding themselves in my knees,

including the knee I'd mashed when I was with her last. The only show in town was my frenzied dick, which I kept pushing and shoving and thrusting in until, like a desperate madman's homemade bomb, it exploded without advance warning inside her body, blowing me sky high in the process.

Some time later, after I'd realised I was still alive, my first thought was I should check if Cassandra was OK. I shifted gently off her and sat up, but, after one look, I decided against asking what it was like for her. Still on her back, motionless in the dirt; eyes palely closed; hair spread loosely in a puddle; skirt wrenched up round her waist; mud-stained thighs, still parted wide, exposing her crimson cunt to the cold shrivelling air – it didn't seem possible she could've enjoyed herself. I should've asked her if she was OK, but the truth was, right that second, still swept by after-shocks and first-time pride, I didn't want to know. It had been so out-of-this-world for me, I just wanted to believe it was mutual so we could go on doing it in every gross backyard in London, in every dump, in every filthy gutter. Heart still drumming, I leant back on my hands, feeling the chill breeze on my scorching face. When I looked again, she'd opened her big oddly coloured eyes and was staring at me. It gave me a jolt like a dead person coming alive. 'Help me up,' she said coolly.

Nervous now, I scrambled to my feet, with one hand hoisting my jeans over my trembling knees, stretching out the other hand to her. She got up slowly, stiffly, groaning, standing to brush herself down, adjusting her suspenders and her skirt, complaining 'Oh god!' at the ladders in her stockings. 'What's my back look like?' She twisted it towards me, while trying to see for herself over her shoulder. Her green cardigan was grey-brown with yard-floor slime; leaves and stones were stuck to the ruined wool and in her muddied hair. 'For god's sake, Ferdia, brush me down a bit.'

I realised sinkingly I must've pissed her off in some crass stupid way – done it all wrong, got the wrong idea in the first place, not performed properly, not lived up to her expectations. I rubbed uselessly at her back and tried to untangle the rubbish from her hair. She flinched. 'Sorry.' I was too flustered, hurting her. I was in a rising panic. 'Shit, I'm really sorry.'

Turning on me, she grabbed my wrists, pinching them hard and tight and still. 'Be honest,' she frowned. 'Was this your first time?' Eyes on the dirty ground, ashamed by how fucking obvious it was, I stood with my wrists locked in her hands and answered nothing. She jerked me closer and kissed my cheekbone gently. 'Thank you.'

'Oh, Cassandra . . .' It was like going upwards in Matt's lift – a stomach-turning flight into the open sky.

She put her finger over my mouth. 'Ssh. Oh, and by the way – next time we should use a condom.'

Next time! I wrapped my arms around her grubby body and plunged my face into her thin scented neck. 'Cassandra!' She was offering me a second chance! 'Cassandra!'

'That's me name,' she mocked me, pushing me gently away.

My abandoned schoolbag was still on the pavement, books tumbling out of it, and her car was still double-parked, without a ticket. I couldn't believe I hadn't been robbed, or she been towed; she shook her head laughing at my amazement. 'We've only been a few minutes.' Now that really shocked me. She got her coat out of the car and put it on over her clothes, covering everything except the long ladders. 'Shall we pay that poor woman?' She meant our friend in Pleasant Aromas. I wouldn't've bothered, but Cassandra seemed eager to do it. We got in her car and drove the fifty yards back to the café.

'You stay here, I'll pay,' I offered.

'Don't be daft,' she said, leaping out with her red leather bag. I'd meant because her hair was in such an obvious mess, despite my efforts at tidying her up; tangled and twiggy and part of it stuck in a clump with what I thought might be a blob of grey chewing-gum. She didn't seem to care, though;

she insisted on waiting for me to come in as well. 'We've just remembered we forgot to pay you!' she cried, waltzing cockily through the tinkling door. 'What do we owe you?' The woman was serving someone else, a man in a long grey cardigan, and took a moment to come over. I could see she was really interested in the state of Cassandra; she kept checking out her hair and her stockings, and glancing at me in between – not quite at me, more at my neck. I was dying. She spent ages checking the bill, less than a fiver. When we got out of the shop, Cassandra went into fits of giggles. 'Do you think she noticed anything?' She put her hand over her mouth, sniggering away like mad. 'Do you think she *guessed*?'

Her hyper happiness was catching. From being kind of embarrassed in the café, I was starting to laugh myself. This amazing, beautiful thing'd just happened to me – I was king of the world – I didn't care who knew – I wouldn't't've minded everybody in the universe knowing. I threw my arm around her. 'Who gives a shit about what she thinks?'

Cassandra sprang out of my embrace and glared at me as if I'd tried to stab her. 'Are you *insane*? Don't you realise the danger you've put me in?' She almost shoved me into the passenger seat, ran round the car and jumped in the driver's side, slamming the door, jiggling the key in the ignition, unable to start the car in her agitation. 'Don't you realise what people are like? If anyone – *anyone* – finds out about this, I'll lose my job, I'll never get another job, I'll have to leave London. You'll *never* see me again.' The car revved up. She grabbed the gear stick and shook it, making an outraged face at me. 'Is that what you want – to have me lose my job?'

Mostly, I was horrified at the idea of never seeing her again. 'Of course I won't tell anyone – I'm not like that. I don't want to get you into trouble.'

But she kept on staring me down with blue-green eyes. 'I'm serious, Ferdia. Deadly serious. People make judgements. People are hard and cruel. If you tell a single soul what you've done today, I might as well kill myself at once.'

'Jesus – listen – I'm not telling anyone, ever!'

Slamming into gear, she accelerated away so fast she pinned me to my seat. As she darted through the side streets, it struck me I was in increasing pain, as if some anaesthetic was wearing off. The knee I'd cut up last time I'd been with her, falling on the pavement in the rain, was in crippling agony now. The rough ground had stripped the scabs from off the graze, and gravel was buried in my broken flesh. My neck also stung where she'd bitten me – I touched my hand to it, and Cassandra, glancing at me as we paused at some lights, winced, grinned forgivingly and murmured, 'Oops.' So I guessed, rather proudly, I must have a bite mark. No wonder Bunhead had been staring. Remembering to keep our vital secret, I turned up the collar of my coat.

Chapter Ten

Lily and Aristotle and Matt had agreed the band should meet with that slaphead opportunist, Dickie, and Matt was excited but in a panic. 'I mean, what if he trashes my stuff, man? I could lose my edge . . . Or if he really likes us he might lure us into selling out or something. What if I get so famous I forget the message, man?'

'Right.' I was lost in the moment of entering Cassandra's bony soft-centred body. 'That's great.'

He strongly suspected I wasn't listening. 'What d'you mean, great? What the fuck d'you disappear on me for? I needed to discuss this with you . . .' I struggled for a reply; nothing was in my head but her. It was seriously frustrating, not being able to talk about it, like I'd won a billion on the lottery and wasn't allowed to tell my friends. Or it was like I'd done this dodgy bank job, and had to keep shtum or spend the rest of my life in jail. I realised at last why those pathetic small-time crooks who hang around the big boys in the films can never keep quiet about the mega-heist but go on the razz and blab to drunken strangers. Matt persisted, shivering moodily, 'What was so fucking important you couldn't be here?'

We were crouched freezing on his balcony, floating free above the brilliant city, spacemen in a breezy galaxy. The windows of the other blocks were square stars evenly plastered on the black. Far beneath our feet, an alien craft – the shuttered Evil Eye – fired an occasional pencil-width of light as its battered door opened and closed; some DJ was drawing the crowds. Aristotle had already left, ordered home to some big Greek plate-smashing family get-together back in Golders Green. His drums still took up most of the living room.

Through the closed glass doors behind us came the rattle and hiss of Lily idly messing with his kit. When I looked back, from our freezing capsule into the mother ship, I could see nothing of her but her long black hair, but she was wholly reflected in Natasha, who, kneeling in centre-carpet, was clearly imitating Lily's exact pose, worshipping her freely in her five-year-old heart. 'I'm here now, aren't I?' I said, hoarsely.

'It's eight in the fucking evening, man,' said Matt. 'Where d'you get to, anyway?'

'Nowhere important.' I could've been there ages ago. If I'd gone straight round at half past four, when Cassandra dropped me at the end of my road, I'd hardly've been late at all. It wasn't like the greatest moment of my life had taken up much of anybody's time. But I couldn't even think about going to Matt's so soon. I just staggered down the windy street to my house, and spent forever trying to get the key in the door, like I'd been out on the piss for days. Jason Peckham, in the latest Arsenal shirt, opened it to me, but I was still so stunned by what'd happened I barely registered that some arsehole was letting me into my own home – I was so out of it, I nearly even thanked him. Then he wanted to know if I'd been in a fight – making out he was really concerned, coming too close to me with his bright blue stare.

'Get away from me,' I said, but I was tired, and slightly sick. Actually, I did kind of feel like I'd been in a fight. I went upstairs and lay down on my bed, flat on my back, legs stretched out. Things started to spin like the wheel of a bike dropped on its side. I pressed the wall with one hand to keep me steady. Everything'd rushed by so fast, it was like I hadn't really been there when it was happening to me, so I needed to take the time out now to experience it, going over everything in my head, flicking through the incredible sequence of events, listening to the words we'd said, remembering her serious eyes on me, the extraordinary feel of her body inside and out, that spectacular moment when I blew apart (fuck! fuck! fuck! what's the date? I have to write it down). The nosy woman in the café; bubblegum and shit in Cassandra's hair. When she dropped me off, she'd said cheekily, See you in class. See you, I'd said. (Who is the man that gets to stay for breakfast?) Whenever I went back in my mind to the main event, I was totally chuffed. In fact, after an hour or so thinking about it all, I got a blue biro out of my schoolbag and dug '27th October' in small letters into the paint on the back of my door.

'What's the date?' I asked Matt suddenly.

'24th.'

'Oh. Right.' Then I got suspicious because he hadn't even taken the time to think about it. 'You sure?'

'Yeah, my mum's birthday's tomorrow.'

Lily slid open the glass partition just as he was saying it. 'Your mum's birthday? What're you getting her?'

'What do you get the woman who has nothing?' He jumped up and pushed past her into the barely furnished room. 'A bottle of gin, right?'

I came in off the balcony too, leaving the shining night outside. Neither me nor Lily said anything back to Matt about what he'd just said.

Natasha announced happily to Lily, 'I'm giving my mum a picture I did at school.' And she ran and got it from the bedroom. 'This is our house.' An excellent tower block, a great long squishy rectangle covered in windows, looking about ready to fall over. 'This is me and my mum.' Two leggy scribbles on a scribble of green, at the bottom of the picture.

'Where's your brother?' asked Lily affectionately.

'Up there.' Natasha pointed him out, far above the figures of her and her beloved mum, not in a window but standing right on top of the teetering block, a stick man with a stick guitar, his many-fingered hand melting into the sun. 'Do you want to be in it?'

'Please,' said Lily.

But Natasha selfishly sketched Lily in at the bottom, holding Natasha's own hand, not up there where she might've wanted to be, with sky-high Matt in his sunlit heaven.

Natasha'd left open the door to her bedroom, which she shared with her mum. Through it I could see the sole of Tessa's trainer, her foot drooping off the end of the bed as she slept the unshakeable sleep of the part-time dead. Matt picked up his guitar and broke out in a rather folky un-Mattish way. *'She's the woman who has nothing and you've got to give her something cos she's sick of having nothing to her name . . .'* Lily scuffed the drums and hummed a little, smiling at Natasha, and I, relieved the man was going so slow, plink-plonked a few recognisable notes. Tessa's foot hung like a broken reed. Matt frowned at his frets, shook his scruffy head, and sang, *'She's the woman who has nothing, and you want to give her something, but whatever you may give her it will all turn into nothing, you're just making her a present of the same . . .'*

'What the fuck is that?' yelped Lily.

Matt halted and glared at her, a flushed offended unrecognised boiled-pink genius at work, but it was me she was pointing at – as I bent over the bass I'd dropped my shoulder and now Lily was staring excitedly at my neck. I'd seen for myself in the mirror Cassandra's large crimson bite; it was the mark of an animal; then I'd inspected myself all over; my back and arse were seriously scratched up, like our cat'd been at me; I was alarmed and proud at being so violently branded. I jerked my coat collar up again, blushing as bad as Matt. 'It's nothing. Leave it out.'

She screeched again, for all the world like a year-seven kid, 'Hey, Matt, *look* – Ferdia's got a fucking enormous *love* bite . . . Shit, Ferdia – where *were* you all afternoon?'

'It *is* her,' joked Matt, wrestling with me to get a proper look. 'I fucking *knew* it, you sly dog, Ferdia.'

'Is not! Get off of me!'

'Is not who?' shouted Lily.

I fell over Natasha, who was already shrieking with almost tearful excitement, and now burst into real tears, because she'd got a bash from my guitar. Matt soothed her down and gave her a drink of water and carried her off to bed, tucking her in beside their silent mother.

Lily kept on at me while he was out of the room; I told her I didn't want to talk about it, but she didn't give a damn. 'Come on, tell us . . .'

'I'm not fucking telling you . . .' I picked up my guitar and leant it against the balcony window. I thought – if she knew!

She started running through all the girls she knew were at my school, beginning unflatteringly at the bottom of the Z-list.

'Victoria?'

'No!'

'Fatima?'

'For fuck's sake . . .'

'Pearl?'

I fell on my front on the thin foam sofa, sulking and determined to say no more. Obviously she didn't think much of my pulling power. In the knockabout with Matt I'd caught my bad knee and now it was killing me again.

'Don't tell me it was Kylie.'

'*NO!* Jesus! What do you take me for?'

She came and sat on the floor beside me, giggling and poking me in the ribs while I grumbled and wriggled away from her. 'Cos if it was, I hope you used a condom . . .'

'Fuck's sake, Lily . . . Leave it out.'

'I mean, if you didn't, you wouldn't catch me following anywhere she's been, know what I mean?'

I looked at her, startled, and she actually gasped and slapped her hand over her mouth, as if she could cram the slippery words back in.

'I mean . . .' she protested, muffled by her palm. But she never added anything to explain what she really meant, just staring at me, practically cross-eyed with horror, over the rim of her hand.

'What's up, Lil?' asked Matt, coming out of his mum's room, gently pushing to the door behind him. 'Did he tell you who it was?'

She didn't move at once, but then shifted on her arse and made a show of grinning, a row of small white teeth. 'It's Kylie, innit? Definitely Kylie.'

'Fuck me . . .' choked Matt, trapped between awe and disbelief.

'You dirty little *liar*!' And I hit her with the sofa cushion, restoring normal relations instantly, like a hard slap to a television. 'It's *no one*, right?'

Matt said, 'Just don't go AWOL on us next time, all right mate? Bring whoever it is along with you.'

I broke out into slightly hysterical laughter. 'I don't think so.'

'Whatever.' He made out he was losing interest, messing with his strings, thinking about his tunes.

'It must be serious,' said Lily, 'if he's not introducing her to his friends.'

'It's not serious,' I said. I caught her eye and she gave me a sweet half-smile, kind of held-back but touchingly friendly, wrapping a finger in her long black hair. My raw knee ached. I could feel the cold teatime wind on my bared back as Cassandra wrenched off my coat and dragged my shirt up to my shoulderblades. I rolled back onto my front as my dick suddenly hardened. No one could call such a muddy fuck romantic. 'It's not serious.' Hearing my words, my heart grew hot and trembled under my shirt. 'It's nothing, right?' I could've done with a sharp blow to the head myself, to clear the screen. I propped myself up on my elbows. 'So you're going to call Dickie, yeah?'

'Yeah,' said Lily, delighted to change channels, get away from the subject of possible sex. 'I'm definitely gonna call him. Only, I need his number – you still got his card?' I didn't – I thought Matt had it, but he denied it. Lily said, a bit snottily, to me, 'Didn't you say he gave one to *Cassandra*? Why don't you ask *her*?'

'I don't know if I'm gonna to see her any time soon,' I said quickly.

Matt stared at me like I'd gone completely mad. 'You're seeing her tomorrow.'

'*What?* No I'm not!'

'She been teaching us all week, you dickhead! Haven't you fucking noticed?'

'Oh . . . right . . .'

He gave me an odd, suspicious look.

Lily wouldn't let it go. 'Or why don't you call her – seeing as you're so *friendly* with her and all . . .'

'How can I? I don't have her number . . .' Actually, I did, since four-thirty, when Cassandra wrote it down for me on a piece torn off the bottom of some kid's essay. But I was hardly going to let on, not with Matt looking at me like that. 'I'll get Dickie's number off Abigail tonight,' I promised, just to shut Lily up.

Standing in the hall of my house, receiver in hand, I wondered what I'd do if Harry answered. I hadn't spoken to him since Sisi's party, not since I'd discovered how long that bastard had been lying to us. He'd called a few times during the week, but I always told my mum I'd ring him back, and didn't bother. Taking a breath, I dialled Abigail's number. At the end of the darkened hall, yellow light outlined the kitchen door; glasses were clinking behind it; I could make out the blurred shapes of words but not who was speaking – not my mum, nor Peckham's sharp voice neither. Harry's cat had its nose pressed damply to the crack between the door and its frame, waiting to be let in.

Abigail picked up the phone.

'Hello,' I said, without using her name, because we didn't use her name in this house where I was now.

'Harry?' She gasped it out with love and relief, but fury overtook her before I could set her right. 'Get back here now before I rip your ugly little bollocks off, you unfaithful *prick*!'

'Hang on . . .'

'I know where you're ringing from! Don't think I don't

recognise her fucking number! I'm sick and tired of this, Harry – it's make your pissing mind up time, you prick on a stick, you pompous little arsehole, you . . . you *cunt* . . .'

'It's me . . .'

'Yes, you, you pathetic impotent middle-aged career-on-the-skids *fucker*!!'

' . . . Ferdia.'

There was a long heavy-breathing silence at the other end of the phone. I assumed she was pulling herself together, and was trying to think of a good conciliatory exit line, but she came back at me with such a high-pitched non-verbal shriek, I had to whip the phone away from my ear. I could still hear her, though. 'Well, is he coming back or isn't he? No – don't answer that – let him tell me his fucking self, the selfish coward!'

I brought the handset as near to me as I dared. 'He's not here, Abby.'

'I know he's there! Put him on the fucking line!'

Staring down the hall to the kitchen, I suddenly realised she was right – it was my dad's voice I was getting through the closed door. I experienced an automatic rush of pleasure, of happy recognition, but then felt weird and depressed because I hadn't recognised his voice at once. What had been so familiar in this house now sounded inappropriate, out of place – like a ghost is never really welcome, however much we loved the person before they died.

Reading my silence as the truth, Abigail stopped shrieking and started crying distant buckets. 'I just want to talk to him. Please, Ferdie, please . . .'

I hesitated. 'Wait, I'll just . . .'

Leaving her hanging, I pushed open the kitchen door. My dad looked towards me, falling silent; he was sat sideways to the table, resting his elbow, cupping a glass of wine; my mum was on the couch, drinking and smoking and looking coldly pissed off; Jason Peckham was stood with his back to the draining board, smoking with a deliberately blank expression and flicking his ash into the plate-filled sink. The cat ran in past me and jumped onto Harry's knee, turning round and round to make herself comfortable, clearly relieved that order was restored and her favourite human being come home at last. 'Hi there, Twinky. I hear you've been trashing the old place.' Then he flashed his confident well-brushed smile at me, acting, like the cat, as if everything in the room was normal, 'Ferdia, hi! Where on earth have you been? Your mother and I are discussing what to do when your school fails its inspection.'

'*If* it fails the inspection,' said Annie, sharply. 'Don't forget I'm teaching there, Harry, before you have the place shut down. Don't forget, *I need the money.*'

'There's plenty of other teaching jobs,' he said, making her choke on a mouthful of wine in exasperation. 'It's Ferdia we have to think of. We can't leave him stuck in a failing school.' He said to me, stroking his humming cat, 'You've got exams coming up. You don't want to be caught in the middle of a closure row.'

I was totally speechless at him acting this way, like time hadn't passed, as if he'd never left – especially now I knew how long he'd been fucking about with his new girlfriend. When I'd calmed down enough to speak, I decided cold-bloodedly to drop him in it. 'Abigail's on the phone. She wants to speak to you.'

While Harry stared, stunned, at me, and Jason covered his mouth with the back of his hand, my mum flew up in her seat and spat, 'What's the *fuck's* she doing calling here, that little tart? I don't want her phoning this house again, Harry! Ever! Tell her!'

'I . . .' He couldn't cope with all these demands. I stood back to let him out the door, if he ever decided to stand up. 'Tell her . . .' he said. (What? 'I love you, I'll be back soon?' 'I'm never coming back, you stupid bitch?' There wasn't really any message that would be appropriate for his son to pass on to his girlfriend – even Harry could see that, once he'd really thought about it.) 'Oh, for fuck's sake.' He got to his feet, unhitching the cat's desperate claws from his trousers. 'Sorry about this,' he muttered to Annie, unusually humble.

'Huh.' She smoked her fag disgustedly.

We could hear him clearly in the hall – after a mere thirteen months he'd forgotten how hard you had to close the door, and Twinky sidled after him, forcing it open. Annie put her chin on her smoking hand, with a furious mean-minded expression, and Jason with a small twist of his thin waist set his finished fag on end on the draining board, leaving it to burn down to the filter. None of us said anything. We were all openly listening to his end of the row, and I guess all three of us were playing at filling in the blanks. At this end, Harry was going, in a deliberately low voice, 'No . . . No . . . I can't talk to you about that now . . . Don't . . . Look, this isn't doing either of us any good . . . Don't . . . We'll talk about that some other time . . . Please . . . I'm not . . . . Of *course* I'm not . . . Listen, I'm going to put the phone down now . . . She is *not* . . . If you're just calling up to abuse me . . .'

My mum was now smirking to herself. I sat at the table in Harry's seat and considered how weird it was we were all here, and Abigail alone in her flat, weeping and wailing on the phone.

'Please don't,' said Harry, loud and urgent. 'Please don't! I'll be home soon, all right?'

Annie scowled into the wine glass she was holding balanced on her knees, black curls hiding her soft round face.

When he came back into the kitchen, he was pale and sweaty with exasperation, wiping his face with his hands. I got up from his chair, but he waved me to sit down again and dropped heavily on to the sofa beside Annie instead. The sudden upheaval of cushions caused a little wine to run down the side of her glass. Annoyed, she snapped, mopping the drops with her fingers, 'Did you tell your tart I didn't want her phoning here again?'

'What?' He made an effort to remember which place he

was in, which woman he had to answer to. 'Oh, right . . . Don't worry – she won't.' The cat sprang back onto his lap.

'Hadn't you better be going *home*?'

He grimaced at Annie apologetically, restraining a delirious Twinky from licking his face. 'I'll just stay for another couple of minutes – please?' He slid his arm gently along the back of the couch, behind her shoulders. 'Until we decide what to do about this bloody school thing.'

'I'm knackered, me,' said Peckham, unexpectedly. 'If you don't mind.' My parents looked up at him, my mother with a long face, my father like he was amazed to hear a monkey speak. 'I'll say goodnight, then,' said Peckham.

'Goodnight,' remarked Harry, briefly raising his hand.

Jason Peckham, with an exaggerated wink at my mum – whose pink mouth was trembling, trying not to look upset – strolled with easy arrogance in his Arsenal shirt and Calvin Klein jeans out of our kitchen, along our hall . . . and slowly up our stairs.

Harry craned forward in his seat to see if he'd heard right. Then he looked at Annie, who was now topping up her glass with a complacent smile. 'Did he just . . .?'

'What?' She was apparently concentrating on whether she was going to overfill the glass before the bottle ran out.

'Has he gone to the loo?'

She looked at him, round-eyed, making out like she didn't get what he was on about.

He indicated. 'Upstairs . . .'

'Hmm?' She gulped down a mouthful of the wine.

'So, Ferdia,' said my dad, one ear cocked hopefully for the flush of a toilet and descending feet. 'What are we going to do about your school?'

'Talking of going to the loo, Harry, I need to go myself.' She jumped up and kissed the top of my head. 'Goodness, it's late. Haven't you got school in the morning?' She made a big show of yawning.

'Night, mum,' I said automatically, as she left the room.

'She'll be back down in a minute,' Harry explained to me. Then he smiled warmly, showing his well-kept teeth, crinkling his actorly cheeks. 'What d'you think?'

'I'm *not* changing school.' No way – not now. I picked up Annie's nearly-full glass and took a swig.

'She's coming back for that . . . No, I mean – it's like old times, isn't it, you and me in the kitchen, having a chat? And Twinky here . . .' He stroked Twinky heavily from head to tail, while she arched her back into his palm. 'I've so missed this. It's been so long.' Caught out by astonishment again, I felt, as at Sisi's party, the overwhelming urge to punch him out and glared straight back at him. After a few seconds his smile faded; he took off his black framed glasses and rubbed his eyes, making a tired puzzled expression. With swelling contempt, I thought: How can he possibly claim it's like old times? Weren't there just the three of us back then – no hysterical Abigail on the phone, no hard-faced Arsenal fans upstairs? But – fuck me – I'm so wrong about that, aren't I? Abigail *was* there all along, stamping her demanding little feet, screaming at him to leave us in the past, fucking with our lives for two whole years before the end. She must've been like a poltergeist in the house, but visible only to Harry (right up to the last, me and my mum only noticed from time to time that the air in the room had gone unnaturally cold). 'I just meant,' he said placatingly, smoothing the bridge of his nose where his spectacle frames had marked it, 'it's good your mum and me can talk together again. It's good we met up at that party.'

'Abby didn't think so,' I reminded him. I drank some more of Annie's wine.

He gaped at me, whipping his hand from his face. 'What? What did she . . .?' He stopped, set his mouth in a full-lipped line, decided he didn't want to know, then, heaving a world-weary sigh, invited me to empathise with him. 'I find it hard getting through to her sometimes. She doesn't understand what it's like to have a family.'

'You better have that baby, then,' I couldn't resist saying.

'Oh.' He grinned awkwardly – a virgin youth embarrassed. 'There's no rush there.' He reached for his fine floppy hair, rummaging his fingers through the crown, checking for the distressing signs of age. 'No rush.' He chanced his arm. 'We haven't known each other long.'

'Yeah, *right*.'

'What?'

Instantly, I realised I didn't want to talk about it. 'Nothing.'

Relieved to be off the hook, he cleaned his glasses on his shirt and shoved them back on, muttering and glancing at the door, 'What's she playing at?' He meant Annie. 'Where's she got to?' He again detached himself from his alarmed cat, stood up and lifted his jacket off the chair. 'Look, I'm sorry, Ferdie, I can't hang around any longer.' Old times must be so boring when revisited. 'We'll carry on this conversation another time, OK?'

'What conversation?' I was genuinely confused – it seemed we hadn't talked about a thing.

He winced at my stupidity. 'School. School.'

'Oh. Yeah.'

I and Twinky walked him to the door, she with her paws in his shadow of his heels. He stopped at the end of the hall, nearly stepping on her, dragging on his jacket. 'Look, this is hard for me too, Ferdia. I do . . . really. You know. And your mum . . .' He glared irritably at the darkened stairs, and raised his voice: 'Tell her I'll call, OK?' He huffed and left, but stopped again at the bottom of the steps, squinting up at me against the light from our house. 'I do feel torn, you know.' The wind was long blown out, and his voice carried perfectly in the calm black air, over Twinky's worried meowing. 'What with you here, and . . .' He glanced towards St John's Wood, through the miles of intervening brick. 'You know.' He smiled and straightened himself, one foot still on the lowest step. 'Come round tomorrow, yeah?' Then, doubtfully: 'Or d'you want to come back with me now?'

It was an interesting offer. I actually didn't want to pass my mother's door and hear the ugly cries of fun. Yet if I knew Abby, she'd be waiting for him with a meat axe, and I didn't want to risk being included in that little scenario either. It was a hard call. He wasn't the only one with his soul stuck half way up and down the Abbey Road.

'I'll see you tomorrow then,' he said, without waiting for my long-drawn-out answer.

'OK.' I slammed the door. In the kitchen, I found another bottle, refilled my mother's glass and sat for a while with the cat glaring malevolently at me like it was all my fault. Then I came back to the phone and dialled.

'Hello?'

'Cassandra?'

'Yes?'

'It's me, Ferdia.'

'Oh! You! Hi! How are you?'

'I'm all right . . . Listen, I wanted to ask you something. You know that bloke's card he gave you – Dickie? I'm kind of looking for his number.'

She went quiet for a moment, then said, 'Do you need it now? It might take me a while to find it.'

I thought, she's busy. Anyway, she knows this is only an excuse – I'm so transparently pathetic. 'It's OK. Sorry. Maybe you could bring it in tomorrow. Sorry to bother you.'

'No, it's fine, really – it's just that it's a bit late to go searching around.'

'In your own time, like, whenever you find it . . .'

'I was in bed, actually.'

'Shit. Sorry.'

'Do you want to come round? I can send you a cab.'

Fucking hell. 'Oh . . . OK.' Jesus Christ! 'That'd be great, yeah.'

Chapter Eleven

Matt was urging me, 'Wake up, man! Wake up, you lazy bastard!'

'G'way.' I was sunk heavily in the bed, having this fabulous dream of Naked Cassandra.

'Wake up, man, you're dribbling everywhere . . .'

No, not a dream – shit – a memory. I was jolted awake, every muscle tense; last night she'd come to the door of her flat with nothing on – tall, naked, white and slightly bony. Before I'd even got my breath, she'd dragged me in on top of her, onto the hard carpet of her hall, flat door still open, struggling to work my jeans below my knees, nails sunk into my prickling flesh, hissing in my ear, *Do it to me now!* By the time I'd come, my left thigh was cooked to crimson by her radiator; I was in pain and stank of burning flesh. Remembering, I moaned and shook.

'Ferdia – wake up! You're having a nightmare!' He was bouncing on the edge of the bed, sending shock waves through the mattress, rocking me up and down.

'Am not . . . G'way . . .' My mouth moved feebly on the pillow. She'd sent me home as soon as I'd stood up, and it was the same cab – maybe she'd asked him to wait? – the driver humming knowingly to himself in Turkish.

'Wake up! I *need* you, man.'

I still couldn't open my eyes. All I could see was Naked Cassandra, the newly-installed screen-saver of my brain.

'Listen, I've gotta talk to you, man – it's about the band – and Lily – I think she might be turning her back on the music gods.' He poked me between the shoulderblades, making my back muscles squirm. 'I'm worried how she keeps on about money and stuff. Do you think she's been sent to tempt me from the true path? Like, to test my resolve?'

'Jesus, Matt, I'm asleep . . .' Reluctantly, I peeled my eyes awake. His anxious pink face was hovering over mine.

'Talk to me.' Annoyingly, he was tugging the duvet off me. 'I'm feeling really strange about this. I need to talk to you . . . Hey, why're you dressed already?'

I'd crawled fully clothed to bed, Dickie's card tucked in my pocket like a tip. I pushed myself into a sitting position with a pointedly jaw-cracking yawn, licking away the tears of sleep as they ran down my face into my stretching mouth. 'What the fuck's the matter with you, man?'

He jumped up and hurried up and down the room, hands jammed into the pockets of his jeans, forehead crumpled, scowling. 'I came round as soon as I woke up.' The back of his tatty old jacket was soaking black, from running through the morning rain. 'Because I've been thinking,' he said, in a rising panicky voice, 'I don't want to do this, man – I want to keep it clean – I don't want some breadhead giving me an opinion, like, making me do commercial shit . . .' He argued, pleadingly, 'OK, at I first I thought it might be a good idea for the music, spread the word and that, and Aristotle's well into it, but maybe that's because Lily's been drawing him towards the dark side . . .'

Blinking desperately, still damply yawning, I made a real effort to concentrate on what he was saying, to push my pulsingly bright Naked Cassandra to one side of my inward monitor. 'Sit down, man – chill.' I swung my feet to the floor, patted the bed, then asked, confused, 'Why've you got this thing about Lily? I thought you really liked her?'

He sighed, throwing himself back down beside me, shoulders slumped against the wall, rapidly working a packet of ten out of his top pocket. When he peered into it, there was only one left – he offered it me insincerely, then, without pausing, lit it for himself. 'Yeah, I mean she's a beautiful girl and all that, and she's got a wicked voice – but, you know, underneath she's just a rich-kid and she can't help thinking about money – it's, like, a curse she's born under and I thought I could free her, but I guess it's stronger than me, and maybe, you know' – he wrinkled his scruffy eyebrows at me – 'I have to cut loose from her and go my own way? I mean, maybe I need to be playing to my own people? Tower-block rock for tower-block people . . .'

It struck me that he was still dreaming on about Peckham's offer to get us a gig at the Evil Eye, and butted in quickly: 'I think you're being really hard on Lily, man – she just loves your music and wants everyone to hear your songs. I mean, you don't have to worry about this bloke turning us into fucking tweenie pop idols or anything – you know, he's just some crappy little nobody – Abigail ditched him straight off, and so can we, if we don't like him.'

He hesitated, acting like I was trying to trap him with some really complicated cunning argument. After nearly starting a few sentences, he countered weakly, 'Yeah, but . . . what if we start making loads of cash and get corrupted?'

I laughed. I couldn't believe how flaky he was getting – like there weren't better things in the world to get worked up about. Things like . . . well, Cassandra, for instance. *Naked Cassandra* . . .

'Seriously, Ferdia. What if we start worshipping Mammon and that?'

'Jesus, Matt – for starters, there's no way that's going to happen, and next, if you make some money you can buy Nat some really nice clothes and if you make loads of money you can buy your mum a really nice big house to live in.'

'What, turn my family into *ground-dwellers*?' He sounded genuinely shocked. I felt this massive surge of irritation with him. Matt always stuck up for that fucking awful flat, how close it was to heaven and that, but no way did I believe that's all he wanted. He might've banged on like Jesus Bloody Christ about the evil of money and power and how it destroyed your soul, but he still hung around with me and Lily and Aristotle, none of us exactly tower block types to be honest, and he was always on the scrounge. I think he would've liked the good life, if he was only honest with himself and stopped this new thing of acting so weird and hung up and strange. Frustrated, not knowing what to say, I drifted back into dreaming of last night's sex, though I didn't realise I had until Matt started shoving me in the shoulder again, saying, 'What's with you these days, Ferdia? Are you getting your end away, or what?'

'NO.'

'I fucking *knew* it.' He snorted hysterically till his nose bubbled, back to his normal self. 'Go on then, tell us, man. Come on, I tell *you*, right?'

It was true, he did. 'Yeah, well, I'm a bit more fucking discreet than that, OK? I've got a bit more fucking respect than to go into details, know what I mean?'

'Look at me . . .' he whispered, mock-hypnotically, thrusting his pink face into mine, straining to keep his pale blue eyes wide open (though the smoke from his fag forced both of us to blink). It was this stupid truth game we'd played when we were kids – first one to look away and that. 'Tell. Me. Her. Name . . .'

I pictured telling him – his stunned respect – him begging on his knees for dirty details . . . Last night she'd totally freaked me out, grabbing my arms in a killer grip, fingertips buried in my biceps: *Don't tell a soul or you'll never see me again! I'll kill myself if anyone finds out!* I got up, went impatiently over to the chair and sat sideways on it, scowling out of the window into the street, counting the bright wet cars beneath the trees.

For a while he went silent, then I heard him shuffle across the room. He stroked my shoulder as if I was an animal, very softly like I might run away. 'Ferdie,' he said. 'Don't be a zombie kid. You're acting really weird, like, strange . . .

Exasperated, I shrugged his hand off me. 'I don't know what you're on about, man. *I'm* OK. It's *you* been acting weird, banging on about this stupid Dickie thing . . .'

His voice came over annoyingly patient. 'No, man, I'm just trying to save my life, fight the good fight, stand up for my soul. Help me, Ferdia? – it's tough on my own.'

I thought, with a heavy thud of my heart – Oh shit – he really is going mad. Then I reassured myself hastily, No, he's just taking the piss. Naked Cassandra flashed brilliantly before my eyes. 'Jesus – what's the time – don't we have to get to school?'

He answered, disappointed, 'Yeah . . .'

Cassandra asked me a question in class. After a few minutes of weakly staring at her, which I'd probably been doing since I'd sat down, I realised she really was addressing me, and answered, 'What?'

She tapped a pencil on her open book, lips in an obvious O of irritation, and bitched, 'Why do you come to my lessons if you can't be bothered to listen to a word I say?'

Now I was genuinely confused. I wanted to protest, Hang on a minute, what're you picking on me for? I'm your . . . I'm the boy you sent the cab for, aren't I? The one you keep telling how wonderful and handsome he is? The one you try to ignore in public? Remember me?

She glared at me bad-temperedly, twitching her long, narrow face, pushing her glasses up her nose. She was wearing her black and white checked skirt, a small black cardigan and bright black nail polish. 'Read the play, Ferdia,' she said nastily. 'You never know – you might even understand it.' What I couldn't understand was why she was going out of her way to humiliate me in public, giving all the crop-headed designer-dressed prats an excuse to fall about punching each other's arms, like she'd made this hilarious joke at my expense. Matt, at my side, wriggled his sandy eyebrows at me.

My jaw cramped up with fury. I flipped over the cheap photocopied pages on my desk, forward and back, and when the lunch bell went I balled them into my bag and took off fast, ahead of the hungry pack. I heard her call my name. I didn't stop. That is, I tried not to stop, but in no time the thrashing, squealing bodies passed me by. Matt was waiting at the distant corner. Cassandra's voice came clearly: 'Ferdia – wait a minute.' I struggled slowly on towards Matt, down the long, long corridor, but slower and slower and finally unable to move forwards, like a dog on one of those elastic leads. Unwillingly, I checked over my shoulder. She was leant in the doorway of the classroom, arms folded, dangling her glasses from her little finger. Naked Cassandra popped up blindingly on my internal screen. I looked back at Matt, who stood waiting, staring impassively at our teacher, his hand pressed lightly to the wall. I couldn't move. With an indifferent shrug, Matt slipped away around the corner. 'Ferdie . . .' She jerked my lead. When I reached her, she took my arm and hurried me back into the room, slamming the half-glass door behind us. 'Why did you go rushing off like that?' she asked, annoyed, perching, thighs crossed, arms crossed, on the edge of her desk. 'Come on. What's the foul expression for?'

I'd thought my face was a steady, angry blank. 'Nothing. I'm fine. Look, is this important? Matt's waiting for me.'

Her thin throat rippled with swallowing aggravation; lowering her head, she fingered one thigh through the black and white checked skirt. 'OK.' She raised her head seriously. 'OK. I'm sorry I got mad.' She added, persuasive now, wide smile tilted to one side, 'It's just, it's so frustrating . . . I know you've got a good brain, if you'd only bother to use it.' I cleared my throat, ready to point out her sad mistake, but she raised one hand to stop me. 'No, listen! None of . . .' – she sunk her voice, holding tight with her other hand to the edge of the desk, dropping down her eyes – 'what's happened between us . . .' – she swung one foot in a narrow black shoe, lifting her voice and eyes again – 'means you're allowed to get away with not doing any work, Ferdia. That's not the deal.' She fed me a bright, unreadable look, rapping her black fingernails on the underside of the desk. 'If I thought this . . . thing . . . between us was interfering in your education . . .'

I felt a breathless slap of panic. 'Hey, no, hang on, I never did any work in the first place, honest.'

She slid to a standing position, reaching out her hand, massaging my shoulder near my neck, rolling my bones beneath her painted fingers. I tensed up further. 'You should read the text at least. And do a few assignments.' She pushed me to arm's length, studied my face earnestly, blinking her long lashes, thick with mascara. 'I'll always be here. I'll help you in any way.'

I swung my heavy unread books from one hand to the other, thinking despairingly, Shit, is she saying it's over already?

'Fancy a coffee after school?' she asked, letting go my shoulder.

I dropped my bag and nearly fell over my feet picking it up. 'OK.'

'Same place as before?' Even as she said it, she was waving me out of the room. 'Go on, get out, Matt'll be wondering where you've got to. Haven't you got music to make?'

As I stumbled to the music room, I had to elbow my way through twenty or thirty members of Matt's growing club of mini-fans, year-seven kids all ripping up each other's exercise books, kicking each other in the legs and generally bundling with shrill squeaks to pass the time until the show started. Inside, Aristotle was attempting to beat to death the school's already seriously injured drum kit, and Matt was sitting quietly astride an amp, replacing a broken string on his guitar. He looked up at me shaking his head, bemused, like I'd arrived before him as naked as Cassandra.

Avoiding his disapproval, I picked up the battered bass in the corner, and thought hazily about tuning it, but before I'd time Matt twanged his fixed guitar, leapt to his feet, yelled, 'One, two, three!' (screams of anticipation in the corridor) and launched at breakneck speed into 'Zombie Kid', without waiting for either of us to catch him up. '*I'm a zombie kid*,

I'm weird because I'm dead; it's not my fault my teacher ate my head.'

'Oh man, that's *deep*,' shouted Aristotle, drumming so hard he was bouncing up and down in his seat.

'She ripped my head off, yes she really did!' Matt danced raggedly across to me, roaring out his lyrics in my face.

I howled right back at him, giving the tuneless bass a whack, *'But I'm not bitter – I'M THE ZOMBIE KID!!!!'* Then I squawked, 'Fucking take it easy, man!' because one of Aristotle's cymbals had shot past my head like a frisbee, gashing a pink line of plaster out of the already well-battered wall.

'Sorry, man!'

Matt started leaping around the room, head thrown back, both feet at a time. *'She fried my brain and spread it on some bread!'*

I pogo-ed after him. *'She said, yum, yum, I LURVE that Zombie spread!'*

'Gotta do the ZOMBIE BOUNCE!' howled Matt breathlessly, another string going. *'Gotta do the ZOMBIE JUMP!'*

'Gotta do the ZOMBIE DANCE! Gotta do the ZOMBIE BUMP!'

Even above our own noise we could hear the mounting uproar in the corridor; the locked door shook as youthful bodies crashed into it. *'Zombie kids!'* They were rioting. *'Zombie kids!'*

'They tell us what to think and what to do; but we don't care, 'cos we are zombies too! Gotta do the ZOMBIE BOUNCE! Gotta do the ZOMBIE JUMP . . .'

'Look out!' yelped Aristotle, as the bolt slipped on the door and several hysterical year-seven kids fell through. Matt and me hurled down our instruments and started chucking out excitable bodies, but they got too many for us in the end, all pogo-ing around the music room, hands flapping, feet together, going, *'Gotta do the ZOMBIE DANCE! Gotta do the ZOMBIE BUMP!'* until we had to retreat to the playground and sit in a row on a bench, smoking Aristotle's filthy Greek cigarettes. Matt didn't seem able to look at me, but I felt oddly happy, like we'd talked something out. Aristotle, flicking ash everywhere, came over all moody and cynical about the price of fame. 'You know, like, if I hear one more little kid murdering one of our songs one more time . . .'

'Innit,' interrupted Matt bitterly, grinding the broken tarmac under his heel. 'I totally hate it when something's just been in my head and suddenly it's out there and I hear other people singing it and just, like, pissing about like it's some huge joke . . . It's like people are stealing my soul and beating it up, kicking it around, I mean, it actually hurts me here . . .' He hit his chest with the side of his fist too hard and winced. 'Know what I mean?'

'Mmm..' said Aristotle unconvincingly, poking his finger up his nose, studying Matt sideways with exaggerated caution.

Matt muttered, head in hands, 'Lily phoned that manager guy and he says to bring him a tape.'

'*Wicked!*' screeched the world's most jaded drummer-boy, leaping up and doing the zombie bounce round and around the bench, flinging his fag end in the air. '*Bad-boy!!* Why the fuck didn't you tell us earlier, you mug? What were you waiting for?'

I glanced at Matt, who went pale and yawned, like he was simply tired. 'You OK, Matt?'

He said nothing.

'We're gonna be huge,' celebrated Aristotle. 'We're gonna be rich! We're gonna rock the world! Let's hear it for *Boybits!*'

'Matt?'

'*What?*' he asked irritably, biting the side of his hand like a dog at a bone.

'You OK?'

'What d'you mean, am I OK?' But without waiting for me to answer, he went on hurriedly, leaning over towards me, keeping his voice right down, 'I'm just a bit confused right now because it seems you're getting interested in doing whatever that teacher tells you . . .'

I muttered furiously back, while Aristotle happily bounced in circles, tunelessly murdering 'Zombie Kids', 'I'm not, I *never* . . .'

He raised his hand, and rushed on louder, 'It's just, if it's true, it's a really bad scene, man, and I think you need to stop, because it's scary stuff. Those teacher types pretend to be your friends, but you gotta remember the song, because the truth is in the music, man. Stay away from her – you could end up without a brain.'

'What're you on about?' I couldn't believe I'd been tempted to tell him the whole truth about Cassandra. 'It's only a joke fucking song, man – get real.'

Instantly, he became really agitated, hair sticking up and pink face coming apart with anxiety. 'What do you mean – get real?' he shouted, jabbing his finger at me. 'What's *real*, zombie kid? *Go on! What's real?*'

Aristotle stopped singing and bouncing around, gaping at Matt in bewilderment. 'Jesus, mate – what planet are you from?'

Matt's head snapped back against the bench. He went a blotchy red. 'Planet? What do you mean, what planet?' His expression was shifty and uncomfortable, as if Aristotle had caught him out in some weird secret. Believe me, I'd no sympathy at all.

'Because you ain't from mine,' announced Aristotle, cheerfully.

'Nor mine,' I added, deliberately cruel, while Matt stared speechlessly from Aristotle to me, worriedly flexing his pink cold-mottled hands.

This time the coffee shop was totally empty. Café-woman was drying a painted cup, so someone must've been in before me, and I immediately worried it was Cassandra. Even though I'd come as fast as I could after school, I still thought maybe she'd been and gone. The flowers were out in their jam jars, unshredded, and the carrot cake piled high on the counter, undisturbed.

'Can I help you?' Then the woman looked up and did a sort of double-take. After a definite thoughtful pause, she said, setting down the dried cup, 'Right. What would you like then?'

I put my fingers in my pockets and found I had no money, only wrappers, fluff and a stone. 'I'm all right, thanks,' I said. I sat down at the back table – *our* table – and observed the purple flowers. When I looked up again the woman had her forearms resting on the high glass top, between the trays of cake.

'Nothing?' She came over amused, not hostile.

'I'm waiting for someone. I haven't actually got any money.'

'I see.'

Behind her the long hand of a big blue wooden clock jerked slowly up the dial from seven to nine. I didn't want to order anything in case Cassandra didn't show. Every time I looked up the woman was still watching me, and every time I caught her eye, she smiled instantly. As the minute hand neared ten, she said, 'I'll treat you to something, if you like.'

I wished I'd waited outside. 'No thanks.'

She said lightly, half offended, 'It's all right, it's my shop.'

'No, really.'

She persisted like I didn't exist. 'Coke was what you had before, wasn't it?' Then she went right ahead and poured one out and brought it over. 'There. Now then.' And sat down opposite me. 'So. What's your name? I'm Bronwyn.' And put her hands on the table between us. Her hair, still in the bun, was shiny brown and streaked with red and grey. Her fingers were freckled to the knuckles. She was really staring at me, her glasses making her eyes huge and distorted, like she was rising up towards me from under the surface of a pond. 'You're a handsome lad . . .'

Cassandra came running into the shop, chimes ringing, cross with herself for being late, wearing a purple velvety hat and her fake fur jacket, small tits puffing in and out. 'Sorry! Sorry! I got stuck with . . .'

The woman was suddenly back behind the counter; I felt weird, disorientated, as if I'd closed my eyes in a lift.

'Great, you've got yourself a Coke, great – been waiting long?' She threw herself into a chair, coat, hat, handbag, arms, legs, a heap of Cassandra, and I felt really warm to see her – excited too, nervous, over the fucking moon, but first this massive hit of warmth.

She ordered tea and then sat grinning at me, elbows on the table, narrow face in her hands, not saying anything, just looking aimlessly pleased to see me. Eventually, after her tea arrived, I felt one of us had to start talking, otherwise it was just too weird, so I said something I'd been dreaming up on the way there. 'I've been thinking about what you said, about doing more work.'

'*Some* would be nice . . .'

'No, wait – listen – I've decided I need an incentive.'

She quirked her pale forehead, puzzled. 'Like chocolate?'

'Yeah, sure . . . No, I was thinking if I did an assignment, properly, like . . .' As I'd hurried to our meeting, under the peeling trees, I'd come up with what I'd thought was a really funny stand-up routine – a sort of Shags for Homework scandal, and that's what I'd been going to say to her, but now I realised, looking at her hopeful, interested face, that it was kind of tacky and rude, and would sound like I considered her to be a bit of a whore, so I hit the fade button pretty damn fast. 'I thought, like, you're right,' I said humbly. 'I'll try and do more work. Like you said.'

'Hmm. And we could grade your incentives according to how well you did in your essay, couldn't we?' she said.

I took a mouthful of my drink.

'A grade C, now . . . that'd be worth . . . a quick shag on the floor, right?'

I choked, and Coke burst painfully through my nose.

'And a B . . . let me think . . . yeess . . .' Her funny-coloured eyes went dreamy, and she began combing out her blonde hair with her fingers, making out she was considering all possible options.

I wiped my bubbling face on my sleeve, looking cautiously over at the counter, worried weird-café-woman was tuning in. But a couple of blokes came blasting through the door, capturing her attention. I turned back to Cassandra, who continued contentedly, 'A grade B would be a nice long session in bed.'

I opened my eyes seriously wide. 'I *will* do my homework, I really will.'

'Good, it's working already. Now then, what would you like for an A?' She added, sardonically, 'Supposing you ever get an A.'

I wasn't sure of the boundaries of her game, but went for something I coveted anyway. 'I get to stay for breakfast?'

'Ah . . . how sweet! No, I was thinking more along the lines of . . .' She paused. She could be a real fucking tease.

I pretended not to care, but then couldn't help myself, and blurted out, 'What?'

She shrugged. 'A blow-job?'

'Oh god,' I moaned, sinking in my seat. 'Oh *god*.'

'But for now,' she snapped briskly, rattling her mug on its saucer, calling me back to Planet Carrot Cake, 'you deserve absolutely nothing. No essays, no – you know what.'

I made some wet pathetic noise. 'No?' I felt flattened, totally fucking ill. And here came that nosy bun-headed bitch, hanging around again, taking my glass. I righted myself miserably on the yellow-painted chair.

'Of course, I know you haven't got anything to show me *today*,' said Cassandra, taunting me, turning her shoulder to the lingering Bunhead. 'So today – but only for today – we'll have to do it in the yard.'

'Oh Jesus,' I said. 'Jesus.' I started to laugh, holding my chest.

'That's . . . fucking harsh!' I couldn't stop laughing for ages.

When I'd finally calmed down, she took my hand with a real show of affection, squeezing it, turning it, rubbing it with her thumb. 'That's what I love about being with you,' she said. 'It's such fun.'

'Thanks.' I thought it was fun, too. I enjoyed this teasing, and mucking about, almost as much as the can't-wait sex thing. 'Me too.' Even so, I was kind of interested in what was going to happen next.

She suddenly pulled and kissed my palm. I slid my eyes to check Bunhead was back behind the counter – which she was, serving an afternoon rush of three. Cassandra murmured, gripping my thumb, very intense, 'You're so gorgeous, Ferdie . . . I've hardly been able to think of anything else. Your eyes are so green . . . Your eyelashes are so damn long . . . Your mouth is so curvy . . .'

I said, embarrassed, 'No, it's you, you're it, it's you that's beautiful . . .' My skin was that sensitised to her, my palm was stinging as if her lips had come dipped in acid.

She said calmly, rising up tall, gathering up handbag and hat, 'I'm just flattered you want to be with me.'

And we headed off, mutually flattered, hand in hand, to that puddled, miserable, hard and heavenly yard.

Chapter Twelve

Dropping me off at the end of my road that Friday, she'd instructed me in her sharpest teacher's voice, 'Be at my flat on Monday, two o'clock sharp.' And I'd asked, genuinely surprised, 'You don't have classes?' She couldn't believe I'd forgotten it was half term. 'My god – you really don't pay any attention in school, do you? It's not just a pose. Now listen, I want you there at two, every day. And don't be late, Mr Daydream.'

All weekend I wandered blindly about in a pinkish mist of Naked Cassandra, falling down steps and hacking my shins on chairs. At night I couldn't sleep – could hardly stay lying down, even. I knew for sure this was going to be the most mind-blowing, unforgettable week – the best, most momentous week of my life, in anyone's life, *ever*. The terrible slowness of time was killing me. Years later, when Monday finally arrived, I was outside her place by half past one and had to spend a desperate twenty-five minutes hanging about in the cold, trying not to be too pathetically early. At five to two, I hit the intercom and she buzzed me in. I was hoping she'd come to the door naked like before and save us some valuable time, but she was stood in the door of her flat fully clothed, looking down through her thin wire glasses at a sheet of paper she was holding in her hand. 'You're early.'

'Sorry . . .' I couldn't wait to get down to it. I made to hug her, but she backed off into the kitchen, and when I followed her she handed me a list of notes and an essay question. I was *gutted*.

The closest I got to her over the next few days was sitting beside her on the sofa, her turning pages, tucking her long blonde hair behind her ear, frowning at me over her glasses, tutting, groaning, digging away with her pen, saying things like, 'We're not out of the yard yet, Ferdia,' and, severely, 'You'll never get a blow-job from me at this rate.' At first I'd hoped it was some kind of incredibly cruel joke, but gradually, to my absolute horror, I realised she was determined to teach me something. And I did learn something too – all of literature, including Shakespeare and poetry, is about people frantically trying to get laid. It totally did my head in, having to read all this kinky stuff with her there beside me, crossing and uncrossing her legs. But if I put one quick hand on her stockings – she was still wearing stockings – she'd say, dry-surprised, 'Can't you take your mind off sex for one second?' Then, if I did it again: 'Excuse me? You imagine you've earned a shag on the floor? I don't *think* so.' The first day she sent me away untouched gave me a nasty shock; on Tuesday I could hardly believe it; I bust a gut to complete a whole essay by Wednesday, and thought I'd cracked it . . . On Thursday, she chucked my desperately worked-over labour-of-lust into the bin without even a catty comment, and ordered me wearily, 'Come on, get in the car.' She drove straight to the yard. I could've wept with delight – I'd thought she was driving me home. 'I imagined I'd feel less guilty, doing it the homework way,' she said, in bad-tempered resignation. 'But for god's sake, Ferdia, you're so gorgeous, I can't wait all year for you to learn how to spell.' She rolled me on my back on the harsh cutting ground, and bit down heavily on my naked shoulder. She even managed to reopen the red slash in my knee. I didn't care. It was nothing compared to the torment of English Literature.

All week, Lily kept phoning me, wanting to know what I was up to, getting more and more insistent. 'Come on, Ferdie, we've got to *practise*, we've got to get this tape together for Dickie. You'll never guess what Matt's got into his head now – he thinks you're having extra tuition!' (She laughed hysterically.) 'Don't worry, me and Aristotle don't believe it!' I didn't ask her exactly what Matt'd said, dodging the feeble effort of denial. 'Ferdie, please, you've *got* to come.'

I joked to Cassandra, in the yard, dragging on my clothes over my shivering dirty skin, 'Does this mean I can stop doing all this work now? I've been missing band practice all week, and Lily's been hassling me on the phone every day.'

'Lily?' she asked, casually, like she didn't know who I was on about, hunting around in the mud. 'Did you see my car keys anywhere? They've fallen out of my pocket.'

'Over there . . . You know,' I reminded our self-styled greatest fan with emphasis, 'the *band*? Lily keeps on at me about making that demo.'

She adjusted her skirt, jingling her dripping keys. She said thoughtfully, 'Actually, I think Dickie was more interested in you than in the band. He's on the look-out right now for nice-looking boys. Why don't you just go and see him by yourself? You don't really need the rest of them, you know.' Turning her long thin back on me, she picked her way carefully through the muddy exit, oddly concerned about where she was putting her feet for someone who'd just been rolling in the muck.

'What, drop the band?' I was totally taken aback. I dogged her through the alleyway to the street. 'But I thought you liked our music?'

In her car, she curved her thin arms round the wheel, resting her cheek on the knuckles of one hand, slitting her eyes at me in a lingering smile as I clambered in. 'Of course I like the band. It's good to see kids enjoying themselves, doing something creative instead of doing drugs. I'm just saying – you shouldn't get too excited on your friends' behalf.' I couldn't think what to answer – despite talking Dickie down, I'd had a sort of background hope that maybe we really were the next best thing, and how great especially that would be for Matt. If Dickie was only touting for pretty boys, then everything about this was a load of shit.

'But he told Lily to bring a demo . . .' A lump came in my throat, thinking Cassandra was laughing at me and seeing this stupid self-deluded kid, when I'd thought before she was so impressed by our great mould-breaking music. Even if I'd had my own doubts, it seemed kind of cruel of her to voice them. She reached over and gently flicked my thigh, sending this semi-painful wave of longing into my groin.

'What d'you want to play with *Lily* for,' she murmured, flickering her pointed blackened lashes, 'when you can play grown-up games with me?'

Good point.

When she dropped me off at the end of my road, she reached into her briefcase and handed me two Hardy novels and an impossibly long assignment. 'That should keep you out of mischief! Don't get distracted!' Then she announced coolly that she was going to Winchester the next day to see her sister for a long weekend. So I was 'reading' (dreaming) on my bed when Lily rang up yet again on Friday morning, and I thought rebelliously, Fuck it, and, feeling like an excited truant, didn't go back to my books. Lily and me and Matt and Aristotle spent the whole day getting a demo together, on quite a flash portable deck Aristotle's nervous mum'd let him borrow. I didn't forget Cassandra for one second, but for those few hours I was really having fun, and the hot stew of lust and panic in my stomach bubbled away on a lower, cooler flame. We laid down in one continuous erratic blast: 'Wanna Rip Somebody's Head Off', 'Zombie Kid', 'Babes in the Air', 'Hungry Poor', 'The Woman Who Has Nothing' and 'Stop that Noise'. Natasha spent ages in her bedroom dressing up to sing 'Stop that Noise', appearing at last looking scary and feeling beautiful in her most loved possessions – pink plastic Barbie high-heels and a small fluorescent pink plastic raincoat buttoned tightly over her vest.

'I'm a princess,' she said, smugly.

'It's only a *tape*, Nat,' said Matt, hunting for his plectrum in the foam craters of his disintegrating sofa. 'No one's gonna see you.'

Natasha rolled her eyes at Lily, like across their years they had some girly connection going, and Lily rose kindly to the occasion, saying, 'It's not about being seen, it's about getting in the right mood, right, Nat?'

Natasha basked.

Aristotle said, coming over all new-mannish, 'It's not about how you look to other people, it's about feeling beautiful inside, innit, Nat?'

Natasha looked at him in disgust. '*No*. Inside me is full of *blood*.'

'Oh – right – I s'pose it is . . .'

'If you poke me yucky stuff comes out.'

'Mmm . . .'

'She's gonna be writing lyrics like yours one day,' I said to Matt, who gazed at me blankly, like he didn't know what the fuck I was on about.

The sun was at the exact height of Matt's flat when we played the tape back afterwards. We sounded pretty damn good. Lily's voice got a bit lost, and sometimes you couldn't hear anything but Aristotle drumming, but on the whole you could pretty much make out everything that was going on. And there were some excellent sound effects, which we hadn't realised at the time, like a helicopter hovering outside during most of 'Hungry Poor', and Tessa blundering out of bed shrieking '*For fuck's sake!*' and slamming the bathroom door, as the perfect kiss-off line to 'Stop that Noise'.

'We should be playing gigs to people who get this shit,' said Matt, listening huddled sideways against the balcony window, staring down at the Evil Eye, his head a silhouette, backed up against the red and blinding sun.

'Yeah. We will. After we've played it to Dickie,' agreed Lily, squinting confidently into the powerful light.

Dickie hung out in a small room on the second floor of a red-brick building in the middle of a pot-holed car park near Kentish Town tube, a dump from outside but inside some pretty clean carpets and laughable office art on the walls. Out on the street, we'd been in a crazy mood, barging our way through Kentish Town, dancing around in the inscrutable crowd, Saturday lunchtime, feeling good. Matt was toting his guitar, and Aristotle had his drumsticks in his pocket. I was dressed pretty normally, but Lily'd glammed herself up, clumping along in metallic wedges, a lace top and embroidered flares, and Aristotle, bizarrely, was wearing a mod-style collarless suit, embarrassingly small, that'd belonged to his dad. Matt ripped the piss out of them for getting dressed up, but we could see he'd done it too, in his own secret way, gear more ripped than ever, hardly a seam not unravelled – Lily made a big show of not touching him in case his clothes fell off completely and left him running bare-arsed down Kentish Town Road.

When we finally found the place, we were late and anxious, had stopped mucking about. A bobbed baby Sloane in reception pointed us towards the lift. Catching sight of ourselves in the lift mirror, I suddenly thought we looked a bit crap – subdued and disorganised. I remembered Cassandra putting down our band, and felt discouraged: maybe this was a childish fantasy trip. .

Dickie had his feet on the desk, short stubby legs in a shiny dark green suit, cupping the lumpy back of his shaven head in both hands. A handful of rain suddenly hit the window behind him, breaking up the panoramic view of the car park and other rubble. He grinned, showing me his dead brown dog tooth, stretching out his hand to me, acting like he was doing me personally this so big favour, letting my friends into his so-important office. 'Ah, Ferdia. Looking good. Glad you could make it.' He added, disparagingly, to Matt over my shoulder, 'You didn't need to bring the instrument with you, kid.'

Matt said, without missing a beat, 'A musician can't travel without his soul, man.'

Dickie laughed, sliding his feet to the floor and standing up. 'Yeah, OK. You write the songs, yeah?'

'I just hear them in my head, man. They arrive. I just play along.'

Dickie was faintly confused, a trace of posh crawling into his voice. 'But it's original material?'

'Like I said, I just . . .'

'Yeah, yeah,' said Dickie, getting it. 'We'll credit God on the cover, OK?'

'I guess I'm the medium,' said Matt, hoarsely.

I'd never heard Matt come out with that particular bullshit before. I wondered if he was serious, or winding Dickie up. I watched him standing in the middle of the room, twisting his guitar round and round by the neck, and realised he was really tensed, to the point of hostility. I touched his arm but he shook me off without looking who I was and took the only available seat, a office swivel chair next to the door.

Lily gave Dickie the tape, and without any chat at all he stuck it straight into a machine behind him and hit play. Matt's legs stiffened and his seat rotated a few degrees; he pounded the carpet with his heel as his badly recorded voice filled up the room. Watching him, I was surprised he cared so much about what this trivial slaphead thought. The tape hissed on, and last night's helicopters roared through the room like lions, and I heard my own frustrated scream as another fucking string exploded, and Nat kept squealing, When's my turn? Dickie stood by the machine looking at me, and Lily and Aristotle leant against the walls with their arms folded and chins tucked tightly into their chests, like they thought they could bury their heads in their own bodies. In the end, to duck Dickie's appraising gaze, I squatted down beside Matt's chair and started listening to the words. Matt laid out in his songs a lot of personal stuff he didn't normally talk about, like his mum being out of it all the time, and him maybe jumping off the twentieth floor. His lyrics always made us laugh, we treated them as a bit of a joke, but if you listened to him ranting on, you could see how he cut himself up for his own material. Then it struck me it must be kind of weird, laying out your life like that with some bald cynical breadhead sat in judgement, ready to tell you if it's worth any fucking *money* .

When the music stopped, nobody said anything or looked at each other. Dickie popped out the tape and spun it up in the air and caught it, then went back to his chair on the far side of the desk and ran one hand over his imaginary hair. He put the tape on the smooth pale wood in front of him, and said, 'Do the kids want punk?'

Matt crushed his fist into the side of his thigh. 'It's not . . .'

'Yeah, yeah, I know,' said Dickie, shoving his chair back against the plate glass window and slamming his feet up on the desk.. 'Not punk – tower-block rock. Urban menace but up in the air. Yah-dee-dah-dee-dah . . . OK, tower-block rock it is. I like it. It's funny. It makes me laugh.'

Matt was speechless, really taken aback. I was knocked out myself, impressed by the man, by his remembering word for word what I'd said to him weeks ago in Abigail's flat. I began to think this particular slaphead was pretty fucking shrewd.

'You can't sing,' he said to Matt.

Behind us against the wall, both Lily and Aristotle released high-tension giggles. Matt shivered, staring at his knees, hands whitening round the neck of his guitar.

'You can't play,' he said to me.

I was still crouched on the carpet next to Matt. It was so true I wasn't all that bothered. 'It'll happen,' I said.

'I doubt it.' He jack-knifed at the waist to get the tape off the desk and flicked it over to me; I just managed to catch it before it hit the wall. 'Look, I dunno,' Dickie said, in his sleazy fake East End. 'There's a few changes gonna have to be made, OK? You need the pretty faces up front. You sing,' he said to me. 'You need to be visible.' (Beside me, Matt hissed faintly through his teeth.) 'Get yourselves a new bass guitarist. What about you?' he suggested, to Lily. 'Ethnic girls on bass are hot stuff right now.' On the point of dismissing her, he hesitated, taking her in. 'Actually, darling, you're quite a looker too. Maybe you need to be up front with Ferdia here. On bass.'

I craned to look at her, perfect oval face in rich black hair. 'I can't . . .' she began, stunned.

He clicked his tongue at her, disapprovingly. 'Hey! It's the new equality. Give it a try. You can still sing a bit if you want to, it's no big deal.'

Aristotle, straightening his back, popped a too-tight button and squeaked in a high strangled voice, 'So . . .' He winced and cleared his throat. 'So.' His voice dropped by a couple of octaves. 'OK then. If we swap things around, does that mean . . . I mean . . . Could we . . .?'

Dickie shrugged, like the world-weary small-time opportunist he was. 'Like I said, it makes me laugh. Makes a change. It's a piss-take of punk, innit? I like the one with the little girl singing. I noticed at the party, that brought them in.'

Beside me, Matt pulled his guitar into his chest, cuddling his arms around it like a precious baby.

'You mean . . .' repeated Aristotle, coming dangerously close to a high-pitched squeak again.

'If it works, we'll take it from there,' said Dickie. 'Maybe fix you a gig at some half-decent venue – plenty of music pubs in Camden.' He winked uncharmingly at me. Suddenly, a classical orchestra erupted in his pocket and he whipped his mobile out, spinning around in his chair with his short fat legs sticking out in front of him. Then, springing up with the phone still flattened to his ear, he flapped us away, turning his back on us, pressing his hairless forehead to the plate glass window, now streaming with continuous rain as you might imagine the green underside of a waterfall.

I had to come back from the corridor to pull Matt up by the arm. He was so tense, so stiff, I could hardly shift him. 'Come on, mate. Time to go.'

At last he registered me, but looking kind of frightened, still furiously embracing his guitar.

Escaping through the downpour, we found a plastic café on the Kentish Town Road to dry off and calm down in, full of dazed hung-over people wolfing down enormous fry-ups. Aristotle was ecstatically smug, bursting out of his diminutive suit. 'Did the man say get yourself a new drummer? No. Did he suggest we get a girl to do the drumming instead? No.'

'Oh fuck off,' said Lily.

'Did he suggest I take up a new career? No.'

'Fuck *off*.' But her Taiwan eyes and Kenyan skin began to burn with deranged excitement, as the whole scene we'd just been through sunk further in. 'He said he likes us. Shit. We're all in this together, right? Do you think we can make it?'

Inside me I could start to feel this continuous thrilling trickle of anxiety and greed. I thought, Yeah, maybe we're going to make it, with me on vocals and Matt writing the songs and playing lead guitar, and the others . . . I still thought I could get better on the bass, though. I was just amazed how things'd gone. 'Your songs, mate,' I said, whacking Matt on the back, nearly knocking his tea out of his hand. 'Sorry . . . Brilliant fucking songs, mate.'

He put down his plastic cup and mopped the plastic table with his tattered sleeve.

'This is so great,' said Aristotle, cartoon dollar-signs of temptation ringing up in his shiny eyes. ' We're gonna be rich and famous. We're gonna have *pools*.' He puffed out his chest and, like wealth had already made him fat, popped off another button. 'Bugger.'

'I'm gonna have a bright pink Jag,' said Lily, sounding like Natasha then looking embarrassed – it must've been a childhood dream she was letting slip.

'*I'm* gonna have a white Rolls Royce,' said Aristotle.

I laughed. 'Shit, that's so *eighties*, man.'

'Who cares? . . . And a helicopter . . .'

'I'm going to live in the Caribbean . . .'

'In Spain . . .'

Lily, sitting opposite me, suddenly reached across and took Matt's left hand in both of hers, black hair flopping down from behind her ear. 'Dickie's an arsehole,' she said earnestly. 'Of course you can sing.'

'Yeah, Matt, your voice is fine, man. It's raw,' I lied supportively.

He whipped his blotchy pink hand out of her slim brown ones. 'It's not that!' he cried. 'It's not *that*, OK? I know I can't *sing*, right?'

'Right,' nodded Aristotle energetically.

Lily asked anxiously, gazing into Matt's heaving blushing face, 'What, then?'

'I'll *tell* you what.' You could tell from the shrillness of his voice he was this far away from tears. With spread fingers, he whacked the plastic table top, making the dirty grains of sugar and tea-stained plastic spoons jump up. 'That ground-dwelling wanker likes my music because it makes him *laugh*, that's what. He wants Ferdia singing my songs because he's fucking *pretty*, that's what. But they're not *supposed* to be sung by some cute fucking ground-dweller with a poncy voice. They're not supposed to make that commercial cum-stain *laugh*. They're for people like *me* – you gotta *feel* them, man, you gotta feel them deep down in your *soul*. And they're NOT FUNNY!'

We stared at him in uncomfortable shock. All around us, sickly people, deaf to the world from clubbing all Friday night, chewed and swallowed. Lily patted sugar crumbs with her finger tip, and pressed them to her tongue. Aristotle said tentatively, cautiously, 'They're not supposed to be . . . funny?'

'NO!'

'But . . .'

'I shouldn't even be playing with any of you,' Matt announced in a hysterical, high-pitched, un-Matt-like yelp. 'You just don't get it, do you?' His voice was shaking; he kept pointing at us, one after the other, jab, jab, jab. 'You're just a bunch of lazy fucking ground-dwellers who think about nothing but money and shit, and you just don't fucking get it, do you? You just don't fucking *get it*.'

I was getting something all right – a bit sick of all this ground-dweller crap. He'd always claimed I'd the soul of a sky-high man, he was always borrowing money off me – he wouldn't have eaten half the time if he hadn't – and now he was having a go like I'd sold him out before we'd even got started. Plus I thought it was seriously insane, him acting like this was so incredibly bloody important, like there was even the remotest faintest slightest possible chance we'd ever be famous millionaires, rather than four kids just pissing about. Dickie was only talking gigs in pubs, and I couldn't see what was wrong with that. It sounded fun. 'Look, I don't *want* to fucking sing, all right? I *like* playing the bass. Jesus, it wasn't my idea. Let's just keep things how they are. Forget about Dickless.'

'Oh man,' complained Aristotle to me, his cheeks going long and thin with disappointment. 'This is our big fucking break – don't spoil it for us, man.'

'Don't talk to me, talk to Matt.' I was well pissed off. 'Either way, I don't give a fuck.'

'Matt,' said Lily. 'Matt. We do care about the music, we do . . . We don't care about making money. But, you know . . . I mean, Ferdie can sing really well, and . . . Matt?' She reached out, stroking his threadbare jacket, but he cringed away, with a strange, mistrustful look.

'You're just a bunch of ground-dwellers,' he whined. 'I don't want to play to trendy indie types in trendy fucking Camden music pubs. I don't want to make ground-dwellers fucking laugh.' He took a trembly petulant breath. 'I don't want to corrupt my soul. I want to do something real. I should've hung around with my own type in the first place. I wanna do a gig at the Evil Eye.'

'What . . .?' began Lily, and Aristotle echoed, '*Where?* Are you out of your nut? That's, like, a rave venue, man – they wouldn't rate our styles. *And* it's full of coked-up nutters – if they didn't like us they'd tear us afuckingpart!'

But Matt came over all persuasive, as if what he was saying was perfectly reasonable. 'I wanna play tower-block rock to tower-block people. I've been thinking about it. Once they

146

hear it, they'll know it's written for them, and they'll love it. A tower-block gig in a tower-block estate. It'll work, I know it will . . .'

'Hang on a minute,' I said, hearing my own voice come out dry with rage, skidding backwards in my seat. 'You know fucking well, Matt, if you're going to start hanging around with that arsehole Jason Peckham you can *count me out*, and you fucking well *know why that is*, so don't fucking pretend this is just about the music, man . . .'

'So is Jason Peckham really fu . . . uh . . . uh . . .? Pass the sugar,' said Aristotle.

Matt lifted his voice defiantly, colouring up a feverish red. 'The Peckhams are my neighbours, man. They're the lights around me every night. It's not their fault if they're a bunch of psychos. I've been thinking about it. I've seen the light. They're my people, man – not types like . . .'

'Oh, great,' I snarled, standing up, booting back my fragile chair. 'I get it. Jason's your real sky-high man. He's your kind of people and I'm not. I get you a fucking audience with a real fucking manager who could make your fucking career, but Jason Peckham's your *real* fucking man.'

Then, while Lily and Aristotle crouched miserably behind their plastic cups, I could have *sworn* I heard my best mate saying under his breath, or at least I could tell he was thinking it in his eyes, and anyway I heard it full volume in my own head, and it was his thought I was hearing, I swear, not my own, *And he's your mother's real man.* Gasping, nauseous, I bolted out into the bucketing rain, beating my way down Kentish Town Road, deafened by that shouting in my head, gutted by his treachery and his madness.

'Ferdia! Ferdie!' She wouldn't have caught me up, but the crowds were bad; she got me by the back of the coat, and held on like mad. 'Wait up! Don't just go like that!'

'I gotta go, Lil. It's pointless talking to him. He's lost it. He's totally fucking out of order.'

'I know, I know. He's in a weird state right now.'

We turned face to face, bundled closer and closer together by the pressure of other hurrying people, hit repeatedly in our backs and sides by bodies and wet bags of supermarket shopping, steel umbrella spikes sticking in our ears, until we were forced up against each other. 'Oh Ferdie,' she said, squeezing her arms around me, her face lifted openly to mine. 'He loves you, he really does. And he does want the best for the band. He's just a bit confused. Don't fall out with him. He needs you. You're a great singer. He's scared of what's happening. It's all so fast.'

'Nothing's happening,' I protested, leaning into her. 'Dickie's some poxy jumped-up nobody. We were only doing it for a laugh. Who does he think he is? Kurt Cobain? He's in the wrong fucking universe again.'

She kissed my leather coat, hugging me mournfully, cheeks freckled with bright drops of water, beautiful eyes peering up at me through the open V of my turned-up collar. 'Come back, don't go, I love your voice . . .' She rose on her toes and kissed my throat, her lips that soft.

I looked over her head straight into Cassandra's wide icy smile, and by sheer brainless instinct shoved Lily's young body away, unnaturally hard, so only the solid crowd kept her up on her feet. 'Cassandra! Wait!' But she wouldn't look back, forcing a passage through the damp human swamp, a clutch of rain-sparkled carrier bags in one hand. I struggled after her. 'Cassandra! Wait! Wait!' On her head was a green velvet hat, and she held high a dripping purple umbrella with which she viciously knocked aside its rivals. '*Wait!*'

She glanced stabbingly over her shoulder, met my eyes in the crowd, jerked up her chin and faced away. Then I realised it wasn't she hadn't heard me shouting – it was just she wasn't going to stop. I couldn't believe this was happening, that my whole existence was being ruined by such a crappy stupid piece of bad luck – her seeing Lily kiss me in the street – that single childish unreturned kiss – that stupid *stupid* kiss. Stranded wretched in the human flood, I could hardly get my head round the irretrievable totality of this fuck-up, couldn't physically believe that something so fundamentally awful could happen to me – I was a stunned passenger with seconds to survive on a plane going down.

But then she stopped, and I surged from astonished despair to desperate optimism, catching up with her, sinking my fingers deep into her thick wet fur before she could run away again. 'Cassandra . . .'

'Exactly *what* are you doing, chasing me down the street?' She lifted her elbow preparatory to shaking me off, but I tightened my grip. Her umbrella, tilting, poured water over my hair, down my forehead, into my eyes. Blinking furiously, I was frantic to say *What you saw, it didn't mean anything*, but realised how crap that would sound and just stood holding tightly to her fur. Annoyed, she stepped backwards, me determinedly following, into the poor shelter of a pub doorway. 'Let me go, please.' I stared at her mouth as it moved offensively. She was wearing pale flesh-coloured lipstick. Viciously, she shook me off.

I clutched at her again. 'I thought you'd gone away . . .'

'Oh, I could see *that*,' she bristled, baring her teeth with their dark hair-line gap, fake fur standing up all over her body in damp grey tufts. 'Now, why don't you go back to kissing *Lily*. Don't let me spoil your fun.'

'No, no – I wasn't – you've got to let me explain!' Oh Jesus, I sounded so pathetic. 'Please let me tell you – I didn't do anything . . .'

For a dreadful moment she just stood glaring at me, eyes like large smooth marbles coldly protruding, then, to my hysterical relief, she snapped shut her purple umbrella with a freezing explosion of silvery spray. 'At least let's get in out of this bloody rain.' And she barged through the stained glass doors, leaving them slamming murderously behind her. When I caught up with her, she was dragging her bags and umbrella clumsily with her into a corner seat, leaving watery trails across the leather bench. 'Get me a vodka and cranberry juice.' She ripped a tenner from her purple purse, nearly tearing it in half. I got myself a pint but, too anxious to drink, I sat on a dark wooden stool opposite her and watched as first she slugged down half her crimson short, soft green hat nearly tipping off, then twisted to stare out of the streaky window, chewing her pale flesh-coloured mouth, crossing her long thin legs sideways. Beneath her coat, a bright green hem showed over shiny black stockings; a rising tidemark darkened the heels of her green wedge shoes.

After waiting ages for her to demand an explanation, I dived headfirst into her freezing silence. 'You see, me and Matt'd just had this huge fucking row, and Lily – she's Matt's girlfriend, actually – was trying to get me to come back.' I pictured Lily trying to keep her balance after I'd shoved her off – her face ashamed, bewildered – and wondered, briefly, what she was thinking now. Cassandra, knocking the rest of her vodka back, showed no sign of having even heard me. I swallowed a large mouthful of uncomfortably fizzy lager. Bubbles streamed slowly through my gut, threatening me with a farcical burp. I released it as softly and cautiously as I could.

Cassandra turned on me suddenly, flicks of blonde shaking out from under her green floppy hat, sneering, 'And Matt was where? When all this was happening?'

Encouraged, I launched into a long and convoluted explanation about Dickie and Matt and everything that had happened to me that day; I even told her about Jason Peckham, which I'd kept quiet about before. Cassandra meanwhile sat revolving a dribble of red liquid in the bottom of her empty glass. I appealed to her, 'Listen – Matt was well pissed off about Dickie wanting me to sing instead of him. And I fucking hate this Evil Eye idea. I dunno what's going to happen now. What d'you think – should I make up with him? He's a really old mate.'

'I'm on your side, of course,' she answered, after a pause. I was pleasantly surprised. I wasn't totally sure what my side was, but I was glad she was on it – it seemed like a good sign.

I relaxed a bit. She added thoughtfully, 'And I don't see why you should let a self-obsessed boy like Matt keep holding you back. In fact, all your friends sound pretty immature. And I must say, personally I'm not at all comfortable with you seeing Lily. Especially now she's seen you chasing after me, and probably heard you calling my name as well.'

Fuck it. She was right, I'd really blown that one. 'Shit – I'm sorry, Cassandra – I don't think she could've heard me – if she did, I'll explain to her it was about homework or something –'

She gave a faint cynical snort through her narrow nose. 'Well, even if you could convince her of *that*, I'm still not happy about you seeing her. For what I must say are pretty obvious reasons.'

The lager bubbles seemed to have reached my head. I explained, fuzzily, 'No, you see – Lily's in the band. She's Matt's girlfriend. I can't just tell him to get rid of her. He wouldn't do it.'

Cassandra sighed and rolled her black-rimmed eyes, like I was bugging the hell out of her. 'Look, will you *stop* going on about the band? It's pretty obvious Dickie's only interested in it because of you. And I mean it, I *really* don't like you seeing her, not after what I saw today. What do I have to say to get you to understand my position on this?'

Confused, I felt it was her that didn't understand. 'No, see, she's in the *band*. I'd have to stop seeing Matt and Aristotle too . . .' Cassandra said nothing, idly wringing rain from the cuffs of her furry sleeves, leaving me to struggle weakly out of my depth. 'Well, you know, I can't just give up my friends, they're, like, pretty important to me . . .'

Head lowered, she looked up at me under the soft green of her hat; shiny blonde snakes slid from under its rim; her face was genuinely hurt and astonished. 'Am I not important to you? Do I not figure in this?'

'Well, yeah . . .' Feeble answer. 'Important' was the understatement of the year. Of the century, actually.

'But not as important as seeing Lily?' Briskly, she gathered her shopping and umbrella. 'In that case, there's no point to carrying on this relationship.'

Instantly, unexpectedly, out of the blue, I was floored by this unbearable sense of loss, overwhelmed by facing a future without Cassandra. I knew at once it musn't be allowed to happen. 'Jesus! No! Don't go – listen – you're right, they're a bunch of immature arseholes – please don't go . . .' She looked at me doubtfully, not believing me, her incredible arse raised slightly off the seat, preparatory to a permanent departure. The thought of such terrible absence did my head in. 'Look, you're the most important thing in my life, and you always will be, and there wasn't anything important to me till you came along! I won't see Lily again, if you don't want me to – *please believe me . . .*'

She laughed, her hands in the handles of her bags, arse firmly back on the seat, 'Steady on, Ferdia, you don't have to grovel, darling.'

Didn't I? I wasn't so sure. Her threat to cast me off had made me realise an unmistakable truth – she had the power, I was her mindless slave. If I had to dump my friends, then so be it. I'd pay any price that she demanded. Why pretend different? I had no other option. Pass me the weapon, show me the well-insured husband.

She asked, almost sympathetically, 'Poor you. Do you want to come back to my place? We better hurry up – I haven't got long.' I staggered after her, weak-kneed and goggled-eyed in my relief. Outside the silver street was blindingly bright, but it was only the after-effect of leaving the pub – in seconds we were dumped back into a dull grey world, like a set of powerful lights had been turned off.

She immediately started flagging down black cabs. They swept past in short processions of two, three, four at a time, bearing smug solitary people. 'I should have brought my car, but there's nowhere to park . . . Damn it, I haven't got that long.' But miraculously, one was humming at the curb. She yanked open the heavy door and scrambled in, showing off her long, black legs, throwing her bags across the floor practically upside down. As I followed her the contents were sliding silkily out of them, creamy pants and bras and see-through slips – she didn't stuff them back into their bags straightaway, just looked from the price-tagged underwear to me and waited to see if I was going to comment. I smiled faintly, unsure of the best way to react, more nervous than before of doing the wrong thing around her, now I knew how abruptly she could abandon me. As the cab set off, slamming me into the seat, the rain grew hard again and battered our windows. We carried on in stops and starts, through the saturated city. She still didn't pick up her stuff. Glancing occasionally at her, I tried not to rest my feet on her pervasive slippery underwear; our mutual space was faintly scented by the freshly-bought smell of it. The driver's glass panel was shut; his radio sounded far away. 'I bought those for you,' she said, eventually, in a needling tone, adjusting her bright green hem. Previous to our session in the pub, I might've asked her how she knew my size. 'They cost a fortune, you know – it's all real silk. And then, when I saw you *kissing* that girl . . .' And as she hissed out the word 'kissing' she reached for and gripped the muscle in my thigh, squeezing it so painfully that I squawked.

'Hey! I wasn't . . .'

'You bastard. That really hurt,' she said through her fine-gapped teeth.

'You're not kidding . . .'

'*Me*, you imbecile. It hurt *me*.'

'But I *didn't* kiss her. I don't fancy her at *all*.'

'Huh.' She snorted. 'Well, it's obvious she fancies *you*. She was all over you. If she finds out about us she'll try to split us up. That is, if she doesn't already know – thanks to your *crass* stupidity.'

Embarrassed, I fidgeted with a broken nail. She turned towards the window, gazing out straight-faced at the acid rain. Then she reached behind her, feeling for my flies. It gave me such a jolt, I nearly crossed my legs. 'Sit there,' she rapped, swivelling to me, jabbing at the pull-down seat opposite her.

'What?' I was confused.

'Wha'? Wha'? Just *do* it.' She shoved me across the cab, me stamping dirty footprints on her underwear, and when I was seated she shot one sharp glance over my shoulder at the driver and bumped to her knees on the floor, quickly unbuttoning my flies, pulling her fur coat over her head and sinking my dick into her mouth. For a blind stomach-wrenching second, I was fucking terrified she was going to bite it off, but she didn't, she just went right ahead and did the business, while my head travelled on through the rainy city, trying to look calm for the sake of passers-by, as cool and detached as a head on a plate. Unfortunately I came just as an open-topped double-decker full of drenched huddled tourists floated up beside us, and I nearly sprained my brain with the effort of not showing in my face what was going on at lap-level. Yet they were all looking down from under their bright umbrellas, and I don't see how they could've failed to notice this fur-covered woman pumping away on her knees.

Cassandra threw back her coat, adjusted her green velvet hat, wiped her mouth, looked at her watch and leant across me to slide back the glass partition. 'Kilburn first, actually,' she said. 'Sorry, I forgot, I've got to drop something off.'

He swung the cab into long, quieter streets.

'Are you OK?' she asked me after a bit, as she stuffed her lingerie back into the bags.

I couldn't utter a squeak.

'I'm really, really sorry about this, but I truly haven't got much time.' She was frowning. 'I've just got time to drop you home, if I carry straight on to where I was going – I didn't realise how late it was.' She tapped her watch, for sympathy. 'Do you mind terribly? We'll see each other tomorrow, Monday, won't we?' She squeezed my feeble hand, with an earnest smile. 'Look, I'm sorry I was so hard on you just now. I know you wouldn't let me down, I really do. I just got a fright, that's all. Stupid. Silly. It's OK, now.'

I found my voice. 'Good,' I whispered.

The cab roared down my road. She left me standing on the kerb, knees buckling, mouth open, flies unbuttoned.

Chapter Thirteen

Places we did it: the Bull and Gate car park, behind a skip in the pouring rain, while punters streamed punching and kicking into the night – once. Her rough hall carpet, door left open, footsteps threatening on the stairs – twice. That filthy junkshop yard, in various weathers, mostly wet, drying off in stunned silence in our café – seven times. Ethnic rug in front room – thirteen times. Her kitchen table, while eating fish and chips, elbows blood-red with ketchup – once. Bathroom, dangerously slippy – twice. St Mary's church, in a white mist of derelict plaster – once. Bus shelter at midnight – once. Phone box – twice. Black cab – never again. Her bed – never.

I chalked up the following injuries: bites; scratches; radiator burns; a number of weird-shaped bruises, origin unknown; two violent bangs to the head (bathroom sink, both occasions); serious damage to my coat. The gash on my knee became a star-shaped scar for life. We took our joint picture in a photo booth; she put one in her wallet; I kept the other three under my mattress. And still she was making me write those terrible essays, scrawling line after line, boring myself to tears. I never knew if she was going to read my painstaking work. Sometimes she'd spend hours (it felt like) drumming Shakespeare and Hardy and Dickens and other ancient stuff into my head, till I could've gone on Mastermind about them. Sometimes we just fucked on the unread pages, her tossing her spectacles across the floor, whispering her desires into my ear, telling me how great, how sexy, how mature I was. I totally stopped thinking about the band, and Matt, and absent friends, and all that crap. It was good I'd had that row with him after all; now all I had to do was not to make it up. When Lily phoned – which she stopped doing eventually – I pretended I was busy. I didn't want her fucking up my life, and my life was nothing but Cassandra.

In fact, I was so taken up with living I barely even saw my parents for the next couple of weeks. They hardly noticed, they were so involved with their own sad lives. But Abigail strongly insisted I came to Harry's surprise birthday party. She greeted me squeakily, linking her arm in mine, tugging me with her round her little flat, kissing her fingers at freshly arriving people. The front room was alive with faces you couldn't quite put your finger on, and names you wouldn't even try to guess – bit part stars from telly and such, drinking mineral water and smoking draw. I caught sight of Harry behind his handsome smile, flattered and pleased to be so surrounded. But, seeing me, he flinched gloomily. I guessed I was now officially too old to be his son, and wondered what age he'd claimed to be today. 'Dickie's been on to me about you,' confided Abby. 'He was wondering where you've got to. He told me he listened to some tape of yours the other day. He's still hoping to sign you up for this boyband idea . . .'

I protested, slightly annoyed with her, 'No, no, he sounded pretty keen about the band. Said he'd get us some gigs.' Then I remembered, briefly sad, that there was no more band – or not with me in it, at least.

She giggled, pinching my arm. 'Maybe, but I'm sure it's you he really wants. Don't you realise the dustbin of pop music is full of weirdo kids like Matt?' Standing up on her little toes, she stared curiously into my face. 'What is the *matter* with you, Ferdia?' She started examining my skin as for infectious spots, then poked my ribs under my coat. 'Are you ill? Are you losing weight? It's giving you great cheekbones.'

Too right, I was losing weight, with the amount of exercise I'd been getting lately. I thought, *If only she knew,* and blurted out, 'I've got to go . . .' I was due at Cassandra's place later, and felt suddenly anxious about missing her.

'Don't be ridiculous,' Abigail huffed. 'You're helping Harry cut his cake.'

I kept trying to get away, but Abby insisted on getting a picture of me cutting a TV-shaped cake with my desperately embarrassed-looking dad, and I was ten minutes late, and Cassandra was gone, and I was convinced she'd already left in disgust. It turned out she'd been late herself. She was seriously upset. 'Where were you? Why didn't you wait?'

'I did wait,' I protested. 'A whole hour. That guy in the upstairs flat must've thought I was a burglar or something. He kept coming half-way down the stairs to check me out.'

We were in our coffee shop, observed by gloomy Bunhead. Cassandra took my hand under the painted table, driving her painted nails into the palm. 'I *needed* you.'

I could see she meant it, and felt awkward and flattered. 'I'm sorry.'

'Don't you care *anything* about us?'

'Cassandra – I waited an *hour*. I thought you'd gone out.'

'I need you to *care*.'

'I *do* care. Of course I do.'

'Do you, though?' She was still in a foul mood when she dropped me off.

Next day, her class was my last of the afternoon. She lifted her chin at me secretively on the way out; she didn't need to do that because I always hung about after class, every day since the black cab. The first couple of times it'd felt difficult, shuffling on the spot in the corridor, watching Matt's back turning the distant corner. But after those two days he'd stopped coming to school. Aristotle was in the year below, and I didn't hang out with him outside the band anyway, so there was no one around to notice my weird behaviour. Cassandra didn't think I should feel guilty about ditching Matt. 'Anyway, you haven't got time for all that now,' she commented dismissively. I wondered what Matt was thinking. I told myself, Well, he started it, and he hasn't tried to sort it, has he? I hoped and feared he didn't give a shit, and wondered if Lily was practising bass guitar.

After the corridor drained of life, I U-turned into the classroom. She came from behind the door, and hugged me so hard she nearly made me lose my balance – I had to catch the back of a school plastic chair. 'I'm sorry I got mad at you yesterday,' she murmured. But I was nervous of being seen with her; I moved away and she let me go, turning to her red handbag, digging around in it. 'I've bought you a present to make up.' She was wearing a short purple skirt and silver stockings. She handed me a mobile phone, thin as a card. I flicked it open, thinking it pretty nice, a seriously expensive model. 'It's yours,' she said. I looked at her, snapping my head back, taken by surprise. She smiled, acknowledging my impressed reaction. 'There's five pounds in it, in case you need to reach me. Keep it just for us. Don't turn it off.'

'Right, thanks . . . Are you sure?'

Packing papers into her leather briefcase, she added, with cool teacherly efficiency. 'You don't have to have the ring on – it vibrates. Nobody needs to know you've got it. Don't give anyone your number. If you keep it in your pocket, you'll feel it go off.' I slid it into my trouser pocket. She paused, with her hand inside the bulging bag. 'I'll always be able to find you, now.' She gave me this look that verged on coy. 'I've got you electronically tagged.'

She had that all right. I was on call. I even slept with it under my pillow, just in case she ever needed me in the middle of the night. Mostly she contacted me late afternoon, but some days I'd be in someone else's lesson when it leapt and trembled against my leg. She said not to answer it in that situation, just pretend the vibration in my trousers was her giving me a secret wank from afar. But I never could get my concentration back after she'd rung, so I took to leaving immediately to meet her, going to the bog and never coming back. When she found I'd been walking out of lessons she went ballistic, blaming herself for screwing up my education, wasting my brain, my life, my youth, my soul. For a whole day she didn't call, but then she started up again, never again asking what I'd been doing when she rang. Last Tuesday, mobile fizzing in my groin, I'd walked out in the middle of a test, pinging my pen into the metal bin. It was getting easier, behaving as if I was simply passing through.

Another thing she did was send dirty little text messages which came up on the mobile's screen. I was reading her latest in the street (*Smile if you had it last night*), shading the words with my hand, one Sunday when Lily caught up with me down Chalk Farm Road, wearing this jacket plastered all over in sequins.

'Ferdia! Ferdia!' she called, above the traffic's grinding blare, and I looked up and saw her bobbing glittering towards me in the human rush and I stopped smiling and slipped the phone into my coat. She washed up against my side, but was careful not to press herself against me, fighting to keep a little physical distance, getting gently knocked about by passers-by, a shiny bottle bobbing on the waves. 'Where have you been? I keep leaving messages with your mum . . .'

Trapped, I couldn't think what to answer. The last time I'd seen her was three weeks ago, when I'd shoved her away, after her soft kiss on my throat, into the arms of the crowd. I checked furtively around me. It frightened me we were on Cassandra's turf; that she might see us standing together, being too close; that things'd be like the last time, only worse. I wished Lily would just sense the awkwardness and move on, but she didn't.

She bobbed a little closer, eyes all round concern. 'Have you been ill or something? Is something the matter? God, you look awfully thin.'

I winced. 'I'm fine.' Too thin! First Abigail, then her. 'Nothing's the matter, OK?' And I thought how it was hard for me never being able to mention anything to anyone about Cassandra, never being able to share this proud exciting secret eating my brain and noticeably burning off my flesh. Instead, I had to put up with this soft pouting girly poor-you-are-you-ill sympathy thing. For a weak moment I was pathetically keen to boast to Lily that I was having mind-blowing sex with a drop-dead woman.

She raised her hand, in a fingerless golden glove, and nervously tightened the thin green scarf she was wearing around her neck. 'Well.' She became suddenly unhappy and tense. 'It's great to see you.'

'Yeah.' I shifted my gaze to the edge of the pavement, watching the rain-filled gutters swell as cars rolled by. 'Sorry, I'm in a bit of a rush, actually.'

She answered, humiliated but determined, 'I'll walk with you . . .'

'No!' But I hadn't meant to sound so hostile. She was glancing at me awkwardly, nipping her soft bottom lip with small white teeth. I apologised, 'Look, I'm sorry, I didn't mean . . .'

'Ferdia, can I ask you a question?' She took hold of my arm and pulled me out of the river of moving people, into a backwater down the side of an old red telephone box. Through the kiosk's dirty little panes, I could see the receiver dangling, disembowelled. Squashed by our feet, colourful crisp packets heaved up filthy water. She said, fixing me with her sloping eyes, 'Remember the last time I saw you . . .'

I screwed up my face, ashamed to be reminded. 'I know – I'm sorry for pushing you like that . . . it wasn't anything to do with you. I just had to get away, that's all.' But I tried to ease my arm from out of hers without making it look like I was brushing her off again, and asked, without pausing to put my brain in gear, 'So, how's the band?'

She groaned, sighed, shrugged, dragging again on the silky scarf, winding it round and around her small brown fingers. 'Since you went . . . Nothing, really.' But she touched my arm gently, like she didn't want me to think she was blaming me. 'I've been up to see Matt a couple of times, but he won't even come out of his room. He just lies on his bed all day, doing nothing at all, going on about hell and stuff and the twentieth floor. It's like, he's really tired and depressed all the time.' She picked a loose sequin off her glittering jacket, and rolled an empty can of Coke backwards and forwards under the arch of her foot. 'It's scary, it's really hard to talk to him.' She added, hurt, 'I don't think he even wants me coming round.'

I never could understand how that unwashed ego could be so careless of his string of adoring rich-girls. I gave her a quick comforting hug, because she was sweet and obviously upset, then hunted guiltily behind me for Cassandra. 'I'm sure he does. He just . . .'

'It doesn't matter,' she interrupted, stroking at my torn leather coat with her fingertip. We both watched her cute gold-painted nail, jutting out from her fingerless golden glove, gently scratching me up and down. Inside my protective coat my flesh drew back, prickling nervously all over. On cue, Cassandra's mobile spasmed against my hip, and I was gripped by the terrible heart-stopping certainty that she was observing us from across the grid-locked road and messaging me to say she never wanted to see me again. I hadn't forgotten how casually she could cast me off. I snatched for the phone so fast it spun out of my hand and skittered out of our space across the pavement between the kicking feet, surfing puddles in the direction of the gutter.

'Oh shit, *shit* . . .' I was down on my knees, groping at arm's length through the slow stampede of shoes, retrieving it. Rising to my feet, I scanned the text message fearfully. *At home. Come now.* Still trembling with adrenaline, feeling at the same time on top of the world, I stepped back into the shelter of the old red box, holding out my hand to say goodbye. 'Lily, listen, I've *got* to go.'

'Wait! There's something I've got to ask you!' She took hold of my forefinger, bouncing up on her toes, energetically enlarging her eyes to stress this *something* was urgent. I made to resist, then briefly, grinning, gave in, deciding maybe I had a moment because Cassandra couldn't realise I was so near. Lily asked, 'That tall skinny woman you chased after down the street – was she the teacher Matt was on about?' From being on a high, my blood ran colder than the weather; in startled reflex, I yanked back against her velvet grip but she held on extra tight. 'Because Matt thinks maybe you and her – I don't believe it for a second – *don't get angry with me.*'

I didn't. Instead, I made this massive effort to look relaxed, letting my finger lie heavily in her grip to prove how totally unfazed I was. 'What d'you go listening to Matt for?' In my own ears, I sounded suspiciously unsteady. 'You know what he's like – he's fucking off his nut.'

'I know – poor Matt . . .' She rolled her deep brown eyes. 'He's just got it into his head, like that insane music god shit he's always on about. He keeps on calling you the Zombie Kid; I tell him, he's talking rubbish . . .' She frowned. 'You feel so *cold* . . . come here . . .' She gathered all my fingers in hers, massaging them to warm them up, then came directly to the point, smiling up in shy apology. 'But I *did* hear you calling her "Cassandra" . . .'

Snatching back my hands, I turned to face the phonebox, cooling my forehead on an icy pane. I thought, She's guessed . . . I had a scary sensation of enemies closing in. Cassandra said Lily would want to split us up if she knew the truth. Yet Lily kind of knew already, and how could I stop her gabbing about it, if I didn't come clean and explain why she had to keep shtum? I thought, Maybe she can help, she can stop Matt mouthing off to Aristotle – fuck me, supposing Stotle starts on about it, he'll never let it go, it'll be round the whole bloody school . . . To be honest, I was glad of the excuse to talk to Lily. I was tired of keeping secrets. I wanted Lily to know I was a man, that I'd grown out of childish company. I found myself squaring my shoulders.

She commented kindly, like she wanted to make me feel better, 'I had a crush on my science teacher once – all the girls did. I don't know what I'd've done if anything'd happened. Been terrified, I suppose!'

I closed my eyes, shoulders slumped again. 'I don't have a *crush* on her,' I growled. It was as bad as Aristotle's cheerful insult about the dicklessness of boyband types. 'I'm not a fucking *kid*.'

'No . . .'

'I don't have a *crush*.'

Lily started giggling behind me. 'Come *on*, don't be so tense, I just wondered, I wasn't serious.' She plucked at the back of my coat. 'D'you want to get a Coke or something?'

I took several deep breaths. I thought, Lily's OK, she's not a mean-minded bitch; I need her to be on my side, to stop any dangerous rumour starting. 'Lily – listen, it's not a crush.'

'I know – you said . . . Come on . . .'

'I mean – it's *real*.' I turned to study her reaction.

She was stood spectacularly still, her hands in their gold silk mittens interlocked in front of her heart. After a pause, she said, 'What do you mean – real?'

'You know – the real thing. We do it.' I waited impatiently. I guess I was looking for startled feminine admiration.

One hand rose slowly to her helpless mouth. It was clear she hadn't believed Matt in the slightest.

'Don't tell anyone,' I said instantly, in a panic at finding I'd duped myself into telling her the truth.

'Oh . . . my . . . god . . .'

'Because if anyone finds out it'll be a big problem for us . . .'

'Oh . . . my . . . god . . . Jesus, Ferdia . . .'

'You know what people are like . . .'

'That's *disgusting*!'

I was genuinely astonished. I wasn't expecting that. 'What the fuck do you mean? It's not disgusting! It's . . . the best thing that ever happened!'

'I don't *believe* it,' she gasped out. 'I can't believe it!' She clutched absurdly dramatically at her head. 'She's your teacher! It's *wrong*. She can't have sex with you!'

'Ssh . . . ssh!' I checked horrified towards the road. Beyond our sheltered spot, the crowd poured on. 'Someone'll hear you . . .'

'I don't care! It's gross!' Her face contorted like she'd stood in shit. 'It makes me want to *puke*!'

164

I couldn't get my head round the way she was carrying on. I'd really thought she was my friend. I turned on her, hurt, shocked, seriously embarrassed. 'Shut up! You don't know what you're on about!'

Undeterred, she shrieked at the top of her voice, jabbing her finger at my chest, 'Of course I do! It's illegal! Teachers aren't allowed to sleep with their students! She's a skinny old bitch – she's twice your age – how can you stand her groping you?'

'Shut *up*!' Enraged, I seized her by the front of her jacket, sequins scattering everywhere. It was all I could do to stop myself slapping her. I ached to gag her with that thin green scarf. Un-London-like, a few pedestrians were actually slowing down to take a look, emerging as interested people from the undifferentiated flood. Freaked out by their what's-going-on expressions, I tore open the phone box and bundled her inside. 'Shut the fuck *up* . . .'

She wouldn't stop. 'It's disgusting, illegal – she's a bloody paedophile!'

I crushed in after her, letting the door swing shut, folding our bodies helplessly together. 'Are you out of your mind? She's not a pervert, right?'

I could feel the small shape of her pressed against me, vibrating helplessly with fury. 'It makes me ill to think about it! She should be reported! Wrinkly old perve!'

I realised too late Cassandra had got it right: Lily obviously fancied me – why else was she so keen to fuck us up? I gripped her thin bendy wrist and cursed myself bitterly for trusting her. *'No one's gonna report anyone!'* I backed her up hard against the broken phone. She shrank beneath me, gasping with the pain, the back of her head pressed awkwardly against the metal telephone buttons, a silver drop of saliva swelling unlicked in the corner of her mouth, tears starting to hop unevenly down her cheeks, leaving starry shiny trails. I was glad she looked so lonely and afraid. I lowered my voice to make it threatening. 'If you say one word to *anyone*, I'll fucking kill you; I'll fuck you up. I'll never speak to you again, I fucking swear it.'

She was crying properly now, with big splattering girly sobs. 'OK, OK – I won't, but . . .'

Pinning her wrist in thumb and forefinger, I squashed it hard between her cuff and glove, feeling the hard veins squirm within her delicate skin. 'But *nothing*. Swear.'

'I swear . . . But . . .'

The mobile in my pocket jerked into life again, and this time it wasn't a message but a proper call. 'OK,' I said, backing hurriedly out the box. 'I've got to go.'

'Don't go,' she said, quickly. 'Don't leave me now.'

Cassandra was right, she was only a jealous cow. 'See you around,' I lied, letting the heavy door fall in on her.

She called after me, holding it open, in a small desperate voice, 'But what about the band?' As if that meant anything to me at all.

'Where are you? Are you on your way?'

'I'm coming now!' Charging down the damp fuming streets between us without stopping, I nearly got knocked down by a bus, and was briefly horrified not by the idea of missing the rest of my life but by the thought I might miss this one meeting with Cassandra. Five minutes later and I was in her street – the house door was open; I legged it up the flight to the first floor, three at a time. At the top, I skidded to a halt, panting, one knee bent, one foot left below me on the stairs. She was standing there in the hall, large as life, leaning in her doorway, talking to that bloke from the flat above. Actually, he was doing all the talking, droning on and on about something under his breath – she was just mindlessly stroking her hair with her hand. She had no shoes on. I watched her slowly realise I was there, raising her head like worried wildlife, sniffing the air. Then whirling away from him, mid-sentence, turning her body like the sun to me. She had no stockings either, not even a dress, only a long Charlatans T-shirt, com-

166

ing halfway down her thighs. When she could think of what to say, she said, 'Oh – you've arrived *early* for your lesson! I'm not even dressed!'

I hovered, heart hammering from the run and the fright I'd had, not knowing what to answer. The bloke wasn't moving, even though he was now obviously a waste of space. Instead, he hung about with his arms wrapped across his chest, staring from her to me, acting like he deserved an introduction.

'Tom. I'll see you later,' she said, gesturing me past her into her flat. Suddenly craving water, I headed for the sink in her kitchen.

'And he is . . .?' I heard the bastard say.

She answered him in a cheeky voice, before slamming the door on him, 'Lovely boy. In need of extra special tuition.' When I came back out of the kitchen, mouth still dripping from the tap, I found her squatting on the floor of the hall, cheeks squashed between her hands, coughing up dirty laughter, one tear running in a long clear spiral down her wrist. 'Oh god,' she was moaning. 'Oh . . . *god*.' She didn't even have any pants on.

I took off my coat.

Ethnic rug in front room, fourteenth time. The sharp scent of oranges flowing from her kiss.

'*Tom?*' I rolled over onto my back, one bare leg cooling on the wooden boards. Always up to now when we were doing it, nothing from other people's worlds came into my head I mean literally *nothing* came into my head, like I'd stopped thinking and was simply me – a sack of violent sensation with no brain to speak of. But this time, for the first time ever, I hadn't escaped from the outside; throughout I'd heard that wanker's voice – *And he is . . .?* I wanted to know: what the fuck's it to him? And I heard Lily too, hassling me – *That's so gross. It's disgusting . . .* Like it was anything to her.

'You should've told me you were so near by,' she complained defensively, propped up on elbows roughened at their points, picking crossly at the fringe of the rug. 'I wasn't ready for you. I was going to . . .' She frowned.

I put in sarcastically, ' . . . finish getting dressed?'

'Finish getting *un*dressed, you idiot,' she smiled, pushing me lightly with her foot. 'Horrible boy. Don't be so suspicious.'

I tried to make a joke of it. 'Standing on the landing wearing *nothing*.'

'Not wearing nothing.' She smirked, arching her back, brushing her hair aside across the back of her neck.

'Wearing practically nothing. Talking to *Tom*.' I heard my voice getting pretty fucking unfunny.

'Oh dear.' She thought this a real laugh. 'Dearie dearie me. Ferdia's jealous of the man upstairs.'

I was usually exhausted after sessions like these, but today the buzz continued, winding me up, making me moodily walk the golden room. She stretched out in patronising silence. Eventually I squatted in her armchair, in my boxers, still wearing my socks, and examined her cool elegant body lounging on the rug, fingers unravelling the fringe, T-shirt thrust up to smooth sharp shoulder blades, the ice-cream scoop of her back, legs extended in the air behind her, long toes wriggling idly. Forgetting Tom, I was swept by a powerful burning rush of devotion, the total loyalty of a dog, the desire to shield her with my very body from her enemies. I shook my head in disbelief that Lily could think such total crap about my relationship with Cassandra, talking like I was a girl being forced by a bloke into doing something I couldn't stop, instead of a walking hard-on in full control.

'There's nothing going on between me and Tom,' Cassandra said at last, with a deliberate lengthy sigh.

'It's not that.' The wintry sun was touching my bare legs gently through the glass. 'I was just thinking, how people would get the wrong idea if they found out about us.'

A spasm of tension ran visibly up her half-naked body. She swung her blonde head towards me, narrow-eyed. 'What on earth do you mean?'

I was kind of surprised at her asking me that. It was her always acting scared of being found out. 'Well, you know, you being my teacher and stuff . . .'

'Stuff?' She was getting slowly to her knees. 'What *stuff*?'

'Hmm . . .' I gripped my socked feet in each hand, bent back my toes, studied them. I'd wanted to reassure her how much her age didn't matter to me, but it was obviously going to be difficult to put in a tactful way. 'You know, um, like you being my teacher and that . . .'

She stalked the room in long pale feet, Charlatans T-shirt clinging to her hips. I crouched in my underwear in the soft yellow chair, watching her, confused by the shocked upset she was giving off. 'You think I'm too old for you, don't you?' She came and posed thrustingly in front of me, one hand on hip, long legs parted, soft and sorrowful and vulnerable. 'You'd rather have a girlfriend your age, wouldn't you? Like Lily?'

'Don't be ridiculous!' I protested. I could see Lily weeping gently in my head, terrified as I twisted back her wrist. 'Cassandra, you're the only one, I swear – I don't care how old you are, you're beautiful.'

She pushed her crotch in my face. 'This is just a fling for you, isn't it? A bit of fun?'

'No!' I was flooded with strange electric anxiety, skin bristling in anticipation. 'All I was saying was . . .'

'Then *don't say it*!' Standing back, she took the twist of polished wood off her mantelpiece, stroking it in her hands. 'Bastard!' I heard the thud of the blow before I felt its pain, the pain in my skull before I realised what she'd done, and then, before I could get out of the way, she did it again – 'Bastard!' – my body crumpling, rolling off the chair, my bare hands clasped over my head, my voice crying out her name in sad despair like when I chased after her through Kentish Town. In uncertain silence, I curled up on the floor, breathing as quietly as I could, my nose filled with the goaty smell of rug. A lorry revving in the street was muffled by the pounding in my ears.

'Ferdia?' She sounded genuinely concerned. 'Ferdia? Are you OK?'

I tried to get to my feet but, when I lifted my head, my brain fell like a stone from one side of my skull to the other; my sight was cluttered with small silvery whirlpools.

'Are you OK? Ferdie – talk to me . . .' She was down beside me, holding me, cradling me, rocking me intimately in her arms, holding my forehead to her shoulder, her thin jaw sharply pressed into my ear. 'I'm so, so sorry. It's just I felt so scared. I couldn't bear it if you left me now.'

I whispered, 'But I didn't want to leave you.'

'Oh god. Poor you. Are you OK?' She folded me into her lanky arms. ' I'm so sorry, losing it like that – it's only because I care so much. Are you sure you're OK? Let's get you comfortable . . .' She helped me carefully to my feet and guided me to the armchair, fussing over me all the way, acting tenderly and motherly. The polished ornament was back on the mantelpiece, neatly arranged among her other trendy Camden Lock purchases.

I fingered the top of my head and then my forehead. The lumps were soft and hurt; I flinched from my own touch, enjoying her guilty gasp – it made a change for her to be the one in the wrong. I felt this pleasurable surge of power. 'Jesus, Cassandra,' I accused her. 'Why?'

Her face falling, she threw herself onto the sofa opposite me, huddled herself into a lonely ball. 'But you make me so unhappy,' she burst out tearfully into her knees. 'I never meant this to happen. The day I met you in the café' – she studied me in pale-faced sorrow – 'I just wanted to make sure you were all right. But then you kissed me! Now I don't know what I'm doing . . . It's all such a terrible, terrible mistake.' She clasped her calves, rocking from side to side. 'I'm only a bit of fun for you, and I'm so vulnerable, so exposed, I'm so scared, I could lose my job over this, ruin my career . . .'

As I remembered it, she'd kissed me first, but what did that matter? Because of course it was me that pushed her down, into the wet dirt on the floor of the yard – I was the male who'd been on top of her, my weight on her; if I hadn't wanted it, nothing could've happened. And it was true, she could lose everything because of me. I looked down at the hands which had pinned her in the mud. 'I don't want you to lose your job.'

After an insufferable pause, Cassandra said patiently, 'You don't understand. It's you I couldn't bear to lose. I'm scared. That's why I hurt you. I love you, Ferdie.' All my muscles, including my heart, went weak with happiness. 'Ferdia?' She held out her long shivering arms.

I slid off the armchair and staggered across to her on my knees. She took my face, kissing it, fingering my skull, pressing on my bruises with her thumb like she was testing damaged fruit; though it hurt a lot, I didn't pull away. So this was love, in all its scary pain. 'I love you too,' I said.

Chapter Fourteen

'What have you been up to, Ferdia?' demanded my mother, later that Sunday afternoon, as I came wandering into the kitchen, drifting along in my rainbow-coloured soap bubble of happiness, brain in my head still banging like a drum but heart swollen with love. 'No – don't lie to me – I know. I heard about it in the staff room.'

I stopped dead.

She was stood with her back pressed against the draining board, hunched uncomfortably over a cigarette, long green dress showered with ash, black curls reddened by the sunset sky. Thin feelers of smoke reached up and stroked her face; awkwardly, she scratched her nose. 'It's so difficult, Ferdia, especially with me teaching there.' Behind her, the clear-cut crimson sun was sliding down, the exact width of the slot between two tower blocks. She pointed, creating a thin lengthy shadow. 'I was so worried, I asked your dad to come over.'

I hadn't noticed Harry till that moment, his arse parked on the rust-coloured sofa and Twinkie coiled throbbingly in his lap, drawing clawfuls of threads from his crumpled linen suit. The moment I saw him he shot to his feet, clumsily spilling his indignant cat. 'We're very worried about you. Very!'

I understood then that Lily had lied – that she'd come right round today and told them. I was totally stunned that she could be so cruel.

Annie said firmly to her cigarette, 'We need you to tell us what's going on.'

'Nothing's going on. Nothing. Leave me alone.' Backed up against the fridge in rising panic, I slipped my fingers into the pocket of my jeans, feeling for the little mobile lying quiet – rubbing it, stroking it, like for luck, like it alone could keep us safe.

Harry leant his sun-bedded knuckles on the table, exhaling impatiently through his handsome nose. 'Come on, Ferdia. We know you keep walking out of lessons without any excuse, and we need to know why. You're our son. We love you. We can help.' He paused for effect while I restrained myself from dancing. They didn't know a thing, and she was safe. The cat jumped up on the table, purring. Harry said bullishly, having psyched himself up for the big one, 'Come on, it's OK, you can tell us. Are you taking something you shouldn't be?'

I groaned. 'Oh, *please.*' But actually I was laughing. Now my initial heart attack was over, I was in too good a mood to be pissed at him for asking. My glorious bubble burst back into being. Outside of its rainbow surface, I could see them flailing around in the shadowy kitchen, wrong-footed by the way I was so totally unfazed.

Annie said, swaying towards the light switch, flicking it on as the sun went down, 'Look, we know there's a lot of drugs going round the school. We're *worried* about you, darling.'

'Don't be. Really.' Humming, I opened the fridge and uncovered a can of lager, snapped the tab, drank it in one, crushed up the empty can and drop-kicked it incredibly neatly into the bin. For a second I was overcome by childish pride, grinning at them. 'Hey – did you see that? Shot!'

Annoyingly, they'd missed it. All they kept staring at was me. 'Ferdia, you look *terrible,*' cried Annie, stepping towards me, her dress floating lightly out behind her. 'What on earth's that awful lump on your forehead?'

Harry, leaning across the table, waves of fine fair hair tumbling out of place, said, 'My god! Have you been in a fight?' Twinkie rose on her haunches and head-butted him softly in the chin.

My happy feelings switched to cold irritation. That was the

same thing Jason Peckham had asked me, meeting at my own door after my first – encounter – with Cassandra. *Have you been in a fight?* Had none of these idiots heard of love? I spun my back on them, sharpish. 'Fell off a skateboard. What's the *matter* with you?' I was swamped by anger, digging out another icy lager. 'Haven't you got better things to do than hassle me? Do you really think I'm a violent drug addict?' All I wanted was for the pair of them to fuck right off. Their inquisition buzzed around my ears, making me feel dizzy, sick and blurred. No wonder my head was killing me. Gripping the lager, my fingers slipped on its cold condensation, and I caught it just above the floor with my other hand, brain hitting the side of my skull with a squelchy thud.

Annie said tentatively, her voice too close, putting her hands on my shoulders, invading my space, making my skin crawl. 'Talk to us, Ferdia. We love you. We want to help.'

I shrugged her fiercely off. 'There's nothing wrong. Now fuck off and leave me alone.' I wouldn't face them again, but I could hear them looking meaningfully at each other.

'I think he's still angry about the divorce,' murmured Annie behind my back. 'I think this is a protest.'

Harry snorted disbelievingly, but then pulled himself together in front of his ex-wife and asked soothingly, 'What do you say, Ferdia? Are you really still upset after *all this time*?'

Having been finally asked, after *all this time* – instead of being constantly told that I was fine – I actually took a moment to consider, pressing a few old sentimental buttons. Nothing. Zilch. Smugly, I ripped the can of beer. Over and over, for more than a year, I'd struggled in childish pain from one end of Abbey Road to the other, rain and shine, fumes and pigeons, never arriving in the right place ever, dragging my heart behind me like a rock. And now, at last, I didn't give a shit. Even the sight of them in this room together didn't seem to bother me any more, as if the past crappy year no longer mattered, nor the future neither. I took a big mouthful

174

of beer, grinning to myself. 'Nope.' I'd come untied like string from a stone, free at last, ballooning into the air, the sky-high man Matt thought I'd never be. I turned to face them, a genuinely happy camper.

'He is, Harry, it's obvious . . .'

But Harry kept studying my cheerful face, head on one side, tanned hand on cheek, out of habit giving his puzzlement a theatrical spin – while all the time his other hand was delicately stealing a cigarette from Annie's open packet on the table, with Twinkie, purring, sniffing his scrabbling fingers. 'I don't get it,' he said, backing up to sit on the rust-coloured sofa, sticking the unlit fag in his cupid-bow mouth. The cat jumped down and joyfully repossessed his lap. 'If you're not mixed up in something serious, you're certainly acting like you are.'

I shrugged, bumming a cigarette as well. 'Yeah? Well, how the hell's that?'

'Oh come on.' He plucked at the top of his head, checking unthinkingly for failing hair as he always did when he was tense, staring at the fag in my fingers, deliberately not objecting to it so as not to 'alienate' me. 'You've lost loads of weight. You can't seem to concentrate on anything. You're always going out and neither of us knows where you are. You refuse to answer the phone to your friends. You don't seem even to care about us anymore. When did you last come to see me without me begging you to?' He looked suddenly exhausted by this long effort of fatherhood. 'Just tell me, please – why are you walking out of lessons?'

'Because they're all crap?'

'That's it,' said Harry, with authority, looking across at Annie. 'We've got to send him to a different school.'

'No,' I said, in a quiet firm voice.

Annie flounced impatiently in her long green dress. 'Oh come on, Harry, that's so like you – I'm telling you, it's nothing to do with the school, it's the divorce.'

But it suited him to seize on a practical problem, rather

than wasting time on something emotional he wasn't prepared to fix, or didn't know how. 'Think about it, Annie. The
school's failing. It's in the bloody papers practically every
day. Journalists everywhere. It's a government target. It'll be
closed next year. He needs a change. Maybe it'll help him to
sort himself out.'

I said, 'I'm not moving school, OK? Anyway, it's too late –
I've got exams this year.'

'You told me yourself,' said Harry to Annie, 'you heard in
the staffroom he's not doing any work at all.'

'You can't just pretend this has nothing to do with . . .'

No work? After all those essays I'd been churning out? I'd
never worked so hard in all my life as I'd done (off and on)
this term. I cried, 'That's totally unfair! I've been working my
arse off for weeks, just ask . . .' And stopped, pulling myself
together, remembering what this was all about, finishing in a
fading mutter, 'Well, I've written a shit-load of English
essays.'

'For Cassandra?'

Even spoken so casually in my mother's voice, her name
made me buckle at the knees. I sat down abruptly at the table
with my beer. 'Yeah. I've been doing loads of work for her.'

'I've been meaning to talk to her about your work, if I ever
catch her in the staffroom . . .'

Oh god, the hideous embarrassment of having my *mother*
discussing me with Cassandra, as if I was some out-of-order
kid, some juvenile schoolboy in need of straightening out.
'No, mum. Don't do that. Leave it out.' My hand convulsed
around the nearly-full can. 'You don't need to check up on
me, mum. I'm not a kid.'

'Yeah, right,' said Harry cynically, dragging down hard on
his fag.

'But Ferdie, we really have to work this out. Together. We
need to discuss this with all your teachers . . .'

'No,' I repeated harshly. '*No.*'

'Come on, Ferdie,' argued Harry crisply. 'This isn't about

invading your privacy. It's about being responsible parents who want to help. We need to sort this out.'

'But I don't want you *sorting me out*. Fucking well leave me alone! Sort yourselves fucking out, if you've got so fucking responsible all of a sudden!' I smashed the beer on the table as hard as I could, and a golden fountain whooshed into the air, showering my parents and the astonished cat with glittering dying sparks of foam. I rushed out of the house into the darkening street. Nobody understood how grown up I was – all everyone wanted to do was tear me apart, interfere, destroy my perfect world, force me to live a pointless fucked-up life. In the middle of my rage, I remembered how crazy I'd been, spilling my guts to Lily; I ripped out the mobile and punched in her number. 'Listen,' I shouted furiously when she answered. 'You don't tell anyone about this, OK? Nothing. Nobody. Nobody. Nothing.'

'But I promised, I told you already, I promised . . .'

'Just don't then!' I glanced back at my house and saw both my parents hovering nervously at the top of our steps, and I raced off like a nutter down the road, long shadowy strides under the buzzing street lights. Later on, picturing it, it made me laugh – there was me, in my crack-dealer's coat, yelling down this strangely expensive mobile, warning some unknown contact to keep their mouth shut. They must've thought they were right about the drugs.

I needed somewhere to stay, or just to hang out – it was freezing outside, and I'd no money on me. Cassandra's mobile rang out. I tried her home number, but the answer machine was on. I left a message, saying if my mum spoke to her, don't worry about it – it was just something dumb to do with school. I said, 'I love you,' realising instantly I couldn't take it back, having to leave it lying around written on this distant tape in my choked, embarrassed voice. If she got murdered, the pigs would listen to it.

I didn't think going to Lily's was a good idea, not after the way I'd been behaving to her. I didn't really hang with Aristotle outside of the band but I phoned him anyway; he'd gone to his cousin's for the weekend. All the time I was walking down the road until I came to the entrance to the estate. I stood under the darkness of Matt's tower and thought about Lily telling me he was refusing to leave his room. I tipped back my head, scanning all the way up his cheap misty block, up past endlessly shrinking squares of light, all the way up to his balcony at the top right-hand corner. Then I went in and punched the lift button, and thought that if the lift was out I definitely wouldn't bother. The doors clattered open with an echoing ping, belching a blast of piss-smell into my face. Holding my breath until I got used to it, I stepped into the warm fresh contents of another man's bladder. At the twentieth floor, I wiped my feet along the tattered lino. No one answered Matt's door. I hung around for a while, wondering what to do next. On the long way up I'd become all geared up to tell him how in my head I was as sky-high as he was, no more ties, cast off, sailing directly up. I was keen to explain to him about it all. But no one was in. I wandered back to the lift, but when the doors burst open, Natasha was there, in a yellow dress, standing with her open-toed sandals in the piss, clasping a carton of milk and a packet of Benson and Hedges to her flat little five-year-old chest.

'Ferdie!' she squeaked, looking like she wanted to give me a hug, but couldn't because of the stuff she was holding. 'Have you come to see Matt? He's really sick! Are you coming in? What's that red lump on your head? I'm really cold!'

'You should wear your coat,' I said.

'I know. It was just to the shop.' She kicked Matt's front door in with her sandal, banging it open. 'Come and see mum.'

Tessa was up, in a way, not totally out of it, wrapped in a throw, sitting on the nylon-covered sofa, holding out her hand to Natasha for the cigarettes, smiling prettily at me. 'Isn't she a good girl?' To Natasha, she added, with real loving drunken warmth, 'You always look after your poor old mum, don't you?' and pulled the little girl close to her with one thin arm, hugging her up onto the couch, tucking the throw around them both. Nat snuggled up, cradling the milk as tenderly as a doll, as her gentle drowsy mother was cradling her. 'Come to see Matt?' Tessa asked me, eyes half-closing as she lit a cigarette carefully over her daughter's head.

Aristotle's drums were still cluttering up most of the room. I shuffled about in the limited space. 'Is he around?'

'Sure.' She nodded at his bedroom.

'He's very sick,' said Natasha.

'He's fine, Nattie. He's just being a typical bloody teenager. Don't worry about it.' She said to me, 'He's a bit down at the moment, just slobs around in bed all day, not saying anything. Typical teenager, innit? Go in and cheer him up a bit.'

Natasha said, trying to open the milk to drink it, 'Tell him I'm sick of always being the one to go to the shop.'

Her mum smiled down at the top of her head. 'I love you, Nat,' she said, overflowing with emotion.

Matt's darkened room stank of unchanged boxers and old breath, enough to make you choke. I switched on the light. He lay in a bundle on his mattress, a tea-stained duvet with no cover wrapped over him, chip wrappers and brown mugs heaped around his head. Posters of unrecorded bands peeled off his walls in long torn strips. I'd found him like this before, loads of times, normally on Sunday mornings. 'Hey,' I said, feeling cheerful to see him again. Everything in my life was so swamped by Cassandra, I hadn't realised how much I'd missed him. He didn't move. 'Oi, anyone there?' I couldn't even hear him breathing. 'Come on, Matt.' For a sick-making second I thought, Fuck it – this is what death looks like: sleep. But at that moment his hand came creeping out from under the duvet. His guitar was crashed out next to him on the mattress, and his fingers wandered rapidly over it, skating like insects up and down its neck.

'Hey, how you doing, man?' I said, relieved. He muttered something. I couldn't make it out. I went towards his corner and bent down. 'You what, mate?'

He said, 'The sun is a music god.'

I squatted next to him, among his rotting socks. He kept his face turned to the wall, his fingers trotting up and down the strings. I wasn't sure I'd heard him properly. 'Say again?'

After a while, he repeated patiently, 'The sun is a music god.'

I stayed in my position. A minute or two later, he flipped his head to face me, and announced quite clearly, 'In another universe the twentieth floor is at ground level.'

I wasn't certain if he wanted replies to these statements. He waited. I said, helpfully, 'Ground level, yeah?'

He shot up in the bed, bare-chested, shivering. 'That's it. You can just walk across the air and right into the sun. Everything under the twentieth floor is sub-ground level.' He glared at me challengingly, like he was expecting me to deny it. '*Everything* – geddit?'

'Yeah, I get it.'

He made an impatient screwed-up expression. 'No. You don't get it. Everything under the twentieth floor is in hell.'

I answered, cautious. 'Yeah? Even my place? I s'pose it has been a bit of a mess lately.'

He tutted in disgust, dragging the duvet up to his chin, letting his guitar slide half onto the floor. 'No. Listen. Hell is underground, right? You gotta understand that.' He stared hard at me, over the duvet. I thought uncomfortably that he must be stoned or out of it on something. It felt a bit sad. I kept waiting for him to make it safe, just say he was writing a song about it. He said, kind of wistful, 'If I could find my way to that universe, man, I'd just walk out across the air, I'd just step off the balcony and walk on god's blue air, right up to my music god and shake him by the hand.'

'Your music god?'

'The *sun*.' He glared, exasperated. Then he lowered his

voice and added, glancing over my shoulder at the door, like it was this big amazing secret he wanted to keep between us, 'I'm learning to look at it.' Startled, I couldn't help trying to check out his eyes, to see if he'd scorched little holes in them. He turned his face instantly away, resting his round naked shoulders against the cracking wall, his unwashed head hanging down and to the side. I settled my arse on the side of his mattress, and sighed, and flicked a string of his guitar. He flinched at the sound of it, and muttered, 'Don't.'

'Look, Matt,' I said, vaguely annoyed by all this shit, making an effort to get him out of it. 'When're we going to do another band practice?' Seeing his guitar made me nostalgic for a jam. I'd kind of forgotten about some stuff in the past few weeks, but being around him again was tugging at me, bringing things back, reminding me of the fun we'd always had. He said nothing, just looked at me suspiciously. For a few seconds, I was puzzled by the way he was acting all pissed off and mistrustful, then it came to me. It seemed so long ago, it'd gone right out of my head. 'Oh come on. Don't worry about Dickie and all that fucking sell-out shit. Forget about it. Let's write a new song. Just us. Just have a laugh, like we used to, right?'

He looked up at his window, uncurtained. 'I dunno,' he said.

'Come on, Matt, lighten up. The music god won't like it if you just stop altogether.'

He reached for a T-shirt and pulled it on over his head, stretching out his pink-skinned freckled arms. 'I dunno,' he said, sadly. 'I'm not writing my own songs anymore.'

'What?' I was almost stunned, felt the empty gouged-out shock of loss almost like when my dad walked out the house with his final suitcase. 'You've stopped? Why? You shouldn't take that Dickie shit so seriously!'

He said kindly, seeing how troubled I was, 'It's OK, Ferdie. It's not like it was ever me, anyway. I thought it was, yeah? We all did. But it was the music god.' Throwing back the filthy duvet, he rose and crossed to the switch, turning off the light. In the dark, he leant his forearms on the windowsill, standing in his T-shirt and boxers, staring out. In the high black night, directly opposite, the moon in the clouds was a nasty blue-brown bruise. With one finger, he started tracing thick black lines through the silvered condensation on the glass.

'What are you doing?' I asked, bewildered.

'Waiting,' he said.

'What for?'

'The sun to come up.'

'Oh for fuck's sake,' I said, losing it. 'It's only seven in the evening.'

He turned and looked at me steadily through the shadows. 'You should listen to the music god, Ferdia,' he said after a while, really seriously. 'Don't try to tie him down, man, with Dickie deals and dosh and flashy cars. All that shit you think you want. You can't tie the sun god down, man. He's too strong for us. Too high in the sky. Your ropes won't work.'

'I don't want *nothing*.' I got to my feet. I was fed up with being accused of all this materialistic crap. 'You're totally wrong, man. What about that boyband thing I turned down? Anyway, what's bad about having a bit of cash? Everyone's got to eat.'

I could hardly see his face at all, only the scruffy outline of his hair. He said gently, 'Yeah, I know. For a bit, I thought cash was really important too. It was a real temptation. I guess, if I'm honest with myself, that's why I went to see Dickie in the first place. Did you see Nat out there?'

'She went to the shop without her coat,' I said, harshly. 'I don't think she even has a coat. That's what having no cash means to her.'

He groaned like I'd given him a slap, resting his scruffy head upon the sill. Then he straightened up and said with renewed determination, 'Everything is a rope.'

'Jesus,' I said, with bitterness. 'If you say so.' I shuffled across the floor, kicking his guitar by accident, making it hum. 'Shit – sorry.' Pausing in his doorway, letting the light in from the living room, I said, trying to get some reality back, 'Look – are you coming to school tomorrow?'

'School is down there, man,' he answered in a worried voice, squinting at me. 'It's for zombie kids.'

'So, you're not coming then?'

'It's *down* there.' He slapped his hand on the wall, his voice getting agitated. 'Why won't you listen to me? You're letting your teacher eat your head. She's got her claws in you. She'll suck your blood. She'll fuck you up. You'll die inside. Trust me. Listen to me, man.'

'You're wrong, mate,' I said, from the door. 'Nothing ties me down. I've been set free.'

Tessa and Natasha were asleep on the sofa together when I left, folded neatly into each other, looking very sweet and the image of each other. Going down and down in the lift, in the heat and stench, head violently aching, I got smothered and dizzy; the doors shuddered open for a madman in a hat, who violently cursed god as we descended; then opened again to let in this scared skinny twelve-year-old, lugging her tiny baby in a sling; then again for some paranoid nutter with a Doberman on a short thick leash and a spider web tattooed across his face. We all ignored each other on our way down the rumbling, creaking, stinking, over-heated shaft; I remembered Matt saying that all below the twentieth floor was hell; in that case, we were a doomed crew going down together. Thinking that way, it shit me up badly when the lobby seemed alight with flickering flames. Some pre-school arseholes were tossing lit fireworks into the row of metal bins outside.

Walking towards the fire, I tried Cassandra again – still no reply. My mind was still on Matt, but when Cassandra wasn't there immediately all I could think about was her, like the lift doors had opened on her face and closed Matt off dead with their metallic clang. Her absence filled my world. Unable to concentrate on anything else, I wandered home, and the weird thing was – I found her in my house.

I came into the kitchen, expecting shit and recriminations about the splattering. But everyone was smiling, and there was Cassandra sat on the kitchen sofa with my mum, sharing a bottle of wine, nodding away, exclaiming, all bright eyes and parted lips, 'Ferdie!' like everything was totally OK, while my dad sat at the table, unable to take his eyes off of her, fondling Twinkie for a substitute. My battered head gave one massive thump; weakly, I put my hand to it. I knew now what Matt meant, about waking up in totally the wrong universe. Ignoring my failure to respond, Cassandra turned back busily to my mum and said, 'Of course, everyone's so demoralised now what with the school failing its inspection, and it being all over the papers, and those dreadful reporters crawling all over the place for the last couple of weeks, following everybody around . . .'

'Bloody reporters,' said my dad, slavishly.

' . . . it's not surprising kids like Ferdia don't feel the teaching's up to much. I know it's not our fault, Annie – the teachers try so hard, and there's bloody little support. But, you know, like I said, he's doing great things with the work I set him. Get him to show you his essays – you'll be proud.' Yet she'd never even given me an A. Unless the black cab counted.

'It's ridiculous that they're talking about closing it instead of putting in more funding,' said Annie. 'All that experience among the teachers – it's far harder with kids from those sort of backgrounds. Look at the others, creaming off all the middle class children – even when they *know* they're lying about living in the catchment area. It's so fucking unfair.'

Harry said, mildly, 'But it's OK complaining the government's doing the wrong thing, OK, let's fight that – the fact is, in the short term, he's still got to get a decent education, and I'm worried about the quality . . .'

Cassandra looked at him, raising her thin fair brows, making her prominent eyes sharply threatening.

'I'm not complaining about what he's learning from *you*, Cassandra,' said Harry hurriedly, downright obsequious. 'And it'd certainly be a pity if he lost that. You're clearly a great opportunity for him.'

'He's very talented,' she purred, winking at me, and sipping her wine. 'Any teacher would be glad to have him.'

'Ferdie – come in,' said my dad, suddenly welcoming me home. 'What're you standing around there for? Come and sit down.'

I thought if I moved at all I would fall down.

'Come, sit,' said Cassandra, poking at a kitchen chair with her green pointed shoe. She was wearing black stockings and a small black cardigan, and a dark green skirt that came in tight below her knees, forcing her to perch sideways on the couch. 'Relax. This isn't a lynch mob. We've all been singing your praises here.' She smiled sweetly up at my face. 'Goodness – what is that nasty bruise?'

'He *says* he fell off a skateboard,' explained my mum.

Cassandra laughed. 'What dangerous games our children play!'

I edged my way round the far side of the table and sat down. All three of them faced me, my father swivelling in his seat to do it. He was going to say something, but Cassandra got there first, and with un-Harry-like deference he didn't interrupt.

'What your parents are worried about, Ferdia,' she said, leaning forward, her long thighs pinched together by the skirt, 'is that you're not giving enough time to the lessons that don't interest you as much as . . . say . . . other ones. Yeah?' She paused as if she wanted a genuine reply. I just kept staring at her, dizzily, ears singing, my thoughts swamped by a million little images of her naked blowing like heavy rain through my hollow head. I heard her say, 'It's a difficult time for the school – we don't want to lose you – I don't want to lose you . . . What do you think?' Loudly, like to get my attention, she said, 'Ferdia – can you try harder? It's important.'

I shook myself, and rubbed my eyes and ears. 'Yeah,' I said. My voice sounded blurred to me. 'Right. I'll try . . . harder.'

'That's all we wanted to hear,' she said, laughing. 'That's all we need – god – look at the time – I've really got to go.'

They all stood up, and Cassandra plucked her grey fake fur from the sofa's arm, and shook it out.

Annie said, 'Thanks for coming round, Cassandra – that was really sweet of you, you really shouldn't have . . . I didn't mean to bother you, I rang on impulse, we were just feeling so terribly worried, and I thought, you being a colleague, you wouldn't mind . . .'

'I know. Don't worry. It makes a change talking to clued-up people about what's going on at that bloody school,' said Cassandra. She was smiling and nodding at them, sliding her coat over her narrow shoulders. 'Lovely talking to you. I'll see you tomorrow, Annie. We must get together for a chat outside school. Go for a drink or something. See you again, Harry. Nice to meet a concerned father.' She held out her long thin hand to him, and he shook it lingeringly.

'I'll walk you to your car,' he said.

'No, no – Ferdie can do it,' she said, looking past him to me. 'Come on, Ferdie, I'm parked right down the street – come and save me from the muggers, you nice tall boy.'

Harry laughed, disappointed, suspecting he stood accused of being too short. 'Go on, then, Ferdie – come straight back.'

'Don't worry, he will,' promised Cassandra from the kitchen door.

'Yes, let's have a drink together,' said my mum, 'this week.'

'That'd be great – come *on*, Ferdia, jump to it.'

I trailed her shakily down the hall, and she made me open the front door for her, standing aside against the wall, leaving this narrow space through which I had to force my way, rubbing up against her friendly fur. I hardly took in who was standing on the step, with the Yale key ready in his hand – Peckham in a black bomber jacket and jeans, long curly blond hair misted with faint rain.

'Hi,' he said, looking off to one side. 'Is Annie in?'

I was so out of it, I actually spoke to him. 'Yeah. My dad is too.'

He shrugged, pretending not to be bothered, then glanced at Cassandra as she followed me out and repeated 'Hi' before sliding sideways past her into the house.

'Hi,' she said after him, in a liquid voice, pausing and staring him up and down as he stalked unhurriedly into the light. She said to me, 'Who is *that*?'

'Nobody important.' I pulled the door sharply to behind us, but she still stood staring back at the house until I took hold of her arm and ushered her jealously down the wet shiny steps. 'Who's *that*?' she repeated, craning her head over her shoulder. 'You haven't got a brother, have you?'

'No. Jesus. Leave it out.' I was pissed off at her for staring so blatantly, so obviously checking him out. 'He's my mum's boyfriend, all right? I told you about him.' Which I had, in that pub in Kentish Town, the time she threatened to break up with me.

'My god,' she murmured slowly, as we walked up the pavement through the damp night towards her car. She was computing that information so hard, she didn't even take my hand. 'You didn't tell me he was . . . How intriguing. My god. Annie. Attagirl. I'm impressed.'

'With *what*?' I nearly squeaked. 'He's a total wanker.'

'I hope not – for Annie's sake. He's gorgeous. I wouldn't mind having a pop at him myself.' She grinned rudely at me while unlocking her car, her teeth lit up by the street lamp over her head. Catching the miserable expression on my face, she shoved me back against the car, kissing me on my eyes, my nose, my mouth. 'Don't be so jealous,' she ordered fiercely. 'Silly boy. Don't be so insecure.'

Still hurt, I slipped my mouth away from hers. 'What were you doing coming round like that? You nearly gave me a heart attack.'

She giggled, resting her hands each side of me, her head

tipped cheekily to one side, hair and lashes luminous in the strong white light, bright with glitter from the misty air. 'Well, Annie called in a bit of a panic, and – you know – I've been waiting for you to introduce me to your parents . . .'

I slapped the metal behind me; stung my palm. 'Fuck's sake!'

She frowned and ran her hands over her hair, brushing off its temporary brightness. 'Relax, OK? I was doing you a favour. You should be grateful.' Grabbing my chin, she held my face under the light, touching the colourful lump she'd inflicted. I jerked away. She said, 'I had my work cut out, convincing them you're not on drugs. Especially with how *rough* you look right now.' She flashed me this humorous 'I'm-sorry-about-that' grimace. 'How's the head?'

'Fine.' But it made me uncomfortable, her talking about it in that jokey way – I thought at the very least she'd be more embarrassed; it was kind of humiliating for me. Personally, I'd rather we both just left it.

'Poor you. Bad bruise,' she said, still sounding amused.

'I rang you,' I said, curtly. 'When I was walking around.' I wasn't going to risk telling her I'd been seeing Matt.

'I know.' She smiled and stroked my arm. 'I must've got home just after you rang. I'd've called you back, but then your mum rang up . . . Thanks for the message. "I love you." Very nice. I love you too, my darling Ferdia.' She kissed me fiercely on the mouth, and pressed her knee between my legs.

Everything left my head but Naked Cassandra. I'd totally forgot the way she'd eyed up Peckham, the way she thought smashing me with a lump of wood was somehow funny, the way she'd turned up at my mum's house without warning me. I offered promptly, as soon as her lips left mine, 'Let me come home with you now.'

She laughed and teased me: 'Ferdia! What would your parents say?'

'I'll call them, I'll say I've gone to a friend's.'

She was grinning the widest of her many grins. 'Go *home*,

Ferdia – I've things to do.' She slid into the car, then wound down the window and murmured, winking up at me, 'I left a kiss on your pillow – you don't mind, do you? I had to go to the loo, and when I was upstairs I couldn't resist taking a peek. You've been in my flat so many times, but you live this life I've never even seen. I didn't know you'd got a West Ham poster on your wall.' She touched her fingers to her mouth. 'I didn't even know you were a West Ham fan.'

I met my mother on the stairs as I headed straight for my room to see what sort of a hideous state Cassandra'd found it in. 'You took your time. Your dad's already gone.' She added, smugly, 'He stormed out when Jason got here.'

Inside my stinking, cluttered room, I lay down on my unmade bed and gathered the unwashed pillow in my arms, running my mouth repeatedly across it, closing my eyes, searching obsessively among the stains for one imagined taste of Cassandra's kiss.

Chapter Fifteen

Because I was in the middle of having sex with Cassandra, I was halfway across the school yard before I realised I wasn't being knocked about accidentally in the rush, but deliberately barged by jeering kids, all calling me insulting names. Stopping to face them, I found to my alarm about twenty hard types in ironed designer shirts had me lined up in their sights, smirking and digging each other with their elbows.

'What?' I yelped irritably, not getting it, shifting my school bag from one shoulder to the other, getting ready to run for cover. 'What's your fucking problem?'

They laughed and prowled around a bit, and one of them, a tiny little one, ran up and hawked up on the ground at my feet, frothy pale green slime. 'My mum says you're *sick*,' he sniggered, with a babyish sneer. I went to give him a slap, but he scampered back twittering to the safety of larger mates.

'What's she like, Turdia? Is she a good fuck?' called a scrawny, spotty, seven-foot-tall guy from my year, flapping his limbs at the back of the pack. 'Does she give good head?' And they all shrieked and choked and nearly died laughing at his razor wit. 'Is she a beast in the bedroom?' So somehow that shit about my mum had spread all over the school. Remembering Peckham's entrance into my house last night, *holding a key*, I pictured again Cassandra's eager eyes checking out his sleek departing body. My rage at him flared up a billion times. The little one ran up and spat again. 'Does she like it up 'er?' Now I was in the mood for blood, even my own. Forgetting about running, I threw down my bag and stripped off my coat.

'Wait for me!' It was Gary's hoarse rampant voice, howling

like a jungle beast in the distance, scrambling through the crowded yard, using people's shoulders to swing him along faster, urging the gathering morons, 'Wait for me!' A cheer went up at his ape-style arrival. He elbowed his way through to the front row, and threw his arm protectively around my shoulders, though he had to stand on tiptoe to do it. 'Leave'im afuckinglone!' he bellowed into their disappointed mugs. 'You're a bunch of fucking arseholes!' Much confusion in the pack, which'd been making up its mind to charge. 'All right, mate?' he asked, giving me a friendly squeeze.

'Come on, Gazza,' protested some junior shithead. 'You know he's knobbin' a fucking teacher!'

Staggered by the suddenness of this exposure, I stumbled off a few paces, resting both hands on the slimy wall of the bike sheds to steady myself. I thought, OK, calm down, how do I deal with this? She'd said she'd end it if this happened, and now it has, no doubt about it. So, what now? I thought, No, I can't deal with this. My knees began shaking way too much; I eased down carefully to my heels, my hands sliding down the coldness of damp brick. I pictured her in her flat, packing bags. I started pleading pointlessly with her: Don't leave! Don't leave! while watching her folding up her underwear. My eyes filled stupidly with water. Outside my desolate internal world, I heard the general universe carrying on – Gary berating the voyeuristic mob: 'Like you wouldn't bone her yourselves, you desperate wankers!' Don't leave! I shouted, but I could feel her slipping – now she was going, now, this minute, the door clicking firmly shut behind her. Everything in life I'd ever wanted. Already left. This was what it felt like. Gone. I wiped my eyes with the back of one hand.

Someone, a man, was saying to me, kindly, 'Ferdia? Ferdia? Look at me,' as if I'd been in an accident and he wanted to check was I still alive. I looked up at him, a middle-aged bloke in a knee-length raincoat, and a flash went off in my face. The next second, Gary ripped the camera out of his hands and started trashing it on the tarmac. The man was yelling at him, jumping up and down, nearly in tears, 'You can't do that! That's my property, you little hooligan!', while long thin guts of film curled out in knots.

'Now fuck off out of here, you porno cunt!' howled my self-styled best mate, Gary Peckham. 'Oi, Fatboy – give us a hand, let's give this poof a kickin'!'

'Oh, for fuck's sake,' swore the bloke, walking off angrily towards the gate.

Gary was crouched beside me, yelling 'Show's over!' to the excited crowd, trying to get me up with encouraging words, acting all wise sympathy. 'Come on, mate, why don't we take you back home for a bit? Have a lie down. Have a cup of char. Take it easy. Fuck off, you lot!'

I muttered, surprised to hear my own voice, 'Who was that bloke? '

'You don't know?' he exclaimed, gripping my arm. Startled, the freckles on his nose stood out like biro dots on his white sunless skin. 'You mean – you haven't . . . .? Fuck!'

'Why the fucking hell was he trying to take my picture?'

'Shit, you don't get it, do you?' We both stood up. I looked him hard in his bull-necked, blue-eyed face. He handed me my coat and bag. 'Come with me, mate. Oi, Fatboy!'

I trailed at his sturdy elbow through the yard, amazed at the exclusion zone his presence generated for me – at least two metres on every side empty of kids, like walking under a massive umbrella in the rain. Out the school gates and down the gusty road, he stared with wide swivelling eyes, jerkily around, back and forwards, up and down, Fatboy rolling along reluctantly behind us. 'What're you looking for?' I asked.

'Paparazzi.'

I snorted with nervous laughter, and he shot me a deeply serious look. 'Stay here, mate. Be cool, yeah? Fatboy – you're in charge.' He shot into the newsagents. Fatboy waited at a distance, morosely counting cars, well-fed hands in half-ripped pockets. Left to myself, I took out the mobile she'd given me and stood with it undecided in my hand. The wind was really getting up, blowing my hair into my eyes, making the streets of lively rubbish dance. Peckham came out with a tabloid, rifling through it, throwing its spare parts into the gutter. At the sight of the newspaper, I thought I knew what was coming, and was bounced sickeningly back to seeing that crappy tabloid pic of my dad outside some stupid night-club, with Abigail's tiny tongue stuffed down his throat. (Pulling the tabloid – not our usual delivery – from the let-terbox, I'd turned the pages carelessly, looking for football results. Harry, coming down the stairs, had glanced inquir-ingly over my frozen shoulder, said nothing, gone back up and packed his bags). The pages in Gary's grasp bugged him by blowing like kites in the wind, tearing themselves away from him into the air. 'Hang on. Hang on,' he kept shouting, punching paper furiously. 'There.' He folded the printed sheets into a tight package and held it out to me. My guts were tied in slippery knots. I took the rag, keeping her mobile in my palm.

The biggest picture on the page was of me and Cassandra, lying together on the ground. My coat and schoolbag in a heap beside us. My face tucked into her shoulder; her arms around me like she was comforting me; one of her long stockinged legs, suspenders slightly showing, wrapped over both of mine. We weren't doing anything. We were in our own back yard, our private filthy yard behind the never-open junk shop; our special place, our lunchtime and after-school fuck-stop. Our lovely, secret place. The bastard who took the picture must've been looking calmly down on us – from a window, or maybe the junk shop roof, treating the readers to a ringside seat. There was a smaller separate photograph of Cassandra's face, laughing in the distance, captioned *Phillips: Seducer*. And there was the woman who ran the carrot-cake café, smirking, posing for the camera. *Price: Disgusted*. Bunhead: Bitch.

In huge type, below:

SEX LESSONS IN SCHOOL FOR SCANDAL
Teacher and GCSE student in shocking liaison

The school at the centre of the latest closure row has been slammed for letting a woman teacher seduce a pupil half her age . . .'She brings him in here every lunchtime,' said café owner Bronwyn Price. 'It's completely obvious what they've been up to. She's old enough to be his mother. It's disgusting.'

Blah, blah, blah . . . *Cassandra Phillips, 33* . . .

Was she? Was she old enough? I was in too much of a panic to figure out simple sums.

'You're famous, mate,' said Gary brightly.

I dialled her number three times – no reply, only the answer phone. 'Call me,' I said, every time. I stuffed the mobile back into my pocket. I thought, OK, OK, let's face it, she's ditched me like she said she would if anyone found out. What am I saying, Anyone? Everyone in the fucking world, more like.

'No one answering? Come on, let's go.' Flipping at Fatboy to get lost, Gary took the paper off of me and binned it in passing. He covered my despairing silence by chattering on all the long way home, and he insisted on walking me through the very centre of his estate, between the windswept grey-streaked concrete blocks, down alleys made brilliant by swirling fluorescent graffiti, blindingly pink and green and mauve and blue. There were plenty of kids about, spraying their gaudy tags on any available space. They stopped what they were doing as I passed by, quiet frozen figures in Calvin Klein. Gary put his arm around me, letting his own know I was untouchable now. 'Y'know,' he said, waving to his startled audience, 'I always thought you were a right snobby stuck-up prat, to be honest, know what I mean, no offence. But that band was fuckin' well good. You still doing that shit? It's not rave or garage or nothin', right, but it kind of said something to me anyhow . . . You ever need a lead guitarist –

well, I can't play shit, but I got this rough new red guitar . . .'
He looked at me, and hurried on, 'I mean, screwing that classy bird Cassandra, though – that's fuckin' impressive. I wouldn't mind giving her one myself, know what I mean? No offence.' He added, almost humbly, 'Course, she's a bit tall for me.' He said, after whistling a few bars of some unrecognisable garage, 'Cheer up, mate. Don't let the bastards grind you down.' After a while, and more shrill aimless whistling, he said, 'Look, mate, it ain't the end of the world. So you're shaggin' your teacher and you got found out – big fuckin' deal. Who gives a fuck? I know someone who shagged a *dog* once. A *real* one. He was a nutter, d'you get me? The bloke, I mean. Dog was all right. You wanna know who I'm shagging right now?'

I looked at him – I couldn't help it. Even though I'd been thinking about nothing but the end of my world, his words got through and I looked in amazement at this short-arsed geezer.

He smiled triumphantly at me. 'My aunt.'

'*Aunt?*'

He looked pleased with himself, then alarmed, saying hastily, 'That's, like, a secret. Keep fuckin' shtum about that one.' After a while of walking on in silence, he added thoughtfully, 'She's lovely, actually. She gave me my guitar.' Ahead of us, Jason sloped into view, combing out his blond curls with his fingers, tucking in his white silk shirt, zipping up his black bomber jacket. He was going to pass right by us without seeing us, without me saying anything, till Gary, turning a yellow shade of pale, muttered, 'Forget what I said, all right? Oi, Jacie!'

Jason glanced irritably over, not remotely pleased to be disturbed. Gary leapt childishly from foot to foot, over-anxious to ingratiate himself. 'I'm doing what you asked, bruv – looking after Ferdia, right? He's in the paper for boning his teacher, right? I took care of him, though – didn't I, man? I smashed this prick's camera, yeah? Should've seen him duck.

He was brickin' it.' And Gary laughed insanely – left foot, right foot.

'Issit.' Jason glanced sideways at me, and quickly away again. 'I'd go in over the back wall if I were you, mate. Your house is fuckin' surrounded.' He straightened himself up, sticking out his chin, squaring off his shoulders, firming up his voice. 'I'd've stayed to help her if she'd let me. But she told me to sling my hook, OK?' I registered, behind his blue-eyed stare, he was totally gutted.

'She dumped you?' gasped Gary, passing his hands across his head, his millimetre-long hair standing up on end. 'Shit!'

Leaving them behind, I sprinted towards the red-brick wall, swung myself over and dropped into my garden. Before going in, I stopped to ring Cassandra again, foot resting on the upturned wheelbarrow which by now had nearly disappeared into two feet of grass. It took forever for her not to answer. 'Call me as soon as you pick this up!' When I crashed open the kitchen door, Annie jumped up with half a scream, saw it was me and threw her arms around me, her old purple dressing gown sweeping round our legs. 'Those ghastly reporters won't stop ringing the bell! Just like when your bloody father did a runner!' She clung to me harder, face down in my neck, then pushed me away, suddenly awkward, as if in the shocking excitement of it all she'd gone and hugged a total stranger. 'Ferdie . . . Honey . . . Is it true?'

The bell kept ringing and ringing. I hurried into the hall. Up against the yellow and red stained glass, flat noses pressed like squidgy putty; nail-polished tentacles jutted sharply through the letter box into our house; a rabble of voices, male and female, droned: 'Annie! Tell us your side of the story! What's it like to find your son's been seduced by a colleague? Will you be suing the school? How old is your boyfriend, Annie? Younger than Abigail? Do you have any sympathy for Ms Phillips?' No wonder my mum wanted Jason out of there. But I couldn't help thinking it was a shame – we could've used him, at a time like this. 'Is poor Ferdia upset? Will he be getting professional help?' I slammed down the flap of the letter box ultra-hard on the wriggling fingers, delighted to hear one of those dirty fuckers shriek. Fuckers who'd ruined my happy blissful life. I reached up and ripped the wires from out the bell, then pressed my face to this side of the glass, a couple of millimetres from the many-headed enemy's grossly distorted red and yellow eyes.

'Is it true?' groaned Annie, tugging on my arm, pulling me away, shepherding me back down the hall into the kitchen, slamming the door against the imploring voices. 'Did she . . .?' I answered nothing; I had no intention of rolling out my personal feelings to be shat on; I pulled out a chair and sat down backwards on it, legs each side of the seat; I stared through our window at the tower blocks. She wept, 'Oh god! That evil monster!' and spooned instant coffee into dirty mugs. 'You should've told me,' she complained, rattling the spoon in the cups not to stir them but because her hand was shaking so badly. 'You should've let me help you, honey – I'm so sorry this dreadful thing has happened to you – we can get through this – I can't believe I didn't realise – you've got to talk about it, talk to me, honey . . .' Sliding one hand into my coat, I touched the mobile; it lay so still it was like I'd something dead in my pocket. While Annie agonised and prattled on, I sat in private silence, waiting and waiting for Cassandra to call, knowing in my deadened heart she never would. The hacks had finally figured out the bell was no longer ringing, and were now bashing on the door with their fists. 'Listen to those evil bastards!' Annie fell into a chair, gathering her dressing gown round her knees, and dropped her head to the table top. 'It's a nightmare, just like the last time!' Then, sitting up, resting her chin on her palm, wiping her round green eyes with her round white forefinger. 'I can't believe it. Coming round here. Your teacher! Poor you. Oh god!' She made a wincing face. 'Taking advantage of you like that. *Disgusting!*'

I said, 'Nobody took advantage of me.'

She looked compassion at me. 'Honey, you can't blame yourself, she was old enough to be your mother . . .' Then glanced distractedly towards the hall. It sounded as if whole bodies now were thudding against the vibrating door. Annie hid her freckled face fearfully in her hands. Easing open the kitchen door, I saw an envelope land on the mat, crept down and picked it up. Inside was the ripped page of a reporter's notebook.

Ferdia, I want to offer you a real chance to tell your side of the story. If you sign a exclusive deal with my paper, we can make sure you and your family are left in peace. You can be sure the truth will be told, sympathetically, in your own words, rather than in the words of unreliable witnesses. And we will pay you five thousand pounds. Please think about it. In friendship, Gayle

I couldn't believe they were offering me money to betray her, like they offer to those embarrassing girls who brag about sucking off some rancid star. Did they think me and Cassandra were that pathetic? I thought, Those wankers have to go. I went back into the kitchen.

' . . . and they kept on asking me how *old* he was,' sobbed Annie despairingly, still with her head in her hands, not having noticed I'd left the room for a while. 'Everything's gone *wrong* since the divorce. Look at what's happened to you. Ever since your dad ran off with that tart . . . Oh god, it's just like then, all those bloody reporters camped on our doorstep, horrible, horrible, don't you remember?'

Of course I did, though I'd tried my best to shove it out of my mind. My dad and his miserable hunted expression struggling up and down our steep front steps with heavy bags, snapped at by the pack of small-fry hacks, me watching from my bedroom window, staying invisible behind the curtain, left behind and feeling nauseous. I opened the back door and went out in the garden. It struck me if those bastards hadn't got pictures of my dad leaving the nightclub with Abigail, and plastered that earth-shattering non-event all over their crappy brain-dead rags, then my parents would probably be together now. It was clear Harry didn't have the guts to make life-changing decisions without serious outside pressure being applied. I ran down towards the back wall, pulled myself up, and dropped into that other world. Walking on under the looming blocks, every footstep a gun-shot crunch of broken glass, I scanned nervously to left and right while pretending to stare steadily ahead, a civilian crossing enemy territory. But no one came towards me; no one spoke. The Peckham exclusion zone applied.

I went right up to his flat, an empty ride in another pissy lift, and rang the bell. His mum came to the door and looked at me sympathetically – very very blonde hair like his (but in a girly plait) and his unnaturally bright stare. She seemed to know who I was. Her and five million others, of course. I asked for Jason, and she sent me smiling down the Evil Eye.

Because the rest of its terrace was gone, it was possible to walk right round the Evil Eye, the only ground-level red-brick building to be found in this upright concrete world. I did walk round it, several times, trying to find a way in. The windows all were boarded up; any cracked and jagged glass still in the frames had once been painted black from the inside; the doors were MDF as if the originals'd got kicked in. No one came to the main door when I banged on it. I tried another door. I came back to the first door and leaned on the bell. After a good five minutes I was giving up, but then locks started popping, with whoever it was starting at the top of the door and working their long slow way to the bottom, swearing their heads off the whole way down. Finally, just when I thought they were taking the piss, this little Nigerian-looking shaven-headed guy whacked open the door, bright yellow eyes threaded with red like I'd woken him up, and croaked, 'What do *you* fucking want, for fuck's only sake?', not letting me in.

'I'm looking for Jason Peckham.'

'In there.' And he stood aside, jerking his thumb behind

him and let me slide past before he slammed the door and, with an exasperated sigh, started zipping up the bolts again.

The pub was empty and almost completely dark. One small bar was opposite me, a couple of optics and a few peculiar bottles. In the distance I could hear someone messing around on bass. I listened for a minute, puzzled, thinking after a bit – I know that tune. Then I had a really weird slow moment of recognition. It was one of ours. Whoever it was was playing 'Watch Out for the Hungry Poor'. I remembered Matt lying up in his bed, coming out with a bunch of crazy stuff, and thought, Shit, he's in here – he's OK, and hurried round the corner into this long narrow section of the bar, where at first I could hardly see. 'Matt?' Gradually my eyes got used to it, and I could make out this slim guy sitting on the edge of a stage at the far end of the room, hunched over a bass guitar, head down, concentrating hard, gently picking out the song with a plectrum. He had very blond hair. He was wearing a white silk shirt. Even before I saw him I knew it couldn't've been Matt, because why would Matt be on bass? And he wouldn't be having to work out the tune. Jason was having a bit of difficulty with it, but he was getting better as he went along, and the bastard knew how to play all right. I stood and watched him, until he looked up and saw me, and he continued to stare at me while his fingers gradually stopped moving.

'Hi,' I said.

He looked down and picked up the guitar and started playing again, softly. This time it was 'Babes in the Air', and he seemed to know it pretty damn well. 'Gary's always playing these on his new guitar,' he said. 'It's his sort of music. Your band was good at that party.'

'Look,' I said. 'You've got to help. These fucking reporters – we've *gotta* get rid of them.'

He wouldn't stop playing, but he glanced at me coldly from behind his long blond silky hair. 'Where's your dad? Can't he sort it out?'

'Look, my mum's *really* upset,' I said. 'I'm not fucking joking.'

'Why you askin' me?' he asked, suddenly switching to 'Gonna Rip Somebody's Head Off', but slowly and quietly. 'You think I'm scum, right?'

'No . . . Look . . .' Suddenly I was sick of myself for even trying. 'Forget it.'

But as I walked away, he slammed the guitar down on the stage and said, 'Oh, for fuck's sake.' I turned round. He was coming towards me. He wasn't as tall as me. He was slight, blond, curly-haired, blue-eyed and fucking hard. 'Come on, Casanova. I'll do your dirty work.'

As we walked back through the estate he kept jerking his chin at other youngish blokes who dropped whatever vague artistic vandalism they were passing the time with and drifted over to us. He kept introducing me as Annie's kid. 'This is Annie's kid, the one with the name, he's all right – this is . . . Kevin . . . Winston . . . Leroy . . . Aziz . . .' (and they all grinned and bottled up their laughter, nodding at me, 'Nice one, mate – shame about the papers') and so on till there were going on twenty of them climbing over our back wall, scraping their knees and falling into the brambles with shouts of cheerful agony. Annie ran out the kitchen door, fearfully, to see what the fuck was going on, black curls flying, looking frightened and confused. But then she saw Jason wading knee-deep through the long wet sea-green grass, and waited where she was, and pressed her hands to her chest. He stopped when he reached her, standing as close to her as he could without his shoulder touching hers, and neither of them spoke, but she just kept looking longingly at him, cheeks flushed behind her shower of fawn freckles. 'Catch you in a mo',' he said, after a while, touching her wrist with his forefinger; he carried on into the house followed by me and the guys.

In the hall, someone's mouth was practically squeezed through the letterbox, rubbery lips actually visible, gurgling, 'Annie! Annie! Do you feel any sympathy for Cassandra

Phillips? Can you say what it's like from your point of view, having a relationship with someone young enough to be your son?'

Jason whipped open the door, and this fat bloke fell in flat on his face. Then the rest of the pack, men in knee-length raincoats and women in knee-length boots, were all smiles, shouting our names, some of them calling Jason 'Ferdia', the ones at the back hurrying forwards, pressing up the steps, so fucking happy we'd opened the door and then . . . pausing, noticing Jason's unimpressed expression, noticing the hall choked up with hard young men, and . . . not so happy.

'Bye bye,' said Jason.

'I . . .' said a woman with puffed red hair in a short black skirt, desperately appealing to him. 'I'm Gayle.'

'Bye *bye*,' said Jason.

'I . . .' She was backing off down the steps, and the fat man was wriggling, big bum in the air, backwards out of the door on his hands and knees, and the others were shuffling away as well, with pissed-off frowning this-can't-be-happening looks. They were leaving, but too slowly for Peckham's liking.

'Get 'em, boys,' said Jason.

And it was great. All the men in raincoats and women in tall boots turned and ran, and Jason's mates went howling and bounding after them – dramatic, heart-warming sight – a pack of terrified ground-dwellers fleeing down the road, jumping frantically into their shining cars, pursued by the scary shaven-headed who ran along beside them roaring threats and driving their fists deep into metal bonnets, snapping off windscreen wipers and snazzy aerials and waving them in the air like looted weapons – 'Come back 'ere or we'll 'av ya!'

I watched from the steps till the last of the hack-pack screeched away, then headed back into the house. 'All right, now, mum?'

Jason and my mother were blocking the hall, wrapped round each other in some gross embrace. My dad suddenly walked into the house behind me, 'Ferdia! What in god's name ...?' I turned to him, but he'd already lost interest in me and was stood staring in sad desperation at Annie and her unusual lover. Automatically, his hand went to his head, fingering his own less white, less silky hair.

'Dad?' He shuddered, pulling himself together as if with a stiff whisky, and slowly re-focused himself on me. He cleared his throat. I said, 'You want to go out and get a coffee?'

Jason's mates were overflowing the pavement outside, looking well pleased with themselves. I nodded to them as they parted to let us through. Harry looked vaguely puzzled by them, clearly not having witnessed our splendid urban hunt. We walked rapidly down the long red street, under the shadows of the concrete blocks, up to Abbey Road. 'Do you want a Coke, or what?' he asked, standing outside a café, examining wrinkled pictures of faded food. 'I'm really hungry. God, but it makes me sick.' Strangely, he took my hand and squeezed it, without looking at me. 'I'm really sorry, Ferdia. I'm so sorry about all this. Do you want to talk about it?'

Like hell. 'No thanks.'

He made eye contact with me via my reflection in the window, translucent face slightly raised to mine, handsomely troubled. 'You OK?'

I shrugged. 'Fine.'

'I mean, look.' He was already embarrassed at asking such a stupid question. 'I know you're not OK.' He pushed open the café door. The place was empty. A guy with a gold-studded smile shuffled to the counter. 'I know what it's like, getting your name in the papers. I'm surprised the hacks aren't camped outside your house yet – I'm afraid they probably will be before long. It's in the news these days – schools – teachers ... And of course, you're the son of someone who's, you know, quite ... well, it's a problem, having one's face in the papers ...'

'I know,' I said. 'They were there already. Jason saw 'em off.'

In glum silence, he gathered his greasy breakfast and took it to a table in the sunless window. Then he ate like he was genuinely starving, stabbing repeatedly at two small sausages which skipped adventurously round his plate. 'All right,' he said, after he'd finished the lot, scraping his full curved lips with the paper napkin, leaving it crimson with superfluous ketchup. 'Look, I realise you were upset about me and Abigail. I just want to say I'm sorry – OK?'

'For what?' I was genuinely puzzled.

He shrugged and spread his hands in the air at elbow height. 'Everything,' he said, a tad dismissively. 'Whatever. Anything you want me to be sorry for. Whatever you think is my fault.' He sighed. 'That sounds wrong. OK, I admit it, I'm no good at talking about this stuff. What I mean is, I'm sorry for everything that made this happen.' He paused and rattled his cutlery on the plate. 'Everything that *bitch* has done to you. Coming round to our house, flaunting herself like that . . .' He inhaled slowly, released his breath again. 'What a bitch . . . I'm sorry, I'm finding this hard to talk about in an unemotional way.'

'You fancied her,' I mentioned.

He answered bitterly, 'Crazy *bitch*.'

In protest, the mobile in my pocket shook – at last! I reached for it like I was going for my gun, springing to my feet and joyfully turning my back on Harry. 'Hello? Is that you?' It could only be her. 'Can you hear me?' It struck me in the stomach – suppose she was ringing to say goodbye? My hands shook so much it was hard to hold the phone to my ear.

'Oh Ferdia,' she was sobbing. 'What are we going to do?'

'Where are you?'

'There were *thousands* of them outside my flat this morning. It was *horrible.* Tom came out with me and yelled at them. I'm going to resign. Oh god! What are we going to do?'

'Where are you?' Thinking, she better not be with that wanker Tom.

'The Railway Hotel, King's Cross, in the bar. I'm having a

drink. I don't care, I fucking need it. I'm going to phone up the school and resign. God, I need to see you. When can you get here?'

The sun came out in my head, blinding my thoughts – despite the worst thing happening, she hadn't dumped me yet. It was still my world. 'I'm coming now.'

'Take a taxi. I'll pay you back. Unless you think the tube will be quicker. No, take a taxi. I don't know. Maybe a taxi to the tube, then the tube. Oh god, no! That's ridiculous. Get a cab to King's Cross and it's the hotel behind the station. Ask the driver. Shit, my credit's going, shi . . .' and she was gone.

Harry had also stood up, long-faced. When I looked at him, he made a move towards me, as if he wanted to touch me. 'Was that her?'

I said, backing away, 'I'm sorry, I've got to go. I'll talk to you later, dad.'

'No, you can't . . .' He reached to put his hand under my elbow. I slid out of the door into the chilly street; he chased after me. 'Stop! Where are you going?' I was flagging down a cab. 'That was her, wasn't it? Ferdia, talk to me! Don't just walk away!' A taxi pulled up. 'You can't! She's an evil bitch! Don't go!' As I leapt into the cab I had to push his pawing hands away; he even ran along beside the cab as it pulled out – poor Harry, sweating, panting, long coat flapping, legs pumping, trademark hair getting all messed up.

'Some of those older geezers,' remarked the cabbie, 'can go all soft and sentimental on you.'

It struck me with sweet vengeful pleasure, that my dad was letting me go with far less dignity than I'd let him leave me behind last year, when I'd watched him through a crack in my bedroom curtains, battering his grim-faced way through the yapping reporters on our steps.

Chapter Sixteen

She was sat on a high wooden stool at the empty bar, drinking a vodka and cranberry juice rapidly down. She had on a pale brown jacket, unbuttoned, old straight jeans and a white shirt; her blonde hair was loosely tied back in a brown silk ribbon. She was watching me in the mirror under the optics; her face was tired and pale without her make-up; she looked so beautiful it choked me up. Coming up behind her, I wrapped my arms around her. In the mirror, our faces stared back cheek to cheek. Neither of us spoke. After a while of lingering like that, I dragged across a bar stool next to hers. Turning on her seat towards me, elbow on the polished wood, she stared closely at me for ages, still saying nothing, just tilting her empty glass backwards and forwards like a clock. Through the high pale green windows, black cabs came and went, picking up travellers from the yellow-brick station. She said, 'I'm painting your picture in my head. To remember you by.'

Tears jumped to my eyes, like she'd stuck a mugger's knife in me. '*No!* What? Don't be ridiculous. Why should we have to end it, just because other people are such arseholes?'

'We were so bloody careless, weren't we?' Tutting, she brushed the hair back from my face and touched my chin, and clucked and murmured, 'What a sad, sad face. What are we going to do with you?'

'Don't go . . .'

'I never meant this to happen,' she said, showing her teeth. 'But you were irresistible. Now my life is ruined.'

'Mine too . . .'

She said, punishingly, 'I'm moving away, somewhere a long way away.'

'Don't go! I'll come with you. Why not, if you're leaving anyway? I'm not a kid. I could get myself a job.'

Leaning across the bar, the buttons of her undone jacket clicking softly on the wood, she shouted to the absent barman, 'Excuse me!' He came round the corner from the other side. 'Do you have a room?'

On the fifth floor, with her back to the hotel bedroom window, she dragged off her jeans and shirt and trainers and threw herself down on the flower-patterned bed, stretching her arms above her head. 'Usually I hate goodbyes,' she said, coolly. 'But this one might turn out to be fun.'

Without undressing, only taking off my coat, I lay down beside her, and hugged her in her clean white underwear against my chest, both arms around her, one hand pressed firmly to her stomach, one to her bra-covered breast. 'Let me come with you,' I said. 'I want to come with you. We could live together.' I kissed her neck, over and over again, spitting her hair out of my mouth, pushing my knees into the backs of hers, folding her into me. I just wanted to prolong the moment – if this was genuinely goodbye, to stretch it out and out forever.

She wriggled impatiently. 'Hey! Don't you *want* to fuck me?'

'Ssh. Let me hold you.'

She kicked and snarled, 'What's the matter – am I too old for you? Don't answer that!' She threw herself on top of me and wrapped her long thin limbs around me. 'Just fuck me, Ferdia. Make love to me like you want to be remembered.'

But I ended up hoping she'd forget that particular fuck. She bit and scratched me so much, it was hard to concentrate. I wondered if she was trying to permanently mark me, scrawling her name in scars across my flesh, like the star-shaped one on my knee which never faded, like the bitter kids with their fluorescent tags. It was hard to enjoy it, being torn apart. Afterwards, shaken in my bloodied flesh, I stood leaning my forearms on the double-glazing, floating high in our rented hotel bubble, way above the soundless sealed-off city. Dinky taxis came and went, bulging with exhausted people, and crowds of tourists rushed as one down the steep slippery steps of King's Cross tube. It was barely lunchtime, but the sky seemed dark already. Everyone in a mad panic to be off.

'All right,' she whispered wearily. 'You can come.'

'What?' I wasn't sure I'd heard her right. 'Sorry?'

'Come with me.' She was rising on her elbow, treating me to a defeated smile. 'Let's go to Spain. Or Italy. Somewhere hot.'

Stepping back from the window, I blurted stupidly, 'Spain? Isn't that a bit far?' Immediately, I couldn't understand my own question. For weeks I'd counted every second I wasn't with her, lost count of every second when I was. 'I mean – Jesus, that's so great.'

She mocked me, lifting one eyebrow, 'There is a world outside north London, you know, parochial boy.' She murmured, tugging on her clean white pants, pointing her long thin toes, 'Places where we can disappear together.'

I was thrilled, flattered, totally terrified. 'Well, I'd have to tell my mum where I was. And dad.'

She shrugged scornfully, doing up her bra. 'What have they ever done for you? Send them a Christmas card if you like. Last chance, Ferdie – coming or not?'

Was she serious? Shit! To disappear completely out of my own life – my stomach sloshed over like a washing-machine. It was hard to imagine my future without me in it. For the first time ever since I'd fucked Cassandra, I was gripped by my trademark urge to walk away. 'Yeah, absolutely. Great. OK.' I told myself this time I couldn't walk away. I had to stop walking away from things, especially the things I really wanted.

As if indifferent to my answer, she was already rummaging about in her brown jacket, pulling out a wallet, tipping me a ten pound note. 'Good. That's settled then. Now, I'm starving. Get dressed, go get chips or something from the station.'

I did strongly fancy a walk in the open air, time out, space to think about this weird Spain idea. And now she'd mentioned it, our shag had made me incredibly hungry and my body was crying out for chips. I strolled in a daze through the railway station, ignoring the herds of early-cut commuters sneaking pale-faced out of work. Finding my way to Burger King, I waited blindly in the endless line, fretting about somewhere hot and blue, somewhere of endless sex and sand, somewhere called Spain frothing with Naked Cassandras. I thought, I *have* to go with her – how can I risk not going? What if I never get over her? All I've thought about for weeks is her. What if it's always going to be that way? What if she's ruined me for anything – anyone – else? What if she's permanently fucked me up? I bought four bags of cooling fries.

On the way back, passing a news stand, I spotted the lunchtime edition of the evening paper, and queued to buy it, shoving chips unthinkingly into my mouth, because it struck me we might be in it. Only at the point when the newspaper bloke thrust my change into my hand, did I realise with a vicious smack of reality that I was as ever a fucking moron, and legged it, not skirting but hurdling the ranks of rolled-up homeless, showering them with a rain of luke-warm chips, knowing this waste of twenty minutes had ruined my life forever – that she'd sent me away so she could leave without me. Sweating in my speed and fear, flying up the hotel stairs, I banged on the door without an answer, then turned out my pockets for the other key, dropping the unread tabloid to the floor. I knew in my heart I'd find an empty room, and I was right – there was no one there, only the duvet scrunched darkly on the bed.

The heaviness of my distress was too much to bear – I had to kneel on the floor, doubled over the edge of the mattress, nose rammed into the bed, chewing the sheet. I thought, OK, OK, so it's over now. It's done, it's over. Take it easy, man. Now you just have to get used to being alive without her. But

I opened my eyes and saw with a sickening shock that she *was* in the room after all – her colourless eyelids, a wisp of her pale blonde hair, peeping out from under the flowered duvet only a foot from my disbelieving face. Dizzy, I gazed at her, panting, licking my lips, waiting for my heartbeat to subside to normal. 'Cassandra . . .' I whispered.

She didn't move or speak. I tiptoed my hand forward, pushing the duvet off her sleeping body. She lay on her back, long and flat, head still turned towards me. Ultra gently, I fingered her bony shoulder, then her bra-strap; one of her hands lay across her throat, thin fingers crumpled like an insect's legs – they slightly curled beneath my touch. Kneeling up, I patted her shallow stomach, her hip-bone thrusting up under the skin; stretching out, I smoothed her elongated thigh. Leaning very close to her narrow face, I could just make out the breath visibly coming and going, nostrils and lips trembling with it; I fondled the butterfly pulse in her neck. She twitched and sniffed. Leaning over her, I tucked the duvet back in around her, cocooning her in comfort like a kid. I was lonely without her, but willing to let her sleep; while she was asleep, there was no weird unknown future to get used to. I stood up, then sat carefully down on the bed, to wait for what was coming next. She slept and slept, heavier and heavier, quieter and quieter, breathing fading. Yawning, I remembered the unread paper, and fetched it from where I'd dropped it outside the door, and sat by her, flipping slowly through its pages.

Her picture stopped me first. I thought, resignedly, OK, now the other papers are running with it. There was a fairly unrecognisable shot of me with my arm around her – at least I thought it was me, until suddenly I realised that it wasn't. Confused, I glanced down at her face. Still she lay immobile, the skin of her face smoothed out by sleep. I studied the grainy photograph closely, bringing the page up close to my eyes. No, I was right, it wasn't me. He was sort of like me, though – dark, tall, longish black hair. Peering, I read the caption. *Victim: Fifteen.* I scanned disbelievingly up to the top of the page, to the beginning of the story. And it wasn't the beginning, it was only half of it – continued from page one. I laid the paper out on the bed and turned back to the front.

SHE'S DONE IT BEFORE

The woman teacher accused of steamy sex sessions with a schoolboy has been in trouble before – for having sex with three pupils at her previous school. Following complaints from one victim's parents, the headmaster allowed Cassandra Phillips, 33, to resign, leaving her free to take up another teaching job. The victim's mother said yesterday, 'I feel guilty now for not pressing charges, but my son was so upset. He only told me about the other boys later.' Changes to the law in the new year will make it a criminal offence for teachers to have sex with any student up to the age of eighteen.

I turned back to his picture. There were quotes from him all down one side of the page. *We had sex in people's gardens. She said she loved me. I told my parents I was staying the night with friends, but I was at her flat. She'd get upset if I didn't stay. She threw a knife at me. She ordered me to give her oral sex.* I'd never stayed the night with her. She'd never asked for oral sex. *Then she had sex with my best friend. Then . . .*

I scattered the tabloid to the floor, a heap of printed rubbish. I needed to wake her up and scream abuse. It did my head in she could stay asleep, while all this shit was going down around us. Then I thought, No, no, let her sleep, then I don't need to deal with all this crap. In the dull overcast light of noon, her face was faintly yellow, nestled in the soft duvet I'd tucked around it. I touched her cheeks, and they were cold; I wondered suddenly if she was dead – I couldn't make out her breathing anymore. Maybe she'd taken pills because she was so upset about us – hadn't she said she'd kill herself? Maybe she'd really meant it? I thought, I can't cope with this, I'm not old enough, I'll never be old enough, I should call the doctor; I lay down in my clothes and coat beside her; I imagined being buried in the same coffin as her. She opened her eyes in that slow scary way she had. 'Hi, Ferdia. Still here?'

Now I knew she was alive I couldn't believe I hadn't run for a doctor instantly.

'Did you get the chips?'

I couldn't say, because I didn't know what would come out of my mouth – if it was anger, I didn't want to hear it. All I knew was, I didn't want to be around. It was a relief, realising I couldn't handle this shit anymore; that I had to get off the ride; that this was my cue to walk, without even bothering to discuss it.

'What's the matter?' she asked, suddenly sitting up. 'What's the matter? Why are you staring at me like that?'

'I'm sorry, I've got to go.' I expected her to complain, like my parents always did, 'Ferdie, you're always running away', but of course I'd never walked out on her before, not counting Sisi's party before it all began. I'd never run away from her; I'd always been the one to go after her, trotting, scrambling, pathetically after her. She was the rope that tied me down. I slid off the bed onto my feet. She said, sitting naked in her bra and pants, puzzled, pale, defenceless. 'Go? One minute you say you want to come . . .'

I stood there, looking at her, hands dangling by my sides. The light from the window was yellow-grey. She reached suddenly for the lamp on the bedside table; I flinched and stepped hastily back. All she did was turn it on, but I found I couldn't face her anymore, and turned away. 'I'm sorry, Cassandra, sorry, I've got to go . . .'

She cried in horror: *'Why are you running away?'*

For the longest time I wandered up and down the Abbey Road, my long straight road to everywhere, as if I'd never left off doing it, thinking about which home to go to – such is habit, I suppose. Eventually I let myself in the door of Abigail's flat, but it was only her eating toast in the kitchen, wearing lavender silk pyjamas. 'My dad in?'

'Ferdie, I don't know if I want to even *speak* to you right now, Harry's gone fucking ballistic about what you've been up to and he's acting like it's all my fucking fault . . .'

'Bye, Abby. Gotta go.'

She called after me, 'Remember – never trust a wrinkly!'

There was a crowd still occupying my mum's steps, but it was Jason's gang, all in bomber jackets and Calvin Klein jeans, smoking spliffs and wolfing down packets of chocolate hobnobs, untroubled and by now completely stoned. They gazed at me blearily as I climbed over their legs, throwing me thumbs-up signs. 'Awri'?'

'Yeah. I'm cool.'

'Just keeping an eye on things, mate.'

'Great. Nice one.' Then I changed my mind about going in and sat down on the steps with them and had a toke or two, until to my now blurred surprise I saw Lily and Aristotle coming up the road, and got up unsteadily to let them in.

Jason came out of the house as I went in, pointing up the stairs to indicate Annie was asleep. 'Don't rush off again just yet,' he said. 'She needs to find you here when she wakes up.'

Lily sat on my bed cross-legged in pale green flares, linking her fingers backwards round her knees, green beads around her neck, denim jacket stitched with green and silver flowers. 'We had to come round to see how you were doing,' she said. 'We kept ringing and ringing, but nobody was answering. We thought maybe you'd got the number changed? You must be feeling really awful.'

Aristotle swung himself up onto my desk under the window, sitting with his elbows on his knees and feet on the chair, scratching the side of his nose. 'Hey, Ferdie,' he said slyly. 'What was it *like*?' I stripped off my coat, crashed down on my bed behind Lily's back and stuffed my face into the pillow. 'I mean,' he said, 'Matt said something about it, but I thought it was his crazy bullshit – I mean – *you* . . .'

'Shut up, Stotle,' hushed Lily, anxiously. 'He doesn't want to talk about it.'

'No, come on, man,' persisted Aristotle. 'You gotta tell us –
I bet it was really wild! Are older women hot?'

'Stotle! Leave him alone!'

'I wouldn't've kicked her out of bed for eating biscuits.'

'Just fuck off,' I said, my eyes tight shut. 'Fucking idiot.'

'Mind you, sounds like she's been around a bit. Are you
going to sell your story, like that kid in the paper today? Did
anyone offer you any dosh yet?'

'Five grand,' I told him. After a bit, when still no one'd spoken, I turned my head to see how he was taking it.

Aristotle's mouth was so wide open he was dribbling. 'Five
what?'

I dug the hack's message out of my back pocket and passed
it to Lily, who was slowly stroking her long black hair. She
read in silence, then handed it to the salivating Aristotle, who
for some reason held it up to the light like a dodgy twenty.
'Well, fuck me sideways,' he said, at last, awestruck. 'What're
you gonna to do with it, man? Can we all go to Spain for a
holiday or something?'

'Give it here,' said Lily. She passed it back to me. 'Are you
really going to take it?'

'No way,' I said. 'I wouldn't do that.'

'Oh come on,' said Aristotle. 'Don't be a moron, man.
That's five thousand fucking quid for doing fuck all. Tell 'em
something interesting. Tell 'em she raped you. She's definitely weird. I wonder if you'd introduced me . . . Did she throw
knives at you ever, like that other one? Did you have, like –
you know – did you go *down* on her?'

'Oh, for god's sake,' said Lily. 'You're such a kid, Aristotle.'

Embarrassing myself, I started to cry, pathetic, my face
pushed hard into the bed, painstakingly crumpling the torn-
out page in my hand. I heard Lily ordering Aristotle out the
door. 'Just get out!'

'Why? What? What did I say?'

'Out!'

I felt the pressure of her hands upon me, rubbing my back,

my arms, my neck, feeling my hair. She kissed my neck and a pain shot from her lips down my right side into my groin. I groaned and sobbed aloud.

'Come on,' she said. 'Everything's OK. You're going to be OK. All those horrible things in the papers. I bet it was really strange, being with a teacher. I told you, I really fancied my science teacher once. I don't know what I'd've done if he came on to me, though. Got the fright of my life! Maybe not, though. It would've been kind of flattering.' Her hands went up and down, stroking my hair, my elbows, the backs of my knees. Uncomfortable waves of chill flowed from her hands, flooding like water over my skin, raising tiny hairs. 'I kind of wonder what it would be like, doing it. I often think . . . Me and Matt,' she said dreamily, 'never did it. And now he's kind of scary, lying in his bed all day; he's got some weird stuff going on. I can't seem to talk to him any more. Do you think he's all right?' She kissed my neck again. When Cassandra kissed me, it was hard and mad. Lily's lips were so light, I didn't know what to make of the sensation. As she kissed me, my nerves sparked all over my back, hurting me like I was being jabbed by a fork, making me tense. 'Relax,' she said. 'I'll take care of you.' But then she turned onto her back, lying beside me, doing nothing. 'Is sex OK?' she asked. 'Is it really nice?'

I raised myself on one elbow and looked at her beautiful face, and couldn't think what to say to her. The last time I'd seen her I'd treated her like shit. I was always treating her like shit.

'I'm sorry about . . .' I said, 'getting so heavy with you. In the phonebox.'

'It's OK.' She sighed, arching her back. Her embroidered jacket fell open, and I could see her nipples through her thin white shirt. She wasn't wearing a bra.

I said, 'Things were kind of awkward at the time.'

She turned to put her hand on my shoulder, tits falling gently sideways. 'Ferdie . . . Don't you like me anymore?'

'Of course I like you.'

'You never call me, though.'

I felt like confessing to her. 'Yeah. Listen. Cassandra didn't want me to, that's all.' At the sound of her name, I got a violent pain in my stomach.

'Oh!' She was delighted. 'She *was* jealous of me! Was she? Why?'

I groaned, 'I don't know. I really don't know. She was just ... like that.'

'You don't know?' She was disappointed, now. 'What was she like?'

'Oh ... Nothing.'

'Nothing?' she asked, kind of hopefully.

I put my head back down on the pillow, and she started kissing my upper arm, just touching me between my shoulder-blades, lightly, nonsensically, a weird, unsexy touch. Almost bad-tempered, I turned back towards her and took her in my arms and kissed her. She sighed and moaned and went all floppy against me, and I hardly knew what to do with her. I pulled down her trousers, and she sort of opened her legs a bit, still with her pants on, her hands by her sides, nervous and undemanding – quite sweet, I suppose, but it was like being asked to fuck a doll. I wasn't really used to running the show. I knew I had to have sex with her, and I thought it would be all right. Maybe that was what I was for – having sex with whoever wanted me. Perhaps it would've been better if Lily'd bit or scratched me. I was so used to Cassandra's furious, nasty nature – the way she marked me; the way my skin was in tatters now, under my clothes which I wasn't going to take off. Lily stroked me softly and asked me to go slow. I got up, leaving her lying on the bed. I stared out of the window into the back garden, the big wet floppy trees and waves of grass, and repeated over and over again to myself, not aloud at all, *Cassandra, Cassandra, Cassandra*, picturing her long naked body in the hotel. The phone in my pocket started vibrating, her answering touch, humming and trembling against my thigh, a distant wank from my disgraceful lover, and while the tears ran down my face, my dick grew hard. Then quickly, before it could go away, I opened my flies, lay down on top of Lily and pushed it right in. She gave a shrill tiny scream and burst into tears, but she wouldn't let me go, she wrapped her legs around me, so I fucked her until I came, Cassandra's distant calls massaging my thigh, despising myself, thinking about Cassandra, both Lily and me crying and hating it, but not hating each other – both of us hoping next time it wouldn't be so bad.

Chapter Seventeen

Lily begged, 'Come on . . .' She wanted to get the morning-after pill, rapidly brushing her disordered hair, looking shy but keen to hurry me along.

I was having a problem trying to make sense of what she was saying. I was reeling from the speed of my unfaithfulness. I couldn't get Cassandra's body out of my head, not since I'd drummed her up to get me hard, her urgent calls vibrating in my jeans. Still her phone wouldn't let me alone, jarring repeatedly against my hip, trying to reopen our connection, humming my name with electronic lips. 'Wait . . . wait a sec . . .'

'But we've got to go?' She smiled unsurely at me. She couldn't understand why I still remained there stiff and frozen like I'd had a stroke – a genuine zombie kid. I awkwardly moved my hand over my pocket to finger the mobile's violent throbbing.

'Wait for me downstairs – I've got to go to the loo.' The second she left the room, I punched *reply* to her mobile number which she'd left repeatedly in my phone, all the time I was fucking my poor sweet friend. Then I cancelled it before it rang, not knowing what to say. Next, as I was crouched over it, it spasmed furiously, and coughed up a text message into my hand: *Have read the paper we must talk.* Again I hit *reply*; again I cancelled. I was a coward; I was too shaken to speak to her after what had just happened with Lily, the girl I'd been ordered not to see again; I suppose I'd been getting my own back for all those others, for finding out I was only one of a kind. I pictured the queue of dark-haired boys in front of me, and, sweating with chronic jealousy, I imagined a ghostly queue stood at my back, waiting for me to move on, to let them take their turn. I should've known, from Harry and Annie, that love was a fucked-up impermanent thing. Look at me – I'd just proved it myself. I thought of Cassandra in sunny Spain, sipping vodka and cranberry juice and dancing with black-haired boys to Abigail-style pop songs.

I could hear Lily screaming for me up the stairs. 'Ferdia! Come quick!' I wondered through my mental haze why she was so frightened. She shouted, 'Ferdia! It's Matt!'

Still in Spain, I came reluctantly out on to the landing. Little Natasha was leaping up the stairs, chest heaving, coatless as usual, thin dirty yellow dress and sockless shoes. I stared at her, trying to get my bearings. She grabbed me by the knees. 'You've gotta stop him! He's trying to jump off our balcony!' Reacting at last, I swept her up and bounded down to the hall, three at the time. Aristotle and Jason were outside on the steps, standing looking around confused among the prostrate blasted bodies. 'Quick! Quick!' howled Natasha, red mouth frantically open.

Racing down the road, I stumbled on a loose paving stone, and Jason grabbed the five-year-old out of my arms. The lift was standing open in the shaft, and I thought that meant god was on our side, but when we ran in and pressed the buttons, nothing moved. 'Shit, shit, shit!' Up we ran, for twenty solid flights, two hundred and forty steps to god knows what, Jason ahead of me holding Natasha all the way, shaking his head when I gasped at him to give me a turn, never once stopping. I didn't dare stop either. On every landing were immense glass windows crossed with wire, but I never looked out, thinking if I did I'd see his body pass, arms and legs awkwardly flung back, broken by the wind in his final, headfirst dive. Further and further behind me, Lily and Aristotle faintly moaned and stumbled. My own lungs packed in halfway up, the muscles in my legs just fell apart, no oxgen in my blood, nor strength in my knees. 'Hurry up!' screamed Natasha over Jason's shoulder. 'He's gonna jump!' I went on running on my hands and feet.

The flat door was open, and the French windows as well, beautiful cold air filling the room. Outside, he was stood – horrifyingly – on the flat metal railing, holding his guitar with one hand round its neck, leaning on it for treacherous support, looking straight ahead into the dying sky, a tall dark shadow against the pinker blue, scrubby sun-rimmed hair ruffled by the gentle breeze. Jason dropped Natasha on the couch and crumpled dying to his knees. In one final effort, a bloke in a cartoon desert, I crawled on my stomach past Aristotle's sad abandoned drum kit to the open window and lay on the floor, dragging down winter air which filled my empty lungs with burning sand. Natasha bounced off the couch and dashed out into the open. 'Don't jump! Don't jump!'

He looked down at her with mild irritation, still the big brother to her annoying naivety. 'It's not like jumping, Nat,' he patronised her. 'It's different.'

'It is! You'll die!'

'Leave me alone. I'm going for a *walk*. To the sun. The sun is my music god.'

I croaked, 'Matt . . . No . . . Please . . .'

Startled by my voice, he glanced back at me, and in doing so wobbled, and the bottom of his guitar skidded off the smooth metal rail into the open air. He tried to save it, staggering on the edge, reaching out, losing his footing. Nat screamed and wet herself. The guitar dropped. Matt grabbed the sharp concrete corner of the wall with both hands. Several seconds later, we heard the sound of its faint musical impact. Nobody moved.

'Shit,' Matt said at last, peering down. 'I've dropped my fucking guitar.'

I crouched speechless in the balcony doorway, stiff with the terror of nearly making him fall. The mobile spewed out another message into my pocket, knocking against my frozen bones.

Jason, getting his breath back, strolled fake-casual past me. 'All right, mate?' he asked, leaning his elbows on the rail, gazing down on the distant world of the ground. 'You coming in?'

Matt shrank closer to the corner of the wall. He said to me with a sarcastic edge, 'Long time no see. Dropped in to say goodbye?'

'No.' I got slowly to my feet.

'Oh come on.' He was taking the piss. 'You gotta say goodbye. This is a big step for me. It's a totally different universe thing. I'm off.' He let go of the corner, standing holding nothing, stepping sideways along the narrow railing.

'No!' shrieked Nat, an emotional five-year-old tearing her hair.

He sighed, wavering like a shadow in the thin chill current of air. The sun was drawing level with his feet, shining between the next door blocks, the air gone fuzzy with fragmented light. 'OK, OK. Calm down. I've not gone yet.'

Jason asked, lighting a fag, offering one up to him, 'What's buggin' you, man? What's going on?'

Matt waved away the cigarette, retreating to the corner of the wall again. 'I'm in the wrong universe, that's what. It's not working out for me here. I've gotta play the music in my soul.' He cried out, like something was really hurting him, 'I gotta get out of here. Everything's a rope.' The sun sprayed pink light along the balcony. 'The sun is my music god.'

Jason said, 'Look, mate – did you still want that gig at the Evil Eye?'

'No.' He crouched down on his heels, leaning forwards, looking and looking, swaying and shivering. 'I've dropped my fucking guitar. It's too late now.'

'Oh Matt,' whispered Lily, leaning trembling against my back, finally arrived. 'It's not too late.' Matt ignored her, but lowered himself down to perch on the railing, his legs dangling, kicking in the empty air.

'How's it . . . going, man,' wheezed Aristotle, sticking his head out past my shoulder. 'Did you know the fucking lifts were gone again? I'm not joking.'

'I know a quick way down,' said Matt, smiling round at him, rocking on his arse.

'Yeah? Thank god for that.'

Matt laughed. He leaned right out over the infinite pit, anchored by white-knuckled hands to the rail. Lily, Natasha and Aristotle all shrieked girlishly, and Matt, bad-tempered, lifted his head, glaring around at us. 'Will you all just fuck off and get out of my space!' We flinched away from him, hands in surrender position, huddling back into the living room. Jason, getting down on his knees, drew a squealing Natasha into his arms and whispered urgently in her ear, 'Get down to the estate and ask for Gary Peckham. Tell him it's Jason. Tell him to bring his new guitar, now.'

'I can't leave him,' she cried hysterically. 'I can't leave him.'

'*Now.* I'm gonna get him down. Quick. Fast as you can.' He pushed her off. Weeping, she ran towards the front door, ancient sandals flip-flopping. Jason looked up at me from his knees and said, 'I don't want her to see him do it.' A small pink cardigan was lying on the sofa, and I picked it up and ran after Nat. The lift doors were closing on her heels – working again, so she did get a quick way down.

Lily was back at the French windows, arguing with Matt about how great life was for him. 'Remember when you said you loved me? And what about your mum?'

'But you love Ferdia. And Tessa doesn't need me. She never has. She's in another universe altogether. She hasn't been in the same one as me for a long long time.' And he began humming 'Babes in the Air'. '*Sleep, baby, sleep, we're so fucking high . . . Me on my valium, you in the sky.*' He went on through the whole song, and me and Lily hummed guiltily along to the end. Aristotle sat down at his kit, and tapped out a little hushed rhythm. Then Matt sang '*She's the woman who has nothing and you've got to give her something cos she's sick of having nothing to her name*' and stopped, but Lily carried on, leaning her shoulder against the frame of the open French windows, her hair rolling down her back: '*She's the woman*

who has nothing, and you want to give her something, but whatev-
er you may give her it will all turn into nothing, you're just making
her a present of the same . . .' Then I wondered for the first time
where Tessa had got to, if she was going to bother to be part
of all this, and edged open the door into her bedroom.

She was lying eyes half-open on the duvet, vaguely smiling. I shook her over and over, rolling her limply by her
shoulders, invoking her blank body by its name, but she was
too far gone. I was angrily astonished how she could sleep so
deep while her son was threatening to die. For the first time
in a long time, I thought forgivingly of Annie and Harry.
Sitting down on Tessa's bed, I took out the mobile and read
the last message: *Talk to me!* It didn't seem like a good idea.
Before leaving, I folded the edges of the duvet over Tessa's
skinny body, like that morning I'd wrapped up my sleeping
lover. In the living room, Aristotle started screaming with
laughter. Phone in my hand, I hurried out to see what was
going on. Stotle was shouting merrily from where he was sat
at his drum kit, waving a stick: 'Yep! He's been porking his
teacher, man! Mind you, he had to join a queue.' I couldn't
see Jason anywhere, and felt shockingly abandoned, but
even as I was thinking it he came sliding back into the flat,
his cousin following silently behind him, carrying a bright
red guitar. Seeing me seeing him, Jason tapped his finger to
his lips. The two of them slid past like thieves, backs glued to
the living-room wall, and disappeared together into Matt's
bedroom.

Lily, still standing in the balcony doorway, was insisting to
Matt, 'But what about Nat? Think how upset she'll be.'

'Ah, Nat,' he answered softly. 'I've got a special song for
her.'

'Sing it.'

But he gave her a cheeky smile and shook his head. The
sun, rolling down the edge of the nearest block, made orange
flashlights of a million windows. Matt squinted and held one
hand against the glare. 'So, Ferdia,' he announced, raising a

cold hard voice. 'We now know for sure you've been shagging your teacher. Even Stotle here appears convinced, despite his doubts about your sex appeal.' Aristotle giggled noisily, whacking the cymbals. Matt, sat sideways, drew up one knee under his chin, his foot on the flat rail in front of him, one hand gripping the metal bar under his thigh, the other foot still treading air. He said to me, shaking his head disparagingly, 'What the fuck were you thinking, man? Didn't I tell you to be careful out there? Teachers are out to own your *soul*. They want to fuck you up.'

'No, man, she just wants to *fuck* him,' said Aristotle, throwing back his head, well pleased with himself.

Matt scowled, 'I'm serious, man. She wants to eat your head.'

'No, man, she wants to eat his *dick* . . .'

'Ferdia, listen to me. You've got to save yourself. Get out while you can. Cut the rope. Just walk away.'

'I know,' I said. 'It's the only thing I'm good at.' The mobile was shuddering in my hand, demanding my answer. Stepping out on to the balcony, I hurled the silver phone into mid-air, where it spun flickering in the falling sun, reflecting crimson light, then dived like a shining bomber for the ground.

Matt asked, taken aback, peering dangerously down after the phone, 'What the fuck was that?'

Jason suddenly appeared in the balcony doorway next to Lily, Gary's flash red Yamaha in his hand, and roared out, '*I'm a zombie kid, I'm weird because I'm dead; it's not my fault my teacher ate my head.*'

Matt grinned approvingly, jabbing his finger at me, joining in, '*She ripped my head off, yes she really did.*'

Aristotle bashed away, laughing inanely, '*But I'm not bitter – I'M THE ZOMBIE KID!* That's you, right, Ferdie?'

But I was in the grip of terror, trying not to look over Matt's shoulder. Gary's small freckled hand, glowing pink in the last of the light, was groping the smooth tower-block wall, stroking its way up and down the red-stained concrete, trying for a grip on the corner behind Matt's back. His Reebok hung suspended in the air, twenty floors up, toe waving around, lace undone, unable to locate the rail. He must've crawled out of Matt's bedroom window. I thought, he's paying his usual dues to Jason. I thought, Fucking *idiot*, this means death for sure. To stop myself giving Gary away, I turned to Lily who smiled awkwardly at me, thinking the song might be offending me. I started singing it myself at the top of my voice: '*She fried my brain and spread it on some bread! She said, yum, yum, I LURVE that Zombie spread!*' I thought, jumping and twirling around, Jesus, up until now everything's been such a fucking mess, I've been in a daze, I haven't been in control, and this is the end, Matt, Gary, death, and here comes the rest of my life, without Cassandra. Gary's round sunset-flushed face inched slowly into view, eyes almost shut in total focus, chest and cheek pressed lovingly to the wall, first foot now on the balcony railing, other foot still hovering trembling out of sight. I thought I wasn't watching any more, but Lily peered questioningly into my eyes, then sharply to her left and briefly squawked, and then Aristotle stood up behind his drums, hands clamped over his silent mouth. Matt, shrugging, turned his back on us all, swinging both legs over the bottomless side. Then he switched his head to the left, now watching, like we all were, Gary step tentatively out onto the rail.

'Matt,' said Jason, evenly, conversationally. 'Gotta do the zombie dance.'

Matt was looking at Gary, who was now standing on the railing. Gary winked at him, folding his arms, chest out, chin up, one foot in front of the other, poised Olympic gymnast, twenty floors up. His number-one haircut gleamed in the dying light. 'Awrigh' mate? How you doing?'

Matt asked in a low, shaking voice, 'Where . . .?'

'Matt's gonna play us a gig at the Evil Eye,' said Jason. 'He's the man. He's gonna do it.'

'Fuckin' blindin',' said Gary. 'Jesus, that's fuckin' wicked news. Well good fuckin' news, Matt.' He gave a little jump, then dropped on his arse on the railing, grabbing it with both hands, swinging backwards and forwards, steadying himself. He stretched one palm to Matt. 'I guarantee the lads'll love it. Put it there, mate.'

Matt just stared and stared at him.

'Come on, mate, put it there.'

Matt said, childishly amazed, 'You walked in the sky, man.'

'That's me, mate,' said Gary, smugly. 'I can do anything, me. Now, for fuck's sake, *put it there.*' And he grabbed Matt's hand in a furious grip and threw himself backwards onto the balcony floor, jerking Matt down with him out of the great red sky back into the concrete box where he belonged.

Me and Lily, and Nat bursting out out from behind Jason, threw ourselves down on his stunned body, shouting without words and holding him down, roping him, weighing him down, never letting him go. 'Fuck's sake, get off of me,' he screeched, thrashing about. 'Fuck's sake! If he can do it, so can I!'

'No, mate,' said Gary, standing up, rubbing the back of his shaven head, dusting himself off. 'Message from the music god. He wants you to play a gig at the Evil Eye. And he's sent you a new guitar.' He snatched from his cousin's hand the guitar he'd been ordered to bring – flash, new, expensive, sun-bright pegs and frets – and waved it triumphantly in Matt's face. 'Look, man – he's done it up for you! Shit, man, it's a red Yamaha! It's, like, a music god's guitar!'

'Jesus,' said Matt, rising to his knees among us, 'you're right' – in a voice of total awe. 'I don't believe it.' Totally wonder-struck, he seized it with both hands, clambering to his feet, turning a shining face towards the winter sunset, the towering red-stained estate, raising the Yamaha way above his head, into the huge brilliant sky surrounding him. 'Thank you! Thank you! Thank you!'

'Now you can play your gig – oh Matt, that's wonderful!' cried Lily.

'Hey, let's have a jam right now!' cried Aristotle, hitting a roll of drums.

'Yep, let's play!' And, still holding his god-given instrument on high, he put one hand on the balcony rail and vaulted over into the great unknown, out of his concrete box into the sky, turning over and over, red guitar hugged in his arms, free fall, unchained, unroped, untroubled, in those few sunlit seconds before his death.

Chapter Eighteen

The last I saw of Cassandra was that crimson spark of her shining phone, pre-empting Matt by minutes into his deep blood-coloured concrete grave. I never tried to ring her, for lots of reasons. For one, if I hadn't deserted Matt for her, been such a crappy friend, then maybe he wouldn't've done the stupid thing he did. Losing her was my punishment. Plus, if I hadn't fucked Lily . . . Sometimes you go somewhere because somebody really wants you to go there, and it turns out not to be a detour off the road but a journey you can never retrace.

I suppose Cassandra left London, but I don't know where she went; the papers dug up endless shit about her; I didn't read it much; my parents didn't bug me about it, didn't try to get me to talk – they knew I had worse things to think about. I guess she met some other delighted boy, some dog-like, eager-to-please, waggy-tailed boy.

Lily kept wanting to make a go of things, and I kind of went along with it. She wanted a relationship so much. I still felt awkward when we were doing it. She never tried to order me about or hurt me in any way, but instead of appreciating her for that I found it left me bored and unexcited. After Cassandra, it was as if I'd come through a war; I was exhausted, different, changed. Yet I really liked Lily and kept on seeing her. I wondered if she saw me as a challenge, and if she'd ever realise how little of a challenge I really was. I was used up – I didn't know how to say No. But I knew she really cared for me. She let me say the most terrible sick things about Matt. I still couldn't bring myself to utter his name. I just kept calling him the Pancake Man.

In the new year, Lily came up with this weird troubling idea of playing a memorial gig for Matt in the Evil Eye. I resisted that. I thought it was wrong, like taking the piss, to steal his show as soon as he'd turned his back, especially when he thought we were such a bunch of materialistic mid-dle-of-the-road ground-dwellers compared to the great prin-cipled no-ties etc Matt Skywalker (but drawn inexorably to the ground, despite his best efforts to walk on air). The real reason was, I didn't want to do it. I hated him. She claimed I should remember him with love, but you know, he'd punched such an unfillable hole in me, making me hear that faint unforgettable sound of him hitting concrete a million miles below. Nat's screams like feedback – so piercing, even Tessa woke up and came out yawning to check was every-thing OK. Our inability to answer her. Her son had the fuck-ing nerve to jump and we didn't even have the courage to put it into words. Unforgivable. I couldn't speak his name.

'You can sing,' said Lily, patting me on my back as I lay in my now accustomed position, face down on my dirty bed.

I shrugged, making her hand hop off my back like a little frog. 'He didn't want me to sing.'

'You're wrong. This is different,' she said. Tentatively, she went back to stroking my shoulder. 'He'd want this. Come on. For Matt.'

'Like he said, I can't sing and play at the same time.'

'No problem. Jacie can play bass,' offered Gary. He was squashed sideways on my windowsill, big Reeboks crammed into the woodwork, feet gradually splitting the rotted frame apart. 'This is wicked. You'll be like a tribute band.' He frowned, struck by a random thought. 'Except . . . you are the band. Sort of.'

'That's right!' cried Aristotle, thrilled to find someone else on his own wavelength. 'Now all we need is a new lead gui-tarist.' Sitting cross-legged on my desk, he looked suddenly ashamed and wasted. 'I mean, yeah, of course we do. I mean, that's the whole point, innit.'

'What about Abigail?' suggested Lily, coolly.

'*Abigail?*' That was me, Gary and Stotle, but only I cried it out in disbelief. The other two were dribbling, just gagging to get into her knickers. I protested, 'She's a fucking Top of the Pops queen, Lil! M . . . that stupid *bastard* would turn in his . . . Have you gone completely mental?'

'And we should write him a song,' she said, tucking her long black hair behind her ears, nodding seriously so it fell right out again.

'No,' I said. 'He wrote the songs.' An intensely bright picture came into my head of him so-called singing, bouncing moronically around the music room at school, metal stands jangling, year-seven kids outside. I thought, And now no one will ever hear him again, the selfish bastard. I said, 'Oh, yeah, all right, I've got a song for him: *I can walk on empty air, oh yes I can! That's why they call me TWAT, THE PANCAKE MAN!*'

'Stop it,' said Lily, sadly. 'You don't mean it.'

But Gary and Aristotle were already cheerfully humming the tune. 'Cool,' they said.

Lily went and spoke to Jason about the Evil Eye, and playing bass, and rang up Abigail, who thought it would be 'inappropriate' for her to play. Gary suggested himself: 'I've got this great new Yam . . . um . . . oh . . .' He ground to a halt, looking a bit depressed, 'Anyway, I'm shit.' Harry leant on Abigail and to my amazement she agreed, providing we didn't sully her fair name by telling anyone – and she meant *anyone* – she was there. She invited us sulkily round for a practice run. I didn't want to go, but Lily got so sad. 'You know,' said Abigail, after she'd listened to the demo a couple of times, standing in her minimal front room, 'this is pretty simple stuff. No wonder Dickie was into it – he likes it basic. He's still quite interested, you know. You should give him a call.' And while we all stared at her, some with renewed disbelief and others with mindless lust, she picked up her own guitar and whacked out a perfect imitation of Matt's inimitable style. 'This isn't really my thing,' she said, setting the guitar down again. 'But just this once . . . I mean, he was almost like family to you, wasn't he, Ferdia? Funny little kid.'

I think she thought she was a modern saint, not charging us a million pounds. Lily was still keen for her to let us use her name, because now she wanted to make it a fund-raiser for Tessa and Nat, but Abigail said No, Jesus! no – absolutely not. Did we want to decimate her fanbase? Our fly-posting team, Aristotle and Gary, compromised between the two positions by setting Abigail's name in extremely small print ('A tribute night by BOYBITS with Abigail Williams standing in for MATT LOFTUS'), and were then incredibly innocently surprised when Abby hit the fucking roof.

Gary offered to sing when I wouldn't, and made a pretty good stab at it I thought – authentically as crap as Matt. But the others refused to play with him, and Abigail especially kept crying with laughter, rolling on the floor with her legs wrapped around her guitar. So I ended up doing it anyway – I didn't care enough to make a stand. I just wanted the whole thing over with. Matt was gone, and all the fun we'd had.

It never struck me anyone much would turn up to Matt's final gig. I thought there'd be about twenty hangers-on. Yet when we were finally standing on the narrow dark stage at the back of the Evil Eye we ended up having to wait forever, silent, self-conscious, smoking to keep our fingers warm, Aristotle bugging us all by buzzing like an insect on the drums. The punters just kept on coming in. All the school showed up – the little kids that used to pack the corridor outside the music room at lunch-hours, and ones my age, and older ones, and some of the better teachers even. Dickie swanned in. I glared at Abigail, but she didn't give a shit. She said, 'It's not his fault your friend was a schiz – get used to it.' Her fanbase was there as well in force – the whole of Natasha's primary school and their friends, swooning and giggling, squealing 'Abigail! Abigail!' cross-legged in long-socked rows just underneath the stage.

My parents had got in early, nodding and waving to all their clever children, drinking together at the bar, looking companionable and trying to ignore the shaven young men from the estate buying cocaine across the counter – the Peckhams had rounded up *hundreds* of them, filling the desperate, filthy dive and spilling out of it into the watery evening light, rolling up their fivers for a quick line before handing them over to Gary for the Nat and Tessa fund. We must've been making thousands. Jason pushed open the double doors at the front, then ripped the boards from broken windows, setting up more speakers to feed the snorting crowd which shuffled around outside in the cool March evening. Abby waved to Dickie and Harry. Tessa was at the bar, drinking and weeping on Annie's shoulder. Jason pushed his way back and climbed up on to the stage. 'Let's go,' I said to him. 'Let's get this over with.'

Gary hit the lights, so only the stage and the bar area were bright. We launched with 'Babes in the Air', and then 'What Do You Give the Woman Who Has Nothing?' I was glancing over at Tessa to see how she was taking it, to see if she realised how sad Matt had been for her, but before long she'd slid down to the filthy floor out of my sight – she'd found the perfect excuse to drown her sorrows, and wasn't going to waste it listening to us. The punters stayed formal and polite – upturned kids' faces and attentive thugs. Then we played 'Zombie Kid'. It was amazing how year seven knew the words, jumping to their feet and doing the zombie dance. I nearly started to enjoy myself, instead of feeling terminally sick. Jason and Abby and Lily started dancing across the stage like maniacs. *'Gotta do the zombie bounce! Gotta do the zombie jump!'* The kids were springing up and down, and then it caught on – hundreds of shaven nutters leaping around playing air guitar and nearly disappearing though the rickety floor, boards giving way like gangland gunshots. *'Gotta do the zombie dance! Gotta do the zombie bump!'*

We were getting hyped, did 'Plastic Man' and 'Wanna Rip Somebody's Head Off', and then, even though we'd taken a decision not to play 'Hungry Poor', Matt's too-sad anthem, I thought, fuck it, he wrote it, he lived it, we couldn't just write it out of history because it made us want to fucking cry – this might be the last airing it ever got. *'Hey, you on the ground, Watch out for the hungry poor! Gonna squash you flat when we jump from the twentieth floor!'* I wrapped my mouth around the mike. *'Gotta jump to my death, Take my very last breath, mid-air . . .'* Lily dropped out and lay down on the stage, but the punters went wild, particularly the tower-block men, shaking their coke-crazed fists and threatening the world, doing the white-thug riot chant (even the black blokes) with one massive voice, a great fierce happy football crowd of a voice. My parents pulled up their coat collars and looked around anxiously. All remaining windows broke and glasses cheerfully flew. Matt would've loved it. This was the audience for him, all right.

Nat wriggled her way to the front of the crowd. *'Stop that noise!'* she screamed up at us, over her head in her compatriots, Abigail's giggling girly hangers-on.

'Oh, Nat . . . ,' said Lily, gazing down on her, still upset from the last song. 'Are you all right?'

'I *want* to do it.' She started hauling herself determinedly up, wearing her small fluorescent pink plastic raincoat and pink Barbie heels, sliding about, looking like a princess.

I slid my arm around her fluorescent shoulders and bellowed into the mike *'Wanna wake the dead, but the little girl said . . .'* and stuck it under Nat's cute turned-up nose as she squealed, *'Stop that noise!' 'Wanna fuck with your heads, but the little girl said –' 'Stop that noise!' 'Wanna make you see red, but the little girl said – ' 'Stop that noise!'* belted out the whole delighted crowd, loving her, drowning her. It made the perfect finale, I thought – the last of his ephemeral repertoire. The punters were howling at us for more. But what could we do? He'd only been fifteen, he'd only just got going. Hardly got started before he'd so suddenly stopped. 'That's it, folks!' I roared at them through the mike. 'Go home! Or get pissed!'

'Fucking more, you poncy long-haired cunt!'

Nat stayed centre-stage, loving it like it was all meant for her. Maybe it was for the only time in her life, but Matt's little sister was a real star. She said to me, cheekily, hands on pink plastic-coated hips, 'Well, come on, why don't you play his other song?'

'Oi, poofter!' There was too much energy going to waste. Fights started breaking out, especially among the tired and emotional primary school girls.

'We've done 'em all, Nat. That's the lot.'

'No, no,' she insisted. 'The one he wrote for me.'

I bent down towards her so I was sure I was hearing her right. 'For you?'

She shouted at all of us like we were mad not to understand, 'He always sung it to me. I wanna sing it now.'

I shrugged at Jason and he stepped forward, flexing his thin hard arms in his white silk shirt. 'All right, you lot. Quieten down. We've got Matt's little sister here, and she wants to sing you a song he made up specially for her.' All the mad stroppy kids and Reeboked heavies stopped fucking about and snorting coke and wrestling each other and paid that little five-year-old the utmost respect as I wrestled the mike down to her level and Lily knelt down beside her to make sure she held it right. I looked over for Tessa, but the proud mum was still out of sight, a hole in the crowd at Annie's feet. I crouched on my heels on the stage, on Nat's other side.

Nat cleared her throat. 'This is the song my big brother made up for me,' she said, quite cheerfully. 'He used to sing it me when I was sad. OK? So listen.' She sang, while we held our breath, '*I'm for . . .*', and stopped, trembling.

'Don't be nervous,' I whispered in her ear.

'Shut UP!' she said, very loudly and shrilly aggressive into the mike. Everyone laughed. 'Stop laughing!' They did. Then she tried again. '*I'm for –*' and stopped, and sniffed, this time to well-behaved silence. '*I'm for –*' Finally she got it together. '*I'm forever blowing bubbles . . . Pretty bubbles in the air . . .*'

I looked up half-grinning at the others on the stage. I knew

Matt was a West Ham fan, which was fucking nutty behaviour on that estate where everyone was die-hard Arsenal – he never did the right thing to belong, even to where he wanted to be. I'd heard him strumming the Hammers anthem one or twice, but I didn't know he sung it to comfort Nat. It was kind of cute, her thinking he'd made it up. I could feel the crowd of coked-up hooligans flexing its muscles automatically, not knowing where to put themselves. Then Jason bravely started following her, wincing a little in his Arsenal socks, playing along with an enemy tune. *'They fly so high . . .'* Now Abigail and Aristotle, also good Arsenal supporters, joined in. *'Nearly reach the sky . . .'*

It should've caused a riot in such a place, but the young shaven-headed all followed Jason's cue, dutifully roaring out together, singing and swaying sentimentally, *'Then like my dreams, they fade and die . . .'* Here we went, cigarette lighters whipped out and held aloft, flickering over the shadowy crowd, outside and in, digging deep for the words: *'. . . dah de dah de dah-dah, dah de dah de dah . . . I'm forever blowing bubbles, pretty bubbles in the air . . .'*

Delighted, overwhelmed, I stood up and looked around – Lily on her knees sharing Nat's mike, Jason and Abigail thrashing out the anthem face to face, Aristotle bashing about insanely. Harry and Annie were singing too, arm in arm. Dickie was leant against the bar beside them, nodding his sleazy head and giving me the thumbs-up sign. I scowled at him and stared away, over the mass of roaring bodies as they spilled right out beyond the Evil Eye, twenty deep outside its battered walls, giving it large, singing their high-rise hearts out, hundreds of tiny flames piercing the blue spring night above their heads. Then suddenly I thought I saw her, hovering casually on the edge of the crowd, her long thin body glimmering in the shadows. Heart pounding, feeling sick and sweaty, I slid without hesitation off the stage and squeezed myself along the wall, climbing out of the nearest broken window, fighting through to the open space beyond. Open, and deserted – shadows and graffiti, erratically lit by all the hand-held fires. Behind me, the song went crashing to the end. Defeated, tired and sad, I turned to face the Evil Eye. All the hot rocking bodies now fell silent, brandishing their brightly burning thumbs. Wondering what was happening back on stage, I climbed onto a concrete bench and saw, through the open double doors, Lily lifting Natasha in her arms.

'Three cheers for Matt!' shouted Natasha in her high sweet voice. 'Hip hip . . .'

The punters exploded, lighters flying like fireworks, and the next minute everyone was hugging each other – the band, my parents, all that crazy crowd, from the squealing school-girls at the front to the most scarily shaven of the shaven-headed. I stayed standing on the bench, shivering in the dark and cold, left alone in the space where Cassandra wasn't. But after a while I had to jump off and run like mad towards the stage, shoving my way to the front as fast as I could, the others reaching down their hands to pull me up, eager for me to join the sky-high cheering.